FADED MOON

BOOKS BY T.L. MORGAN

Faded Moon

Sweet Sorrow

Published as Talli L. Morgan

The Windermere Tales Series

The Oracle Stone

The Savior's Rise

The Master of Time

The Peacebringer Trilogy

Truthseeker

Standalones

Meliora

FADED MOON

T.L. MORGAN

Cover art, design, and interior graphics by Juniper Lake Fitzgerald

Printed in the United States of America

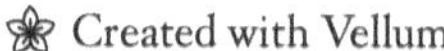 Created with Vellum

For the ones who are told they do not belong: you do.

Given love or given hate determines everybody's fate in life; be careful what you give.

—*"Prodigal Son" by Kamelot*

PROLOGUE
WANING CRESCENT I

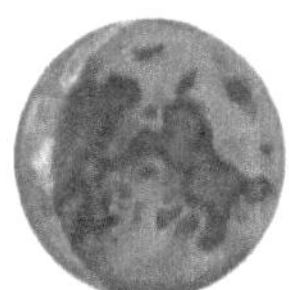

RUNE'S NEXT hit was an easy target, and he was effortless to find. It only took a bit of asking around; Rune loved little rural towns like this for the precise reason that absolutely no one could keep a secret. With a few choice questions, Rune had yet another necromancer in his sights.

One step closer to his own atonement.

Rune instructed his partners to remain where they were concealed in the shadows behind a dilapidated barn. He drew his black hood up over his head, letting the edge fall just to his eyebrows, casting his features in darkness. He tucked his arms beneath the cloak as well, keeping his left hand on the hilt of the dagger at his right. Across a stretch of damp, overgrown grass, a fair-skinned man with silvering black hair prodded through a heap of firewood behind the house.

Golden light from the gaslamps indoors flooded a rectangular patch of grass, but the man stood just outside the light's reach. He wore a gray shirt with sleeves rolled up to his elbows, untucked from his pants, and he hadn't tied his boots. It was lucky — no, a blessing — that Rune had been here at just the right time for his presence to coincide with this man's quick step outside at this late hour.

Rune glanced up at the sky as he made his way across the yard on silent footsteps. Cloaked behind thick clouds, the moon would be just past its half phase, creeping toward its night of darkness when God's power would be at its weakest — and the heretic Jovian's power at its strongest. Rune had promised that his atonement would be complete before this next phase, and God strike him down if he failed.

He had failed enough times already. He could not keep letting these monsters get away.

Rune tightened his gloved hand around the slender hilt of the dagger. *Not yet*, he reminded himself even as his heart jumped with adrenaline. He needed time to observe before he made a move. He needed to gauge the necromancer's strength and agility before he ran in swinging. Rune was no brute; though in his late twenties, he had never grown out of his youthful lankiness — he blamed it on the dark magic that had corrupted his soul — and his build made it particularly challenging to face opponents bigger than him. But he was quick, and he was efficient. And nearly every time, those traits served him well.

He'd be damned if he didn't make up for that one failure.

When he had only a dozen feet between himself and the yet-unsuspecting necromancer, Rune stopped. He let out a silent breath, and closed his eyes. *God, guide my hand.*

"Is someone there?"

Ah, so the necromancer had spotted him. Rune opened his eyes and raised his head, drifting closer so the light caught his eyes. The man jerked back, shoulders going rigid.

"Who are you?"

Rune moved another step forward. "I am God's mortal hand." He gripped his dagger, hard enough for the silver ring on his thumb to dig into his skin. Adrenaline rushed through him, setting a tremble in his usually steady hands. Rune clenched and unclenched them, telling himself to be calm.

"The fuck are you talking about, man?" The necromancer scrubbed his hand through his short hair. "Leave me alone. I won't say it again."

Rune moved closer, careful to stay out of the light. The necromancer moved back a few steps, lifting his hands defensively. Rune smirked to himself. What did he plan to do? His power did not exactly specialize in matters of self-defense.

"What do you want!" barked the monster. He backed up until he hit the side of the house, startling himself, then turned his gaze to Rune with real fear. "Shit, come on. Whatever you need — Money? Is it money? Is that why you're— Look, just— Let me help you. You don't have to do this."

What, he thought Rune was locked into some kind of contract? That this crusade wasn't entirely his own mission? His own *duty*? Anger rippled through him, strengthening his resolve. No one had *ordered* Rune down this path. Rune had chosen it for the sake of his own repentance. His own salvation. His own soul.

But this wasn't for him, not at the core. Rune was a servant of the One True God Illir, not because he wanted something in return, but because God did not deserve for His world to be tainted with the heretic's dark power. The necromancer Jovian had been cast off the earth — even in death — for a reason. Rune was merely finishing God's work.

No, this wasn't for his own sake. This was for God.

"I am not the one who needs help," Rune said, advancing closer to the necromancer. The man's pale eyes widened, and something within Rune curled with delight at the blatant terror in his gaze. It was a rush better than adrenaline, better than any human desire he'd ignored over the years. *This* was what fueled him — this rightful fear in the eyes of monsters meeting their comeuppance.

Rune grinned and slowly drew his dagger. The man had nowhere to run; to his right, a heap of rotting firewood blocked an easy escape. If he tried to dart left, Rune needed only to move a step to the side. Rune had him cornered, and now it was a question of whether the monster would actually put up a fight, or accept his fate.

Rune saw the necromancer's decision harden in his eyes a breath before he made a move. The man feigned left, obviously thinking Rune would move to block him, leaving his forward path open. But Rune anticipated that; when the man lurched to the left, Rune lunged forward and drove the dagger between his ribs, directly into his heart.

One move. One thrust. Rune pinned him against the side of the house and twisted the knife. The man gasped, breath catching on the blood rising to his throat. His eyes remained wide — still with fear, but also with surprise — staring blankly at Rune until the life bled out of them.

Rune grinned. Energy pulsed through him — God's power at work, he was sure. He felt alight, *alive*, his mind and body buzzing as if intoxicated. Rune lived for this rush. He *chased* this rush. In the first moments after the knife drove in, Rune felt the entire universe align in perfect synchrony.

"For God," Rune murmured, and let the body slump to the ground. Blood steadily leaked from the necromancer's chest, soaking into his shirt and gushing in viscous rivulets to the ground. Rune whistled a long, low note, and seconds later the followers he'd brought with him tonight were at his side.

Like all of Rune's followers, Jas and Finn moved soundlessly, like shadows, just as Rune had trained them. The two siblings were younger than others in the fellowship by half a decade — hardly more than children, which had initially given Rune pause, but in the months since they had joined, Jas and Finn had proved themselves as loyal and useful followers. Even if Finn was still clearly put off by the smell of blood; he hung back while Jas leaned over Rune's shoulder to get a closer look at the body.

"Whew," she muttered. "Well done, Master Rune."

Rune hummed with satisfaction. "Pass me the jar."

She tossed it at him haphazardly, and Rune nearly dropped it. He scowled at her carelessness, but it was an issue for another time. Rune had only minutes before the necromancer's blood would begin to congeal.

Rune tipped the edge of the jar against the dead man's chest and let the blood spill in. While he waited for the steady flow to fill it, he looked up at his followers. "You weren't seen or heard?"

"Course not," said Finn. He pushed the hood of his black cloak off his head and shook out his dark curls. "Not a sound from the neighbors."

Rune nodded. Good. It was a risk, approaching a house with so much light spilling outside, and with neighboring houses only a few hundred feet away across open land, Rune had feared the sound would carry. But he'd been quick, the man hadn't made much of a commotion, and if anyone had heard, surely they would have—

"Gabriel? What's taking you— What the *fuck*!"

Rune froze. His followers froze. His stomach dropped. For a heartbeat, the three of them stared back at the woman in the doorway, who stood with steadily growing horror in her eyes. She slowly brought her hand to her mouth, then her gaze locked with Rune.

He reeled in his shock and hardened his gaze to a glare. He clicked his tongue, and without hesitation Jas and Finn lunged at the woman before she could scream.

While they struggled, Rune looked down at the jar in his hand. Only half full, and the blood flow was slowing. *Come on.* He pressed the jar harder into the man's chest.

"No! *NO!*" The woman shrieked, struggling wildly against Rune's partners. "What have you done! *You fucking monsters! What have you done!*"

Rune gritted his teeth and prayed for the blood to pour faster. Just a little more, then he'd have enough. He tuned out the ongoing scuffle and focused, but then a hard shove sent him falling backwards, and sent the jar flying out of his hand.

"No!" Rune lunged for the jar, but the woman kicked him away, landing a hard blow to his shoulder. Rune winced and made for the jar again, but then froze when he saw the woman press her hands to the man's chest.

Time slowed. His heart thundered in his ears. The woman sobbed and begged, clenching her jaw. Her hands clutched the dead man's blood-soaked shirt. She closed her eyes, shoulders tensing, and Rune knew exactly what she was doing.

God have mercy, she was one of them too.

Jas didn't hesitate. She leapt at the woman, grabbing her by the shoulders and then around the neck. She thrashed and fought, kicking and elbowing Jas, but Jas held fast. She whipped out her dagger and had it across the necromancer's throat in seconds, then turned to Rune for the command.

Rune shook himself out of his shock. He scrambled to pick up the jar

— *shit*, too much blood had been lost — and then got to his feet. "Wait," he told Jas. He stood before the necromancer woman, calmly meeting her wild, wrathful gaze. "Don't kill her. Perhaps she can be of use to us."

The woman bared her teeth. "I'll kill you, you fucking monsters. You—" She cut off in a gasp as Jas inclined the edge of her blade against her throat.

"Be calm. We won't hurt you. But we're looking for something, and I have an inkling that you know how to find it." Rune searched her eyes. If she knew at all what he was talking about, she didn't show it.

Perhaps it was risky, and a little bit blasphemous, to invite the very monster Rune was working to eradicate into his close circles. But how did that old saying go? Keep your friends close, but your enemies closer?

If the stories were true, and necromancers — unfortunate souls cursed by witches with the dark magic Jovian had brought into the world — had an inherent connection to the resting place of the first necromancer, this woman could lead Rune and his partners straight to the source of dark magic. If Rune found the elusive tomb and destroyed it, thus erasing all vestiges of necromancy from the world, surely that was more than enough to atone him. And the dark stain would be wiped from his own soul for good.

Rune glanced at Finn and Jas in turn, who eyed him curiously. But he saw not a hint of suspicion in their gazes; they trusted their leader, as they should.

He met the necromancer woman's eyes again. "How much do you know about Jovian's Tomb?"

CHAPTER 1
WANING CRESCENT II

ATHERIS WAS LATE, and Saros was anxious.

He tried to give her the benefit of the doubt: Evyrmyre Academy, where Atheris had spent the past year studying magic, was at the heart of the city of Artunia; Artunia was three miles from the village of Kasvalta, the outskirts of which housed Saros's secluded cabin. The trek from the school to this cabin was approximately an hour on foot, and Atheris *was* only about thirty minutes late, meaning she might have left Evyrmyre at the time she was *supposed* to be here and therefore it would be another half hour of waiting and pacing before Atheris actually got here.

Saros knew that Atheris was notoriously late for everything, but he'd thought she understood how important this evening was. Surely she'd planned ahead so she wouldn't be backed up with work?

Who am I kidding? Saros thought, eyeing the front door with a sigh, *Of course she didn't plan ahead.*

He wished he had a way to contact Atheris and tell her to forget it and come back tomorrow at first light. It wouldn't be *too* late, even if Atheris found more issues with Saros's plans. Unless she found a lot of issues. And that was possible. Tonight really was the best time to solidify his plans, if he wanted to have enough time to revise them, but even still, Illir's Woods was no place to travel alone after dark.

Saros paced the drafty living room, conscious of the winter night's cold seeping in through the windows and under the door, but each time he passed by the hearth, he told himself he'd rile up a fire on the next lap.

Twenty minutes passed — still no Atheris — and he had made no effort to stop and heat the room. The effort of it... *Ugh*, was it even worth it? He had no spare logs next to the hearth, which meant he'd have to go outside and bring them in, and then he'd have to actually build and start the fire, which was a whole other ordeal thanks to the persistent tremor in his hands. He'd rather just get a blanket. If Atheris wanted a fire when she got here — if she ever did — she could make it herself. Saros was used to the cold.

He paused his pacing in the middle of the living room and fished his brass timepiece out of his pocket. Flipping it open, he told himself to look *only* at the clockface, but as always his eyes betrayed him and sought the faded photograph tucked into the watch's concave lid. A tiny, sepia-toned daguerreotype displayed a much younger Saros standing proudly with the person who had gifted him this timepiece — a person whose memory stung just as harshly as this image of his youthful face. Yet despite the tug on Saros's heartstrings each time he glanced at the time, he could not bring himself to remove the photograph. Sure, he could take it out, but then what? Burn it? Tear it into pieces and let the wind take it? No. He would not let go of the past so easily when there was still a slim, foolish chance to regain what he had lost. Each glance at this image reminded him of that.

These days, though, that hope seemed fainter than ever. Saros often forgot how much he had changed, and how much the fading had wasted him away. This photograph had been taken less than a decade ago, but the insatiable curse eating away at him had leeched the brown pigment from his hair, dulled his eyes, and turned his skin ghostly white. For a man of twenty-seven, he could have been mistaken for one of sixty. He hardly recognized the younger man in the photograph anymore; seven years of isolation often made him wonder if his past was merely a dream hallucinated out of desperation for something better than this.

Saros tugged the leather glove off his right hand. He flexed his stiff fingers and grimaced; the fading had worsened again this month. All five of his fingers were reduced to bone, with only a faint shadow of the flesh and skin that should have covered them. His wrists were starting to look translucent, too. If Saros didn't make a move to follow his plans within the next few days, by the next full moon, there might not be enough of him left to go on.

Outside, the wind howled through the trees and rattled the brittle window panes. Saros paced amid furniture and possessions that were not his — remnants of a life that had once inhabited this space and had been left to rot alongside him. The only items under this roof that belonged to him were contained in the single bedroom — day-to-day miscellany, a few books, fine clothes and expensive shoes he'd likely never wear again. There was no point in *living* here when he was likely to be dead within a few moon phases.

Saros had scarcely gotten his glove back on when the front door crashed open. He dropped the timepiece back into his pocket just as Atheris stomped into the house and kicked the door shut behind her.

"Illir's teeth, Saros, it's *freezing* in here! I think it's warmer outside!" She visibly shivered and crossed her arms tight over her chest, making her oversized coat bunch up around her neck as if swallowing her whole. Her freckled cheeks were flushed from the winter air, her ginger hair threatened to escape from its tiny bun on the top of her head, and her round glasses lay askew on her nose. She looked winded; had she *run* here?

"Good evening to you, too, Atheris." Saros suppressed a shiver of his own at the frigid air that had come in with her. *Fine*, maybe it was time to start a fire.

Atheris kicked off her boots, scattering snow and ice all over the floor, but kept her coat on and rubbed her hands together as she crossed the room and flopped onto the sofa. She propped her feet up on the arm, displaying socks with little white bears on them. "Hey, sorry I'm late. I forgot until this afternoon that I had an exam tonight, and I didn't expect it to take as long as it did. This one professor *swore* to us last week that this whole lesson on magic applied to alchemy would *not* be on this exam — which I thought was *tomorrow*, but whatever — but I'll give you one guess of what the *entire* last section of the exam was. The *entire last section*, Saros!" She heaved a groan and dropped her head down on the cushion. "They'd better curve our grades, is all I'm saying. Anyway. I'm here. You look disgruntled. What's wrong?"

Saros waited a second to make sure she was actually done talking. He glanced at the wall opposite the sofa, currently blank and free of obstructing furniture, but on which seven years' worth of research lay beneath a concealing spell. "Nothing is wrong," he said without much confidence. "But I made some alterations to the map since last time, if you'd take a look."

"Sure, yeah!" Atheris sat up and rubbed her hands together again, rings clacking against each other. "What're we digging into? Oh, speaking of which, do you have anything to eat? My expectations aren't high, but you must have *something*, right? I'm famished."

Saros raised an eyebrow. "They don't feed you at your fancy magic school?"

"It's bad luck to feed the roaches." She grinned.

He frowned. Hearing how Atheris was treated at Evyrmyre — by fellow students and professors alike — never failed to surprise him. Atheris had fought to earn her place at the academy just as well as everyone else. Saros was convinced they were all baffled and irked that she had landed a seat *without* a wealthy relative buying her in. But really, if inventing a new type of magic wasn't enough to win their respect, what possibly could? Saros didn't know why she bothered with them.

"Oh, come on, don't pretend you care that much." Atheris hopped off the sofa and strode toward the kitchen. "Don't start worrying about me now. Dealing with those rich snobs is nothing." She disappeared into the next room; Saros listened to her rummaging and knew she would come back disappointed. He had almost nothing stored in there; it was hard to find motivation to keep food in the house when he wasn't certain how much longer he'd be alive.

While Atheris was occupied with her search for food, Saros

grabbed his coat and boots and went outside for firewood. Cold winter wind bit straight through his clothes, and he fruitlessly tried to rub warmth into his numb hands. He grabbed three logs from the pile behind the cabin, brushing snow off them as he went back around front. His hands trembled, muscles straining around the dense weight of the logs. Saros didn't know when he'd lost so much strength, but it was yet another reminder that he was out of time.

He paused at the front door and looked up at the sky. The moon hid somewhere behind a thick blanket of clouds, but tonight it would only be a slim crescent. In a few days, it would disappear behind the shadow of its new phase, and Saros would bargain with fate. Would he survive another progression of the fading? Or would the curse finally claim him for good?

He hoped the new moon brought neither of those situations. If his plans were solid, he needn't worry about fading. He'd be free.

Let's see what Atheris has to say about that first.

Inside, Atheris was tearing into a days-old loaf of bread that Saros had forgotten he still had. She glared at the loaf as if it had personally insulted her — it *was* probably quite stale — but she ate it anyway.

"I'm not even going to offer you some of this," she said around a mouthful, "because it's like eating... I don't know, but not bread. Next time remind me to bring snacks."

Saros dropped the logs in the hearth and grabbed the flint from the mantel, then knelt to light it only to immediately recoil when something moved behind the wood.

"*Atheris*— God damn it!" Saros scowled at the black snake cheekily curled up at the back of the hearth.

Atheris burst out laughing. "Never gets old. It's just Crescent, Saros! She won't hurt you. She's not even venomous."

"I do not care." He sent the creature a disdainful look. "Get the snake out of the fireplace, or it goes up in flames."

Atheris gasped. "You would never."

He wouldn't, but he sent her a pointed look. "Try me."

Atheris narrowed her eyes, but a smirk curled at the corner of her mouth and Saros knew she didn't believe he was serious. She leaned down and held out her hand to the snake, making a kissing noise at it.

Saros grimaced as the creature crawled up Atheris's arm, coiling its iridescent black body all the way up to her shoulder. He had had that snake wrapped around his own arm exactly once, and the memory of those smooth, cold scales made his skin crawl to this day.

"So dramatic, isn't he?" Atheris cooed to the snake. She gently patted her finger on the top of its head, and it flicked its black tongue at Saros.

He scowled back, then returned his attention to lighting the fire. His hand trembled as he went to strike the flint against the hearth's stone floor, and it took him a few tries to get a spark. When the flame finally caught, he sat back on his heels and watched until the fire grew and began to devour the logs.

"I dunno why you bother with flint," Atheris said. "What're you, a caveman? Why don't you get a fire amulet?"

Right, because that was so easy. "Magic doesn't interest me," he lied.

"You are so full of shit." Atheris snorted.

Saros scowled and got up from the floor, dusting off his gloved hands. "They're hard to find. Besides, why go through the trouble when flint works just fine?"

"Because magic is awesome?" Atheris shrugged. The black snake was now draped around her neck like a scarf, intertwined cozily with a white serpent of the same species. "Also, for what it's worth, fire amulets might be hard to find *here*, but they're in every other shop in Artunia."

"How convenient for everyone in Artunia." Saros went across the room to hang up his coat by the door. He set his boots on the floor underneath it, and with a disdainful look in Atheris's direction (which she didn't see), he slid her discarded boots across the floor and placed them neatly beside his own.

Saros hovered by the door and watched Atheris poke around the living room. She always found something new she hadn't discovered before, something to question or fiddle with or steal when she thought he wasn't looking. He didn't care. The stuff wasn't his. His grandmother, who had lived here before Saros did, had collected anything and everything. His parents used to call her Grandmother

Crow because of her collections of random items. No one had bothered to clean or throw anything out when she had died, and certainly not for Saros's sake when his father had sent him here.

Atheris could take or break whatever she wanted. It wasn't her kleptomania that worried him, it was her insistent nosy tendencies. Even an innocent question about magic might have opened the door to many other questions Saros was sure she had queued up.

What's with the gloves?

Why are you so reclusive?

Why are you so obsessed with this research you've roped me into?

What are you hiding from me?

Saros trusted Atheris, but she didn't know the whole story, and he wished to keep it that way. A curious girl by nature, she would ask too many questions. For all her scatterbrained faults and inability to focus on one task for more than two minutes at a time, Atheris was smart as a whip. She unraveled things, and if Saros gave her an inch, she'd unravel *him*. Her help was invaluable to him, and he would never have gotten this far without her, but he couldn't bring himself to tell her anything more than she already knew. He kept conversations about their research focused on the mythology, the history, and the patterns in the sky — the facts, not the backstory that had led Saros to this obsession.

If Atheris was more like a friend and less like an academic colleague, Saros might confide in her. He didn't want to push her away; he enjoyed her company, he liked hearing her talk through his research and theories (even when she was ripping them apart), and she undoubtedly brought some brightness to this dreary cabin. Besides, he doubted she'd leave him alone even if he asked.

Saros didn't mind. It had been a long time since he'd had anything close to a friend. Seven years of isolation would do that to you.

"How are you alive?" Atheris drew his attention back to her. She was at the far end of the room, holding a dusty jewelry box in one hand and poking through its contents with the other. "There is literally — and I mean *literally* — just shit in this house. If none of it's yours, why do you keep it around? Is *anything* here actually yours? Also, when's the last time you went into town? Your kitchen is empty except for that bread that doesn't deserve the honor of being called bread. Good grief, Saros, go to the marketplace. Good *grief*, I sound like my mother."

Saros rolled his eyes and snapped his fingers a few times to summon Zenith, his familiar. He heard a faint *thunk* from his bedroom, where she must have been perched on the windowsill, and a moment later she made her way into the main room. "There you are," Saros murmured, leaning down to stroke his hand along her black fur. She meowed and circled his legs, then darted over to the blank wall running along the front side of the living room.

"You already know what we're up to, huh? Show me, Zenith."

She pressed her front paws to the wall, then touched her nose to it. Ripples ringed around the point of contact, and when the spell dropped, Saros's research appeared. Seven years of careful records, predictions, and scratched-out dead ends became visible on the formerly blank, whitewashed wall.

Atheris went to Saros's side and grinned. "That never gets old."

"Better than pranking me with your snakes?"

"Hmmm... No, actually."

Saros hadn't thought so. But she was right about the spell being extraordinary every time they witnessed it, and it was thanks to Atheris's own brilliance that it worked. Not only had she invented the magic that powered the spell, she had also helped train Saros's cat to understand and work with the magic.

"Nature is *made* of illusions," Atheris had explained while pacing the length of Saros's cabin one windy evening last winter. "Nature conceals, in camouflage and false eyes on fishes' fins and moths' wings. Nature *hides* — with dense foliage and pelts that change to match the brown of autumn and white of winter. We can adapt these illusions for our lives just as we borrow other powers the natural world provides. It just requires a little thinking outside the box."

Apparently, no one else had ever tried illusionary magic before, and Atheris's ideas combined with her success in making it work had won her a golden ticket into Evyrmyre. Saros was happy for her, but to this day he couldn't help feeling a little stung as well.

That was supposed to be his life. He'd had goals, plans, a whole future mapped out. But then the curse had claimed him, and then he'd been sent away to this precipice of Illir's Woods, and then the fading had begun.

Now, no academy would dare accept him even if he did have the energy to devote to academics. Not unless he succeeded in what he planned to do this week.

Despite Saros's lack of formal education, the magic Atheris had taught him came easily to him — with the help of his familiar, of course. Zenith wasn't really a true, trained familiar, but like all animals she had inherent magical abilities, and if there was one thing she loved to do, it was hide things.

She circled his feet now and nudged his ankles with her head until he bent down and lifted her into his arms. She stared at the wall, eyes wide and ears alert, as if there was something for her to find in these notes, too. But Saros doubted that *anyone* other than himself and Atheris could make sense of all this.

To anyone else, this wall looked like the ramblings of a madman. Across the top, as close to the ceiling as he could get, Saros had charted the night sky for the past seven years. Underneath the cycle of constellations, he had drawn the monthly phases of the moon in precise detail. The moon, he had learned, was the map; its shape and its position with the stars determined the appearance of Jovian's Tomb.

It wasn't a literal tomb, not in the traditional sense. Nothing could be that easy. Jovian's Tomb was a lake. Rich with magical properties, it appeared and then vanished every month, relocating as cyclically as the moon. Saros had been trying to track its appearances for years, and after two fruitless searches, he finally understood its pattern.

He thought. He hoped. If he was correct — and this time, he had to be — the tomb should appear five days from now, on the first night of the new moon, somewhere within this very forest.

The only problem was that Illir's Woods went on for endless miles, and was utterly unpredictable. No one had ever successfully mapped the farthest reaches of the Woods, hence the name: only the god Illir knew its boundaries. Saros lived at the edge of the sprawling forest, and rarely dared to venture any deeper unless he had a sharp knife and ample daylight ahead of him. He did not wish to know which of the forest's legendary monsters were real.

If Saros's charts were accurate, the stars should lead him straight to the site of the lake. If that wasn't enough, Saros could feel its power pulling him toward it. It was an instinct within him, like a creeping sense that he was being watched. He felt the lake's presence growing ever stronger as the moon phased toward darkness. It spoke to his magic — his curse — like calling to like.

Saros flexed his hands. He was used to the numb cold, had learned to deal with the constant tremble, but now his bones were starting to hurt. He could not be wrong again. He could not miss this appearance of the tomb. He was out of time. Another passing moon cycle would kill him; he was sure of it.

He glanced at Atheris beside him, whose attention was glued to the notes. Her green eyes darted back and forth behind her glasses, and a crease formed between her brows as she read. Her lips moved in silent whispers as she talked out Saros's map to herself.

He had to wonder what she made of all this. He knew she knew about the lake — perhaps not the *entire* myth, but she had seen it before and obviously understood that it was supernatural. But did she have a suspicion that there was more to it than an interest in proving the impossible? Did she see more than Saros wanted her to see?

Although, she would likely make it known if she drew any conclusions about Saros's real reason for tracking the tomb. If she knew the truth about him and his curse, she'd be able to see it as clearly as Saros could see his own bones through his skin.

He was relieved she didn't know. Hell, if she did, she might not be here at all. Saros would be left to weave his plans all on his own, and he would never know if he'd miscalculated until the moment something went wrong. He owed so much to Atheris, but it did not add up to the price of telling her the actual truth.

It was a crime, after all, to know of a necromancer and neglect to report them to the magi.

Not that Atheris was much of a stickler for following laws like that, but still, with the way she gossiped, Saros doubted she could keep a secret of that magnitude. He didn't trust that she wouldn't let something slip, and he could not afford that risk. Not when he was so close to finding the tomb and finally putting the curse to rest.

Once he found the tomb and his magic was silenced — perhaps even taken from him, if he was lucky — *then* he could tell Atheris the truth.

But by then, what was the point? It was better if no one knew. Once it was gone and he was cured (and hopefully still alive), it wouldn't matter anymore.

"So what exactly am I looking for? Is there more?" Atheris's voice brought him out of his thoughts, and he realized he hadn't really been reading what he was looking at. "What part do you want me to shred to pieces? You know, it really feeds my ego that you value my intelligence so much. Wish those snobs at Evyrmyre saw in me what you do."

She spoke flippantly, but Saros recognized the warmth in her words. He was relieved to hear that she knew he valued her, and that she didn't think he was just using her as a means to an end.

He nodded at the wall. "No, there isn't more. This is everything. So you tell me. What part needs to be shredded? What's a little off, or too much of an estimation, or as you like to say, *utterly made-up bullshit?*"

She snickered and nudged him aside to get a better look at the section of wall he'd been not-reading. Saros nearly stumbled at her shove; he hadn't expected that much strength from a person barely clearing five feet.

"You know, I never thought I'd say this," Atheris muttered, "but I think you've actually got it this time."

Saros stared at her and held his breath, waiting for the joke's punchline to land. But she said nothing more, and when he didn't say anything, she turned to him.

"No, seriously. Like, for once that wasn't sarcasm. I can't find anything wrong with this. If you follow the stars exactly as you've got them charted here, and time your travel carefully so you don't lose the moonlight, you'll walk directly into the lake."

Saros let out a breath and seven years of stress sloughed off his shoulders with it. "Y-You're sure? There's no fatal mistakes this time?"

"That, I couldn't tell you." Atheris smirked. "You might dig your own grave on the way, or eat something poisonous, or get a terrible snake bite" — she grinned as Saros glared at her — "but no, your tracking is flawless. Borderline obsessive, actually. I wouldn't tell you it was solid if it wasn't. I know how important this is to you."

She didn't, actually, but he appreciated that she cared beyond her own academic interest.

"The key this time," Atheris continued with a wave toward the wall, "is that you're not *guessing*. Everything backing up your predicted location — the stars, the exact percentage of the moon's light, the past pattern of appearances — is an educated hypothesis determined by solid facts and careful records. There's no holes in your logic, and no errors in your calculations this time."

Saros sighed. "You're never going to let the math incident go, are you?"

Atheris grinned. "Never. But Saros — I'm serious. You've done it. You've done it!" She clapped. "Okay, I have one question, though."

Saros was so dizzy with relief that he would've told her anything at all. "What's that?"

She stared at him like it should've been obvious. "Uh, when do we leave?"

CHAPTER 2
WANING CRESCENT III

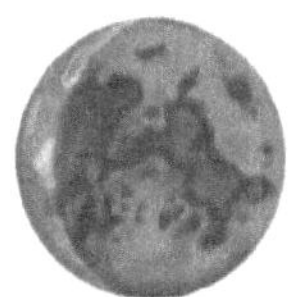

"WE?"

Atheris stared at Saros. "Um, yes, *we*. I thought that was the deal! I tell you about my sighting, I help you solidify your calculations, *I* bring you a goddamned meal every once in a while so you don't *die*, and in return, I tag along." She lifted her hands. "I share the grand adventure! I get to see that lake again so I know I didn't hallucinate it the first time. Tell me that's unfair in any way."

He narrowed his eyes. "Don't you have exams?"

"Last one was tonight."

Saros shook his head. He shouldn't even entertain this idea. "No. No, Atheris. This isn't some storybook adventure. We're not going for *fun*. Maybe it's a curiosity for you, but this is my life."

To Saros's confusion, Atheris grinned.

He frowned. "What?"

"You said *we*."

"What?"

"You said '*we're* not going for fun.' Call that a subconscious slip. Come on, do you really want to go into Illir's Woods alone?"

"Atheris."

"Saros." She lightly nudged his arm. "You act all moody and reclusive out here, but you want to know what I think?"

She paused, but Saros knew she would say it whether or not he wished to hear it. He raised an eyebrow.

"I think," she went on as expected, "that underneath your stormy personality and tendency to hermit, you're lonely."

Saros's heart stuttered with a blip of surprise, but the feeling quickly twisted into anger. He rarely let Atheris's blunt observations sink in their claws — especially since he knew she wasn't wrong — but he didn't like it when she read him so easily.

He turned away from her and snapped his fingers to catch Zenith's attention. "Conceal, Zenith," he said, and the cat touched her nose to the wall. Saros's notes vanished.

Atheris wasn't deterred. "Am I wrong?"

"You don't know a damned thing about me, Atheris," Saros grumbled. He picked up Zenith and stroked his hand down her back, avoiding Atheris's gaze. But after a minute Zenith squirmed and he set her down, then slipped his hand into his pocket and gripped the timepiece. He focused on its familiar shape, its solid weight in his palm. The brass would leave a faint metallic odor on his glove; an invisible bloodstain.

He wasn't unknowable. He knew there were things that bled through the cracks, pieces of him that he tried to hide but Atheris found anyway. He knew Atheris, clever and perceptive as she was, had her assumptions about him — and those assumptions probably bordered the truth. Saros told himself he didn't care what she thought, as long as she didn't say it. A very small part of him wanted to let her know him, but he couldn't get past the barrier that his instincts had raised. If she, too, turned on him once she learned about the curse, the only person to blame was himself.

There had been a time when he wasn't reluctant to let others know him, but it was easier now to hide everything behind a mask. Saros didn't wish to be a phantom, never fully perceived, but what choice did he have? As long as the necromantic curse had ahold of his soul, he could never live a normal life among normal people. The family he'd once had had made that quite clear when they'd cast him away.

Atheris could try all she wanted to dig under his skin, but she could never know everything. As long as he wanted her in his life — and he did — she could not know the truth. That was Saros's one unbreakable rule: *no one* could know everything. Only one person did, and only that one person ever would. Saros had learned, from that very person, that not all of him was worth knowing.

He resented that Atheris saw through him so easily, but after spending a year around someone as chatty and carefree as her, of course he'd let his guard down. Her openness was contagious, and Saros felt lighter around her than he had in years. So yes, of *course* he was lonely. Of course he wanted Atheris to be his friend — with no secrets or walls between them. She had shown time and again that she didn't judge him for his reclusive lifestyle, or his apparent exile, or his secrecy. She certainly had questions, but she didn't push him. He appreciated that.

He just hated giving her the satisfaction of knowing she was correct about him. When he turned to her again, crossing his arms, he saw on her face that she knew he'd caved. He didn't have the energy to argue with her. And after all, Illir's Woods should not be traveled alone.

He prayed that he wouldn't regret this. "You may not ask any intrusive questions. You may not bring any friends, or spring any surprises on me, or turn us into a caravan. We are going to find the lake, and that's it. No detours, no stops to admire the scenery, no tangents." He raised his eyebrows, making an effort not to look amused by the unmasked glee on her face. "Understand?"

Atheris bounced on her toes, nodding enthusiastically. Her grin outshone the goddamned sun. "Yes! Yes, got it, we're good. Oh, this is amazing, Saros! *Thank you*. I can't believe you really said yes. That's a big step for you, you know. Accepting companionship? That's a step toward having, like, an actual *friend*." Her grin softened a little. "Glad it's me."

He looked away from her and down at the floor. Zenith blinked up at him. "Just understand that there is something real at stake here. It's not just an academic obsession."

He felt her eyes on him as she waited for him to say more, and he could sense her curiosity. He knew she wanted an explanation; she was a scholar at heart, as Saros himself was, never satisfied with an unanswered question. But Saros knew her well enough to know she wouldn't press. And she knew *him* well enough to know she wouldn't get anywhere by demanding answers he didn't want to give. In that respect, they understood each other.

When Saros glanced back up at her, her mood had sobered. She caught his gaze and nodded once. "I get it." But she could never stay serious for long, and soon the smirk was back. She shoved her glasses up her nose and then set a hand on her hip. "You are a mysterious entity, Saros Antarian."

He exhaled a vague semblance of humor. "Good. If you're really coming with me, go home and pack. Be back here at dawn. If you're late I'm leaving without you."

He meant it lightly, but apparently his tone failed to convey that. Atheris flinched, then nodded and turned to leave. Uncomfortable silence stretched between them as she stepped into her boots and flipped up the collar on her coat. But she paused before she opened the door, and looked up at him with an odd frown creasing her brows.

"You wouldn't really leave without me, would you?"

Saros blinked, surprised at the emotion weighing her voice. "No. I wouldn't. But... you can't be late like you were tonight."

"Well, tonight it didn't matter because—"

"I know," he said softly. "But tomorrow matters. Every hour matters. We have four nights to track this lake."

And I have four nights to live, he added silently.

"I know."

Saros swallowed. "Okay."

She nodded and opened the door. "Please don't leave me behind."

She left before Saros could find a response to that.

Saros sat on the old sofa across from his wall of notes and stared at his hands. His gloves lay draped over his knee, at the ready so he could grab them and hide his hands when Atheris arrived. But for now his hands were bare, and as he read over the notes one last time, he absently flexed his fingers in a hopeless effort to work the aches out and some warmth in.

It wouldn't actually make a difference; what was faded was gone — at least until he dipped his hands into the waters of Jovian's Tomb. Even still, Saros didn't know if that would cure the parts of him that had already faded, or if it would simply halt the affliction from progressing.

He tugged his sleeve back and eyed the grayness creeping up his forearm. It wasn't as far gone as his hands, but it was still a chilling sight to watch his veins steadily blacken and his skin gradually lose its opacity. There was something distinctly *incorrect* about being able to see his bones through his skin.

What would happen, he wondered, if he were to fade entirely? Would he become an animated corpse, drained of all signs of life? Would he disappear completely, vanishing like a ghost? Would he even survive that long?

Saros didn't intend to find out.

It had been seven years since the first and only time he'd actually used his power, but the fading progressed nonetheless. Every moon phase, it spread, and he assumed his ultimate death would come when it consumed all of him. Or maybe when it reached his heart? For all his research, Saros barely knew anything about his own curse. None of the stories mentioned anything like this affliction he suffered.

Either way, he could feel his body dying. The magic dragged him under, chained him down.. He did not have another month to spare if he failed to find Jovian's Tomb in five days.

It had to be now. It had to be this week. Five short days were all that stood between him and the rest of his life, and it was all too possible that five days were all he had left.

If his theories about the tomb were correct, the lake's water should soothe his restless magic and put it at ease so that it didn't eat away at his soul and weaken his body. That alone would be a welcome change, but Saros's deeper wish — the one he hardly dared to voice lest the gods snatch the chance from his hands — was for the lake to lift his curse entirely.

Necromancy was not a natural force of magic. For normal people *not* cursed with this dark power, magic was an academic interest. Except for in rare cases of being born a witch, magic wasn't intrinsic; anyone could learn to use the powers provided by the natural world. But necromancy was a part of Saros; it was a hunger inside him that was desperate to feed off his life.

According to the family that had sent him away, he had been cursed as a child, though Saros remembered no such incident. But he did remember the aftermath: years of being sequestered away from other children, forbidden from getting too close to anyone. He was hidden and silenced and told to ignore any interest in magic while other children his age were learning and experimenting with nature's power.

As the years had passed and Saros's curse had remained dormant, his family had loosened their control over him. His life had crept back to normal and he'd dived straight into the study of magic, immersing himself in this world of knowledge he'd been deprived of as a child. He'd found a path for his life to follow. He'd started to fall in love with the world again — and with one beloved friend who had adamantly refused to let him be alone all that time.

His life had become so easy and normal that he had all but forgotten about the curse.

Until finally, it had come alive. Seven years ago, the summer he turned twenty, the magic had burst to life within him and yanked itself out of his control. He hadn't even realized what was happening until it was over, but he would never forget that moment of horror when he realized what he was.

Being cursed was one thing. That, he'd lived with. But being a necromancer was a death sentence.

Next thing he knew, his life and everything he'd grown to love had been torn away from him. And this cabin — his grandmother's dusty, drafty old home, still inhabited with all her things — had become his entire world.

To this day, he could not believe that saving his best friend's life — an instinct of deep, selfless love — had landed him in this situation. That the magic was killing him in exchange for the life he had restored was a cruel sort of poetry.

Saros clasped his hands together and looked up at the wall. He scanned the notes yet again, searching for inconsistencies or holes or errors he already knew he wouldn't find. And he was relieved that he had a real chance this time, but it was also strange to think that it was over. More than half a decade of his life had been devoted to this obsessive study, and despite his desperation for it to finally reach fruition, he had no idea what came next.

He supposed it all depended on what Jovian's Tomb could do for him. For all he knew, there was *nothing* coming next.

But no. After all this, Saros refused to believe that it was for nothing. He'd seen enough consistencies in the myths to make him believe that Jovian's Tomb could save him. He knew the stories — Jovian, the first necromancer; witches and their unusually strong power; the lake and its impermanence. He had spent countless hours searching for connections across centuries of mythology and hints of real history among them. A myth was only fiction if enough closed-minded academics decided so; there was a core of truth in every legend if you knew where to look.

Jovian wasn't just a villain in a story; he was a real man who had seized remarkable power, stepping away from humanity into something worse. Upon his death, he had tainted the earth in which he was buried, and the god Illir could not stand to see His beloved earth infected with such evil. He refused to allow Jovian to lie at peace in any one spot, and thus, his tomb appeared in a new location once per month under the new moon.

Jovian's Tomb might not be the direct cause of each existing necromantic curse, but it was the source of all dark magic. Witches alone had the power to draw from the lake to cast their curses, and necromancy was by far the worst. Its practice was a sin, an offense to the gods — no matter which ones you believed in — and its practitioner... practically demonic. Saros didn't know of a single other living necromancer. If they existed, they kept themselves well hidden just like he did. He shuddered to think of what had happened to the unlucky ones.

Looking at his notes now, he wondered if he was the first to search for the tomb, or if he was the next in a long line of fools chasing after a myth.

It's not just a myth, he reminded himself. He couldn't let any doubts creep into his mind. Jovian's Tomb might be a legend, but it was most certainly real. There had been dozens of sightings across the years, reports from travelers and hunters stumbling upon a glassy body of water that they knew had never been there before. When the lake vanished just as suddenly, the sightings were written off as hallucinations scrambling the minds of travel-weary hunters and merchants. Saros had tried to track down and speak to some of those witnesses, but each lead was a dead end. It seemed those who had seen Jovian's Tomb wished to erase themselves from the world.

The only person Saros had managed to find, and who was more than willing to recount her sighting, was Atheris Fay.

A loud *CLUNK* jolted Saros from his thoughts. He pulled his gloves back on just in time for Atheris to burst through the front door, panting and gasping as if she'd run all the way here from Artunia. Her hair was a frizzy, disheveled mess, and her oversized coat flapped open. As always, her serpentine familiars were draped around her neck. "You're still here!"

Saros frowned. "You're not late." Also, he had promised.

Atheris slumped against the wall, catching her breath. "The sun just came up. I thought..."

Saros stood from the couch and told Zenith to conceal the notes on the wall, then approached Atheris. "I told you I wouldn't leave without you. I don't break promises. Let me get my things, and..." He glanced at the wall again, though it was blank now.

He had his instincts, he had his calculations, and he had the stories. He had studied everything he'd been able to get his hands on. He had copied all of the correct charts onto paper so he could bring a physical map. He *was* ready.

But what if it wasn't enough?

"Saros." The floor creaked as Atheris moved closer to him. "Come on, you're the one who threatened to leave me in the dust if I wasn't here exactly at dawn, and now you're staring at that wall like it changed overnight." She let her bag fall from her shoulder and it hit the floor with a solid *thunk*. "I told you, it's solid. Waterproof. *Fool*proof, even. My grandmama couldn't find a problem in there, and listen, if you think *I'm* nitpicky and too perceptive, I am a *deity* compared to Grandmama. I have never met another person so keen to make everyone around her develop a self-esteem problem."

Saros closed his eyes, rubbing his forehead. "Are you ready?"

She nodded.

Saros glanced down as Zenith bumped her head against his ankle. "What about you?" he murmured, lifting her into his arms. "Want to go on a little trip?"

She chirped in reply and climbed up onto his shoulder. Saros took a final look around the main room, eyes scanning across all the old furniture and keepsakes and boxes of things that weren't his. After this week, there was a good chance he'd never have to come back to this cabin. This lonely, secluded place would no longer be all he knew. He could return to the wider world, maybe not here in Kasvalta, but he could go anywhere. Perhaps he would join Atheris at Evyrmyre and return to the path he'd always wanted to follow.

And maybe, just maybe, he could find Rune again too.

As he gathered up his packed bag and grabbed his coat from the hook next to the door, he felt his future opening up before him. His doubts about this journey fled. Something was going to change in the next five days; he could feel it. This was not the end of the line.

Saros shrugged on his coat and dragged the door open, then turned to Atheris. "Let's go."

CHAPTER 3
WANING CRESCENT IV

IT TOOK LESS than an hour for Illir's Woods to show its true colors. While Saros and Atheris traveled in companionable silence, Saros focused on the pull toward the lake and Atheris gazing around with wonder, the Woods peered back. Literally. Giant, round eyes — some with pale, colored irises like those of humans, others entirely black or blood-red or white — rolled in their sockets on the tree trunks and intently tracked Saros and Atheris's movement. Saros tried not to stare back, but dozens of eyes upon him from every angle set him on edge; he found himself startling at every birdcall and snapped twig.

Atheris, on the other hand, was apparently unbothered by the eyeballs embedded in the tree trunks. Saros was tempted to point them out just to be sure he wasn't the only one seeing them. Then again, if Atheris cut through patches of this forest frequently to shorten her trek to Saros's cabin, this was probably normal to her.

The leaves whispered. Birds Saros had never seen or heard before chattered overhead; a glimpse showed some with four wings instead of two, with bat-like claws on the joints where they bent. Furry critters skittered up tree trunks and soared among the canopy, some gliding on outstretched skin, others with feathered wings. Deer and deer-like animals with long legs and twisty antlers gazed at Saros and Atheris from behind the gnarled trees, and canines baring many rows of sharp teeth barked and growled before darting away.

It was a forest, vibrant and alive. The sounds were familiar even if the creatures weren't, but Saros reasoned that as long as he didn't bother them, they wouldn't bother him.

Around midday, they stopped by a clear stream to refill their canteens, and Saros could tell that Atheris was desperate to talk after a whole morning of saying almost nothing. Saros had never seen her be quiet for this long. It was actually a little unsettling.

He twisted the cap back on his canteen and tucked it in the pocket on the side of his bag, then looked at Atheris as they continued their trek forward. "Tell me about your sighting of the lake."

That was all he had to say.

Atheris's face lit up even brighter than it had when he'd agreed to her traveling with him. "I— Wait." She narrowed her eyes. "But you've already heard this story."

"So tell me again," Saros said. "Remind me of the details. Maybe there's something I overlooked the first time."

Atheris scrunched her nose. "Are you sure? Because you are definitely a 'It physically hurts me to hear the same story more than once' type of person."

Saros raised an eyebrow and just waited, knowing she wouldn't be able to resist now that he'd asked.

Sure enough, she let no more than five seconds pass before launching into her tale. "Okay, well, it was a little over a year ago, right, just before I met you. I was traveling to Artunia for school, and I was on the main road coming into the city with at *least* a couple hundred other people. I have to emphasize that because there *were* witnesses. It wasn't just me." She huffed. "Anyway, we were all moving pretty steadily toward the city, and then all at once everyone stopped. We reached a flood of backed up traffic. I kept going and shoved my way through the crowd, thinking I'd find a different road into the city and avoid whatever was going on, but then I got closer to the gates and I saw why everyone had stopped: there was a whole fucking lake in the middle of the outer city. I had never been to Artunia before, but I was *pretty sure* there—"

"Go back to the lake," Saros said. "What did it look like? What did it *feel* like?"

She glanced at him. "You didn't ask that before. How did you know that it felt like something?"

"It's a magic lake, Atheris. Why wouldn't it have some sort of sense surrounding it?"

"Okay, fair. But I dunno... it was unnatural. That's the best word I can find. It was just *wrong*. It didn't belong there. I mean, not only did it not belong *there* outside the city, but it was like it didn't belong in the world." She crossed her arms. "I saw the thing in broad daylight, but it was black as night. No movement. No reflections."

Saros nodded. Sounded right. A place cursed to never occupy any one location surely would give off an energy of not belonging.

"I also— I didn't tell you this before," Atheris continued. "But I felt, like, compelled toward it. I wanted to get closer, to look directly into the water. I... Oh, this is going to sound so crazy."

"No, what is it?"

Atheris was quiet for a long minute. "I felt like it had something I wanted. Like it *knew* that it had something I wanted, and if I just went closer..."

Saros looked at her. She hadn't said anything like this before, only told him that she'd seen the lake, and her description had confirmed it was indeed Jovian's Tomb. "So did you?"

She met his eyes. "Did I what?"

"Go closer. Look in."

"No." Atheris abruptly turned her head as something took flight in the trees overhead. "I found a way into the city as far from the lake as possible, and the whole time I couldn't shake the feeling that none of it was real. It was like the world had shifted a little off center, like in a dream. Like the lake itself was trying to convince me that it wasn't real, I didn't see it, and I'd wake up and be back home. But it *was* real." She shoved her hands into her coat pockets. "It was. Other people saw it. It *has* to be real."

"I believe you," Saros said. He would not have asked for her help if he'd thought she'd made the whole thing up.

Atheris scoffed. "That makes you the only one."

Really? All those people had seen the lake, and... what? Decided to forget about it? Wrote it off as an exhaustion-induced hallucination caused by long hours of travel?

It wouldn't surprise Saros if the magi and town guards in Artunia went out of their way to silence whispers of a sighting of the tomb — they went out of their way to insist necromancy didn't exist at all — but with all those people as witnesses... It wasn't as though they could stop that many people from talking about the appearance. The question was whether anyone *dared* to speak of it.

Jovian was not an unknown legend. He was infamous, the villain of the god Illir's story. Illir's defeat of Jovian was a significant piece of the backbone of faith for those who followed the god; Jovian was the darkness to Illir's light. His tomb, of course, was the vindicating conclusion to the story. Saros could safely guess that most — if not all — of the people outside Artunia that day knew exactly what they had seen, and perhaps that was why so few of them chose to speak of it.

He glanced at Atheris. "When did the lake disappear?"

She was gazing into the trees again, and it took her a second to realize he'd said something. "Huh? Oh. It was gone by morning. When I went back to the outer city the following evening, the lake wasn't there. Vanished, like it had never been there at all. I knew what I saw, but looking out there that night, I doubted everything. I have never felt my memory and my logic battle each other so strongly. I *knew* what I had seen, but my rationality was like, 'How could there have possibly been a lake there twelve hours ago?' Nothing was damaged or disrupted on the landscape. It was like the lake literally did not touch the earth."

"Mhmm." And perhaps that confusion and doubt and fear was what kept most people from seeking out the lake again after seeing it once.

"So yeah, obviously all I want is to see this lake again," Atheris went on. She lifted a hand and fiddled with the amulets strung on a leather cord around her neck. "I want to understand it. I want to know why it's even here. What does *it* want?"

Saros eyed her curiously. He'd never considered that the tomb — or Jovian himself — might *want* something aside from a few precious hours in the mortal realm.

"What has *you* set upon this weird lake, anyway?" Atheris said. "All you've said is that it's important to you, life-or-death or whatever, but that's pretty dramatic, isn't it? What does it have to do with you? And who *is* Jovian, anyway? Friend of yours?"

That almost got a laugh out of Saros, simply because it was absurd and yet... almost accurate. He and Jovian did have something in common, but Saros wouldn't willingly compare himself to a man who had *chosen* to be a necromancer. Saros was a victim; Jovian had dug his own grave.

"Hey, those weren't rhetorical questions," Atheris said. "Those were actual, looking-for-answers types of questions that I *know* you know the—"

"How do you expect me to answer you when you don't let me get a word in?" Saros grumbled.

"One of us has to fill the silence! You take five-minute breaks between every one-syllable reply. Feels like I'm talking to myself." She traced her fingers down the white snake's head. "Gonna start talking to Crescent and Moon instead. Or Zenith. I bet she'd talk to me."

"Unlike some of those present, I don't feel compelled to fill the air with chatter."

Atheris rolled her eyes. "Fine, be grumpy, but I still want you to answer my questions."

And Saros would, but what he was really doing was stalling until he sorted out what he could safely tell her. He was taking a risk talking about this at all with someone as perceptive as Atheris.

He absently scratched the top of Zenith's head. "Jovian was someone who turned against the gods. He wanted power, he reached too far, and he was punished for it."

"Oh? Do I smell a myth? A classic case of 'learn a lesson by watching some guy tremendously fuck up?'"

"It's not a myth," Saros said. "Jovian was a real person, and there are reliable records of his existence. Some of the less reliable stories say he was one of the old gods, but I doubt that."

"Are you implying that the old gods were real?" Atheris said.

"Allegedly." This part of the story bled heavily into myth and theology, and Saros had never been able to pin down the accurate truth. According to the stories, the old gods — Jovian included — were killed by Illir, but Saros was more inclined to believe that it was *mortals* who had written the gods out of existence. History had killed them — history, and a growing movement toward monotheistic belief systems that left no room for any gods other than Illir, the so-called "True God."

"Jovian may have been god*like*, but he was a mortal, no matter how much he tried to deny it himself," Saros continued. "It was because of Illir, however, that the lake — Jovian's final resting place — never appears in the same place twice."

"But why?" Atheris studied Saros intently as they wove through the foliage, and he had to pull on her sleeve so she didn't walk straight into a tree. "What did Jovian—" Her eyes widened. "Oh, shit, did he kill the old gods?"

Saros wished it was that simple, and he almost said yes just to keep her away from the actual truth of the story. But despite everything, he didn't want to lie to Atheris. He wished he didn't have to. "No. He didn't kill any gods."

"Damn. Okay, then what?"

He hesitated. If he told her the whole truth — at least, as much as he'd been able to piece together from the fragments of history he'd dug up over the years — Atheris would easily connect him to the story and thus to necromancy. He had told her, time and again, that his obsession with the lake went beyond a mere curiosity. He'd told her it was personal. That was his first mistake. If she figured it out... Then what? He truly had no idea how she would react.

"*Saros*," Atheris whined. "Come *on*, you can't leave me in suspense like this!"

He shook off his worry. "Right, like I said, he tried to become too powerful, and Illir punished him for trying to be a god." That wasn't untrue, but it was the barest bones of truth and Saros was sure Atheris knew it as much as he did. "And that's probably why some stories say he *was* a god. Whatever he did, it nearly made him..." He glanced at Atheris and found her enraptured. "This sounds dramatic, but whatever power Jovian tried to seize, it truly made him almost divine. You can imagine how the 'True God' Illir didn't like that."

"Illir's a little bitch," Atheris said, and a laugh burst out of Saros. Atheris's eyes lit up. "Oh my *god*, did you just laugh?"

He instantly smothered the humor. "No."

"Shut the hell up," Atheris cackled, "I can't believe you actually laughed! At *me*! This is all I ever needed, Saros, for you to genuinely think I'm funny. If I can make you laugh, especially by accident, I'm set for life."

Saros sighed. "You're never going to let this go, are you?"

"Nope. Just like the math incident."

"For god's sake." Saros shook his head. "You're insufferable."

"Sure, but you still think I'm funny."

"Hearing the words 'Illir's a little bitch' would take anyone by surprise."

"Am I wrong, though?" Atheris chuckled. "Anyway, okay, so Jovian did something stupid, Illir got mad, cursed him to never have a permanent grave. That's actually an interesting story. I want to know how the magic works there. Like, is it an illusion? Is the lake actually... I dunno, somehow metaphysical? Does it really exist? I mean— We know it exists, because I've seen it and so have many other people. It has a consistent pattern, so I can believe it's a... I would almost say a celestial entity, like the moon. We know why the moon has phases and changes appearance every few nights, but I'll bet people a hundred years ago saw a new moon or an eclipse and thought the gods were pissed.

"My point here," she continued, waving her hands as she talked — and narrowly avoided colliding with another tree as she shouldered around it — "is that *we* might not be able to explain Jovian's Tomb now, but there must be a reasonable process behind it."

Saros hid another smile as he listened to her work through her logic. This was why he liked her; everything was a puzzle to her, and consequently, everything had a solution.

"*Anyway*, that was a tangent," Atheris went on. "What I was really getting down to, again, was my question of why this matters to you." She looked up at him. "You keep saying it's personal. But you won't say why."

Saros took a deep breath. He kept his head turned down, his eyes fixed on the thorny branches and dense leaves cluttering the forest floor. He felt Atheris's eyes on him, but didn't look up. "I think Jovian's Tomb can save my life."

Seconds dragged by. Even the forest's sounds quieted behind the thump of Saros's pulse. Why had he said that? Why had he given her even an inch of the truth? It would only encourage her to dig deeper, to unearth the entire truth, and then—

When Atheris replied, her voice was quiet. "Save your life... how?"

The concern in her voice brought his walls right back up. He should never have thought they could be friends, should never have let her get as close as she was. Hadn't he learned his lesson last time?

But he owed her at least one answer, even if it skirted the truth. "You're on the right track, saying Jovian's Tomb has something supernatural about it. It was conjured by a god, after all, so it's supposed to have certain powerful properties. Hopefully those powers are enough to help me."

"But... What, are you dying or something?" Atheris halted. "Wait. Saros. Seriously. What haven't you told me?"

He kept trudging forward. Up ahead, branches snapped as an animal fled deeper into the woods. The trees' eyes blinked and rolled. Shadows stretched across the ground, slithering between tree trunks and leafy bushes; the day was already waning, and Saros wanted to get farther before they stopped to rest. With the night sky as the best map, they couldn't afford to lose too much of the night to sleep.

"*Saros!*"

Her voice was sharp enough that time that he stopped — mostly involuntarily. Reluctantly, he turned his head over his shoulder. "What."

She stared back at him, wide-eyed and slack-jawed. "Is it true? Are you dying?"

He looked down at the forest floor and let a second lapse before meeting her gaze. "Yes. Very slowly."

She moved closer to him. "Why didn't you say that from the beginning?"

"I told you it was life or death."

"But— But this is different! I thought— I dunno. I didn't realize you meant you were *actively* dying. What happens if...?"

"No." Saros shook his head and kept walking. This time, she fell into step beside him. "There's no 'what ifs,' Atheris. I am going to find the lake and then I'll be out of danger. End of story. I cannot afford to raise any doubts when this is already a little insane and extremely risky." He glanced at her again. "Are you still with me?"

It shocked him how much he wanted her to say yes.

She blinked, almost looking a little offended. "Of course I am."

Some of his stress lessened. "Good. Keep up. We've still got a lot of ground to cover today."

ILLIR'S WOODS WAS ALIVE. Which sounded absurd, but the longer Saros spent in the forest, the clearer it became: it wasn't just the trees and plants and wildlife that lived and breathed; the forest itself was a living entity. And Saros had an inkling the Woods were *leading* him.

He followed his map, of course, and kept the correct constellations overhead, but alongside the pull within him that drew him toward Jovian's Tomb, something else guided his direction.

Atheris said it was "incredibly dumb luck" that they found a series of caves to take shelter in when they decided to rest, but Saros had a feeling it was more than pure chance. Something had led them in this direction, shifting and bending the forest to clear their path, but he wondered why. Did Illir's Woods *want* him to find Jovian's Tomb... or not?

Either way, Saros was glad to have shelter that wasn't a canvas tent in the middle of the most unpredictable forest on earth. The yawning caverns were carved into the craggy side of a gorge that gouged a massive rift through Illir's Woods; Saros had been hesitant to descend into the gorge when they'd found it four hours ago, but Atheris had pointed out that the stars would be more visible from here, and Saros reasoned that finding a way around the gorge would take far too much time.

So down they went, stepping carefully among crumbling shale and loose rocks slick with mist from the churning river that slithered down the center of the gorge.

Saros thought the caves were perfect; they'd be out of the elements and hopefully out of sight of anything that might want a quick meal of two people, two snakes, and a cat. But when he went to step inside, Atheris grabbed the back of his coat and halted him in his tracks.

He turned around. "What?"

"You're really about to walk in there like it's nothing?" Atheris's eyes were wide behind her glasses. "What if there's bears? Or something worse? We have seen the *weirdest fucking animals* today. The *trees* have *eyes,* Saros. There could be literally anything in there."

"Bats, at worst," Saros said.

"I repeat: bears. Also wolves. And *snakes—*"

"You are currently wearing two snakes around your neck."

"Not of the venomous variety!" Atheris set her hands on her hips. "Consider also: insects that bite. A really pissed off deer that'll stomp us to death with its hooves. And this isn't even considering whatever fucked-up monsters beyond our comprehension call this place home! There is a *reason* no one has ever successfully mapped this forest, and it's because they walked blindly into caves with fucked-up monsters!"

Saros rolled his eyes and went into the cave. "We'll be fine, Atheris. If you don't believe me, enjoy your sleep out here in the open, *with* the bears and wolves and fucked-up monsters."

Atheris made a frustrated noise, but followed Saros into the cave.

If something lived here, it didn't make its presence known when Saros entered. The air inside was cool and damp, smelling strongly of moss and rot, and vaguely of sulfur. Stalactites stretched down from above, dripping water that plopped onto the rocks below and echoed deep within the cave. Saros peered into the shadows, but if there were bats or anything worse, they were out of sight.

The cave floor widened beyond the entrance, providing enough flat space for a fire and for Saros and Atheris to spread out their bedrolls with more than the two feet the tent allowed between them. The hard, rocky ground would make for uncomfortable sleeping, but at least they only had to endure it for a few hours before they continued on their way.

"I don't like this." Atheris dropped her bag on the ground and kicked a loose stone, sending it skittering into the dark. "Just throwing that out there so it's known by all: I do not like this. I much prefer pitching the tent in the woods."

"The woods," Saros repeated, "where we're pretty much exposed from all sides?" He set his own bag down and dug inside for the jar of fire starters. He grabbed a bundle of the rolled-up kindling and set it on the ground, then fished the flint out of his pocket.

"We might not be exposed in here, but we *are* trapped," Atheris said. "If something were to find us, there's only one way out. The back of the cave is either a dead end or a *bunch* of dead ends, and I'm not about to explore it to find out. Even if we *could* get out through the front entrance, we're still stuck in a gorge. Any way we run, we're dead."

Saros ignored her and focused on steadying his hands enough to strike the flint. It took a few tries, but a spark caught and conjured a tiny flame on the kindling. Saros dropped the flint back in his pocket only for the flame to snuff out a second later. He frowned.

Atheris snorted and tugged her string of amulets out of her shirt. "Here, let me." She pulled the necklace over her head and held one of the stones — a smooth, round amber charm — over the bundle of kindling. "*Ra Ascien.*" Despite the wind sweeping into the cave, the fire caught and blazed. Atheris snatched back the amulet and waved it around to cool it, then put it back around her neck. "You're welcome."

Saros eyed the charm. "Where did you get that?"

"What, this?" Atheris toyed with the amulet. "Had it forever. I think it was my mother's, but my aunt gave it to me when I was a kid." She closed her hand around it. "It took me a long time to get that spell right without, you know, setting my hands on fire."

Saros thought she was joking, but he realized that there was some subtle scarring on her fingers and knuckles that might have been burns healed with magic. He frowned.

"It's fine." Atheris dropped the amulets down the front of her sweater. "Got it eventually."

She scooted closer to the growing fire and warmed her hands. The snakes emerged from under her coat and coiled down her arms to get closer to the warmth, and Zenith climbed down from Saros's shoulders to do the same.

Saros let his eyes slide out of focus as he held his hands near the fire. The heat seeped through his gloves, but his fingers remained stubbornly numb. He opened and closed his hands, trying to work some feeling back into them despite the fading. At this point, he was lucky he could still use his hands at all.

"Hey." Atheris passed him a package of almonds and dried cranberries. "Why didn't you tell me?"

"Tell you what?" Saros poured a handful into his palm and passed the package back to Atheris.

"That you're *dying*."

"Why would I?" Saros tossed a berry into his mouth. "It's not important."

"It's pretty fucking important, Saros."

"Is it?" He flicked an almond into the fire.

Atheris turned to face him. "You think I don't care? I mean, yeah, you're moody and quiet and grumpy and I know I test your patience, but I've also seen the way your eyes light up when we talk through your research. I've noticed the smiles you try to hide when I say something funny — and I *am* funny — and I see the gentle way you care for Zenith. So I know that you're not as cold as you pretend to be. I don't know what happened to make you think you have to hide all of that, but I've seen the heart you've got, Saros. You might guard it with everything you have, but it's there." She reached over and poked his arm. Reluctantly, he looked up at her. She raised her eyebrows. "You are my friend. You are important to me. I care."

Saros didn't know what to do with that. It shamed him to realize that he'd forgotten what it was like to matter to someone else. He'd spent so many years entirely alone; did he even know how to have a friend anymore, much less *be* a friend?

He swallowed down the emotions welling in his throat and turned his gaze back to the fire. "What would you have done differently," he asked quietly, "if you had known?"

"Maybe nothing," Atheris said. "But I understand your urgency now. I'm sorry if I ever made it seem like I didn't take this seriously. And I hope..."

Saros looked down at his hands. Yeah, he hoped, too.

Atheris sighed and stood up, stretching her back. "All right. I'm beat. Wake me up when it's time to go." She grabbed her pack and headed further into the cave, but Saros called out to her and she turned. "Huh?"

He flickered a faint smile. "Thank you."

She winked. "What else are comically misfit friends for? Get some rest, Saros."

"Saros. Hey. Saros, wake up."

He jerked awake after what felt like two minutes since he'd closed his eyes. He felt a hand on his shoulder and swatted it away as he sat up. "Ugh. What?"

Atheris was kneeling next to him, clutching her coat around herself. She held a finger to her lips to tell Saros to stay quiet. "I think there's something outside."

Saros stared at her for a second while his brain caught up. The cave was still dark, the fire long dead, and there was no sound aside from the steady, rhythmic drip of water falling from the stalactites.

Wait. That was strange. Except for the faint rush of the river, there was no sound outside; the gorge and the forest were quiet.

Atheris was right. There *was* something lurking out there. But before Saros could agree with her, Zenith bolted out from beneath his coat and tore across the cave with a yowl.

"Whoa!" Atheris stumbled back.

"Zenith!" Saros scrambled to his feet and darted after her, but halted at the cave's entrance when a loud, deep growl erupted outside.

Atheris stopped beside Saros and exchanged a look with him. *What the fuck?* she mouthed.

Saros had exactly zero answers to that. He crept closer to the cave mouth, realizing too late that he didn't have a weapon on him. More growls and now shouts echoed off the gorge walls, and Saros stepped outside just in time to see a massive black feline swipe a man off his feet, sending him flying into the river.

Saros couldn't process anything in front of him. Half a dozen bodies lay limp on the rocks, slumped in dark puddles of blood. A few were missing limbs, and Saros's stomach turned over when he glimpsed a disembodied arm caught on a boulder in the river.

Atheris announced her presence at Saros's side with a full volume, "What the *fuck?*"

Saros tore his eyes away from the carnage and sought the giant feline. He spotted it crouched on a rock at the top of a small waterfall several feet away, round ears perked and gold eyes wide. Its fur was solid black, and aside from its unnatural size, it looked like a normal panther.

Yet... despite the obvious differences, Saros swore he knew those eyes. He stepped farther out of the cave, ignoring Atheris's sputtered protests, and made sure the panther saw him. It made a low growl, lashing its tail. Saros lifted his hand and snapped his fingers once.

"Saros, what the hell—"

"Zenith," he called, his voice echoing across the gorge, "come here."

"*What?*" Atheris hissed. "Wh— Have you lost your *mind?*"

Saros held his breath as the panther blinked at him. Then it rose out of its crouch and bounded down the rocks in graceful, silent steps. In four quick strides, it stood before Saros and passed its pink tongue over its nose.

Saros grinned. The beast towered over him; his head only barely came up to its shoulder, but despite every impossibility, this was Zenith. Her fur was the same thick, velvety black, and Saros recognized the intelligence in her vivid yellow eyes. He had often suspected that there was far more to Zenith than he'd ever understand — most of nature was beyond human understanding, after all — and it seemed he was right.

Atheris staggered out of the cave. "You... You've gotta be kidding. That's *Zenith?* But how? She was a *cat*. Cats don't shapeshift into bigger cats!"

"Clearly this one does." Saros lifted a hand to Zenith's nose. He was rather delighted that despite transforming into an unusually large apex predator, Zenith still had a kitten's soft pink nose. Zenith nudged his hand, purring.

This was extraordinary. Had Zenith always been able to do this? Was this her true form, and the smaller version merely saved her energy or made her more approachable? Or had she only gained this ability when she had entered Illir's Woods and ate its wildlife and drank its water?

Well, if that was the logic of the Woods, Saros hoped he didn't wake up tomorrow with wings sprouting from his back or horns growing out of his head.

He stroked his hand up Zenith's snout to the top of her head, burying his fingers in her thick fur. He scratched behind her ears in the spot she liked, and in moments she had collapsed to a puddle on the ground. She rolled onto her back, purring, and Saros narrowly avoided a paw the size of his face colliding with the side of his head.

"I wish this was the weirdest thing to happen tonight," Atheris said, "but, uh, who are our unfortunate guests? And why did Zenith literally tear them apart?"

Zenith snorted and rolled to her feet, shaking out her fur. She stepped over to one of the bodies and shoved it with her paw so the victim turned face-up. A swarm of black flies vacated the body, disturbed by the movement, and scattered off to the next one. Saros grimaced and approached the corpse.

"Clearly she was protecting us." Saros noted a wickedly sharp dagger discarded next to the body. The victim's hand, inches away from the weapon, was torn to bloody, broken shreds. Saros wrinkled his nose at the sharp tang of blood in the air, and tried not to think about the puddles and spatters under his feet as he leaned closer to the black-cloaked body. He realized with a twinge of regret that the victim was young; a boy still early in his teens. Practically a child.

"Illir's teeth." Atheris pressed the back of her hand to her nose. "There's four more bodies over there, I think I can see at least two farther down the river, and that's not counting the ones that are likely getting swept out to sea as we speak. Yeah, Zenith protected us, but how did she know we were in danger? Why would these guys be after *us*?"

Saros didn't have any answers for her. He studied the boy in front of him as much as he could without actually touching the body. There must be some sort of clue as to where these people had come from and why they were as deep into Illir's Woods as Saros and Atheris were.

Saros glanced at the other nearby bodies. They each wore the same black hooded cloak as the boy in front of Saros, but as far as he could tell, the garment was plain and free of any defining emblems or symbols.

A few feet away, Atheris spoke the fire spell again and brought a bright flame flickering to life. The yellowish light leapt across the river's edge and drew Saros's attention back to the body before him as something metallic caught the shine. A ring, somehow intact on the boy's thumb despite the broken state of both his hands.

Saros reached across the body and tugged the ring off, holding it up in the faint light. "Atheris, come closer with the fire."

"Whatcha got?" She made her way over to him, and Saros blinked in the sudden brightness. He held the ring closer to the flame, turning it between his thumb and forefinger. He couldn't tell what the material was — silver, maybe, given the shine — but it was well made and carefully engraved with bold lettering.

Saros squinted and turned the ring so the light caught the letters. Barely visible in the flickering glow, he made out the words, FOR LIFE.

"Huh. A wedding ring?" Atheris questioned. "Kid looks young, but..."

"I don't think so." Saros searched for more markings, but found none. "It was on his thumb, not his ring finger. Let's check the others. I have a feeling."

"What, you think they're some kind of cult?" Atheris went over to the next closest body, taking the light with her. She wrinkled her nose. "Good grief. Guess I don't want to piss off your cat." She leaned down and prodded at another victim's hand, then straightened and held up another ring. "Ugh. I can't believe you just made me touch a dead guy's hand. Gross. But look. You're onto something."

Saros thought so. He trailed Atheris to three more bodies and found three more identical rings, all on the victims' right thumbs. Maybe it was a cult, or maybe something more benevolent, but whoever these people were, Zenith had sensed their ill intentions. If the daggers each of the victims openly carried were any indication, Zenith's instincts were right.

But that still begged the question: why had they come after Saros and Atheris? It seemed far less likely that the group's presence in this very same corner of Illir's Woods was a coincidence. Saros and Atheris were being followed.

Atheris snatched up one of the blood-spattered weapons and wiped the flat side of the blade on her thigh. Her grin looked manic in the harsh glow from her amulet. "Can I keep this?"

"Why are you asking my permission?" Saros found another dagger and took it for himself. He hoped he didn't have to use it, but it was better to have something than nothing in Illir's Woods. Giant panther or not. He nudged around the cultist's clothes until he found the leather sheath for the knife, then turned to Atheris with a shrug. "They don't need them anymore."

Atheris grinned and sheathed her own dagger, then came over to Saros with the light. "So what's up with the rings? What have we got?" She spread the three she'd collected across her palm.

Saros held them up to the light one by one. He found another that said FOR LIFE, but the others were different. "For soul." He placed each back in Atheris's hand as he mumbled the words. "Salvation. For peace." Then he frowned at the final one. The tremble in his hand worsened as his pulse spiked.

"What is it?" Atheris said.

Saros forced the words out. "This one says 'for God.'"

"Oh, most definitely a cult. Maybe some kind of, I dunno, self-righteousness thing? Like, 'Join us and we'll solve all your problems' type of deal. 'Join us and you won't go to hell.' Kinda ironic that their idea of salvation involves stalking and murdering people, yeah?" Atheris clapped Saros on the shoulder, jolting him out of his shock.

He closed his hand around the ring. "Yeah."

Oblivious, Atheris wandered off, taking the light with her, and shooed off a trio of large black birds that had gathered around one of the bodies. Saros watched only absently as she spoke another spell and the man's body disintegrated to dust. She brushed off her hands and went to the next one, repeating the spell until each body had returned to the earth.

When there was nothing more to see, Saros reluctantly brought his attention back to the ring in his hand. FOR GOD.

Not *For Illir*.

God.

Saros only knew one person who insisted his god remain nameless.

He pocketed the ring, hearing it click against his timepiece, then followed Atheris back into the cave, hoping to whatever gods might listen that he was wrong.

CHAPTER 4
WANING CRESCENT V

HE USED to be so carefree and jovial. He laughed, fully and loudly, and always had a joke at the tip of his tongue. He didn't take things too seriously. Troubles and worries slid right off his shoulders like water on a duck's feathers. His heart yearned for adventure, to leave no stone unturned, to climb as high as the pines would take him and drink in the world from the birds' point of view.

This was the person I chose to remember. The person I loved.

He was the only one who waved off concerns about my connection to magic before any of us knew what it was. He didn't believe in the curse, didn't let it stop him from continuing to be my friend. He snuck away from his grandmother's cow farm, fetched me from whatever menial task my own family had put me up to, and we spent those endless young days scaling the gnarled trees at the edge of the village until the forest ate up the sunlight. Each time he dashed home, always with an excuse prepared for his concerned yet lenient grandmother, I never doubted we would do it all again the very next day.

I could never pin down when his free spirit started to die, but I knew it had something to do with the winter his father returned from Artunia.

If he and his gentle, studious grandmother were cut from the same cloth, then he and his father were from entirely different sheep. At first, when he still visited, he complained that the man had leeched all the lightness and joy out of his grandmother's house.

46

"*Rotten bastard,*" *he said to me one afternoon as we sat on the roof of an abandoned barn at the edge of town. "All he does is grumble about magicians, drink that disgusting whiskey, and tell us how to do our jobs. As if we don't know our own work on that farm! He's from the goddamned city; the hell does he know about running a farm? Absolute jack shit, that's what.*"

Despite his father's iron grip on the household, he still visited. Our days continued as they always did — wandering the meadows and woods, catching fish only to release them farther down the stream to save them from the village fishermen, studying the wildlife and flora, wondering about magic and all the unknown wonders of our world. But then one day he was late, and when he arrived, the first thing I noticed was the bruise.

"*Nothing,*" *he snapped when I demanded to know what had happened. "Accident. It's fine.*"

It was neither an accident, nor was it fine. The entire left side of his face was darkened reddish-purple, worst beneath his eye. Anger simmered in his silver eyes; I didn't know how he thought he could fool me.

"*He was acting like an ass,*" *he finally admitted, voice quiet and hands clenched tight. "He hit our— He hit Grandmom's dog. The older one, Sunny. I yelled at him. I just... exploded.*" *He turned his head away from me and buried his face in his hands. "And then he hit me.*"

I thought, if anything, he would get more rebellious after that. He was not one to tuck his tail between his legs and accept defeat. But his visits became shorter. Entire days contracted into mere hours — I was lucky if I had an afternoon with him. Soon enough, those hours shrank to sixty precious minutes. I watched the joy leave his eyes, replaced by a foggy exhaustion that even his favorite pastimes couldn't chase away. He stopped telling me how he'd defended his grandmother or snapped back at his father. He stopped speaking of the future, of the academy, of his quest for nature's powers.

And he started talking about God.

Suddenly it wasn't magic that tapped us into nature; it was God. It wasn't the rotation of the earth and its orbit around the sun that made the days and seasons pass; it was God. It wasn't a combination of cells and genes that brought new life into the world; it was God.

I didn't know this God he spoke of. I knew of only one by name — Illir — and He was no god of mine. I was not taught to listen to the teachings of those who followed Illir, and neither was he. His grandmother had instilled in both of us a deep respect for and fascination with the natural world and all its hidden beauties. We grew up on a healthy diet of ancient myths and loving rituals to honor the earth. That was our religion.

Until his father.

Until he started to believe that everything he'd grown up hearing was blasphemy.

Until the things my family said about me started to make sense to him.

"But think about it, Saros," he told me one evening as we meandered from his family's house to mine. "The world is so complex and impossible. How could it be the work of anything other than God? And magic — of course God punishes us for trying to use magic. I'd be fearful if I were you, too."

"Illir didn't create the world," I'd replied, unable to conjure a response to his implication about my supposed curse. "You know that."

"But I don't. None of us do. How can I claim to know anything? I'm nothing."

I'd just shaken my head, unsure what had become of the boy that I loved.

He became scarce. An hour every day turned into two days a week. Then a handful of minutes once or twice a week. I told myself I was lucky he still visited at all, even if it was only to ramble about his newfound god and how great He was. How powerful. How merciful.

But if He was so merciful, why was I cursed? Why did my family shun me? Why did mercy only apply to a few?

By the end of that winter, my love had become a stranger. He was no longer the person I had fallen for; he was someone his father was proud of — someone he'd sworn to me he'd never become.

It should not have been a surprise when he fully turned on me three months later.

"Hey. Saros. *Saros.*"

A sharp whistle jolted him out of his memories. It took him a second to remember where he was, but the immediate sight of bioluminescent plants surrounding him brought him back to the present. Illir's Woods was aglow under a perfectly clear sky, nearly hypnotizing with its vibrance.

He then realized that Atheris was trying to get his attention. "Sorry. What?"

She eyed him oddly. "Nothing. Just making sure you're still here. Looked like you were possessed for a second there. The hell are you thinking about?"

He shook his head, taking a deep breath of the cold night air. "Just the past." Finding those cultists and their rings had dredged up all kinds of memories, and Saros had been buried in them for hours. He'd barely noticed when they'd climbed their way out of the gorge and returned to the dense trees.

"Cryptic," Atheris said. "Must be some heavy shit, because this" — she waved her hand in an arc in front of her — "is extraordinary. I didn't know Illir's Woods glowed in the dark."

Saros nodded absently as a raccoon-like critter with vivid green stripes along its sides skittered up a tree and leapt from branch to branch. Its eyes reflected the glowing leaves around it.

Higher, above the gnarled tree branches and their blinking eyes, the stars traced their patterns across the night's velvety backdrop. Saros couldn't see the moon through the trees, but he felt the lake's pull, stronger than ever. It enticed him closer, persuading him to ignore the need to sleep or rest or eat and instead forge onward until he stood before the tomb.

What do you have to tell me? he wondered. *What secrets do you really hold?*

Saros glanced at Atheris again. A branch snapped somewhere within the foliage, and she jumped. Her shoulders were tensed up to her ears, and she turned her head so abruptly at every sound that she was bound to pull a muscle.

He gently nudged her arm. "Atheris."

She startled. "Huh? What?"

He meant to say something like, *You don't have to worry*, or *We're safe* or *There's nothing to be afraid of*, but none of those statements was entirely true. Instead he reached for something guaranteed to occupy her: "Tell me about the new magic you're trying to invent."

Sure enough, that got her attention. "Okay, yes, hear me out: dream magic."

Saros raised an eyebrow.

"I know," Atheris waved her hand, "I know how it sounds. But dreams are a force of nature, if you get right down to the details. Our dreams are caused by signals and reactions in our brains — the same forces of imagination that let us hope, wish, daydream, whatever. Dreams are memories as much as they're visual representations of our hopes and fears. It's all energy. And the whole world — the universe, even — runs on the same kind of energy. It's cause and effect, but on a cellular level. Following me so far?"

"Sure." But he didn't see how this sort of energy could be tangibly applied to everyday magic.

"Great." Atheris's hands talked with her. "Now, as you know, most of us need a tether to the natural world in order to harness its power. Flowers, animals... living aspects of nature. But did you know it wasn't always like that?"

Saros did not. "Now do *I* smell a myth?"

She grinned. "Indeed, a classic case of 'Learn a lesson by watching a guy tremendously fuck up.' Except this time, it *surprisingly* wasn't a guy, but a woman. A witch, to be exact."

Saros raised his eyebrows. "I'm listening."

Atheris adjusted her bag on her shoulders. Her white snake poked its head out of her coat and flicked its tongue. "Story time, Saros Antarian. Usually I'd give you the short version, since the sound of my voice is apparently like nails on a chalkboard to you, but we've got all the time in the world tonight. Like it or not, we're taking the scenic route through this story." She grinned.

He hid a smile of his own. "Let's hear it, then."

"Right, so, before you form any initial judgments — yes, this woman was a witch, *but* witches weren't always feared like they are now. A long time ago, they were the strongest, most respected users of magic. Witches weren't limited by tethers to the natural world — no one was — and magic-users thrived. Witches were basically at the top of society, but there was one type of magic they had yet to master."

"Fire," Saros guessed. He'd heard stories like this before.

"Nope." Atheris smirked. "Memories. Dreams. The human mind."

"Wouldn't that be forbidden?" He had to wonder how *Atheris* planned to use this magic, should she find a way to reach it.

"Oh, totally. But there was a trio of witches — our main character among them — who wanted to figure it out. Not because they wanted to control people, but simply because they just wanted to know if it could be done."

"Famous last words," Saros muttered. What was that saying? The road to hell was paved with good intentions?

Atheris snorted. "Yeah. These witches vowed that, if they found a way to work with this magic, they would keep it between the three of them. They'd hide their findings so the spells couldn't fall into the wrong hands."

"Hide," Saros pointed out, "but not destroy."

"Uh-huh." Atheris smirked. "Well... turns out *theirs* were the wrong hands. They did figure out how to approach memories and dreams with magic. Our main character witch, Firelei, was the—"

"*Firelei?*" Saros knew that name. "Isn't she that infamous witch who—"

"*Spoilers*! I'm getting there." Atheris swatted his arm. "Let's back up. So, Firelei and her two gal pals — no, for real, they were probably in a polycule — figured out that in order to control mind energies, the mind needed to be in the dream state first. But the spells were never strong enough; they'd *see* each other in their dreams, but no one could take control. Dreams are too unpredictable. Obviously the next course of action was to use some really potent drugs."

"Of course it was."

"Yeah, and it turns out, the shit they used was *so* potent that they didn't just appear in each other's dreams. They all showed up on a different *plane*."

Saros frowned. "That's not possible."

"Someone's never toyed with really potent drugs."

Saros had no response to that.

"But yeah, no, it *shouldn't* be possible," Atheris went on. "This wasn't just a hallucination. They actually *went somewhere else*. And in this other plane — dimension, world, what have you — they met some gods."

Saros snorted.

"No, hear me out!" She smacked his arm again, then ducked as a bird with four wings soared over their heads. Atheris looked back at it suspiciously. "Um. Okay. Anyway, they ended up in this other world, and the gods offered them limitless magical power — for a trade."

"Of course," Saros muttered. "And what witch could turn down limitless power?"

Atheris frowned, but quickly resumed her tale. "The gods said to Firelei and the others, 'Sure, you can know all the secrets of magic, but *only* you three. The rest of humanity will lose its inherent connection to magic, and may only *borrow* but never *have*.' Two of the witches balked at the idea, but Firelei agreed."

"And thus ripped magic away from everyone on earth."

Atheris nodded. "These gods only needed a yes from one of them. Before the other witches could beg them to wait, they made it happen. They gave the witches unimaginable power, and stole everyone else's. They contained all this magic within the natural world, but hid it. It was generations before humans figured out how to get a taste of magic again, and even now, as you know, it's tricky.

"As for Firelei and her partners... It wasn't pretty. They became outcasts, shunned and resented for retaining the power everyone else lost. People went out in mobs to hunt and attack them, forcing them into hiding and to disguise themselves when they had to go outside. At first people were angry because it was unfair that three women had somehow been spared the loss of magic, but when it got out that they were the *reason* for it? Well..."

"Yes, I'm sure everyone loved that."

"Yeaaaaah," Atheris drew out the word. "They, uh, executed Firelei. Well, that makes it sound too official. Nah, they murdered her. And her one partner, Thalia, too. But the third one, Serefine, got away — and took a piece of each of her partners with her."

Saros eyed Atheris. "When you say a *piece*..."

"Yes, like a physical piece," Atheris said. "She took a bone from Firelei and hair from Thalia, and she used the remains to make amulets." She pulled her own amulets out of her shirt and let them roll across her palm. Accompanying the amber charm Saros had seen before were two more: one solid black, and one pearly white. "These were the first tethers that put humanity back in touch with magic. Took Serefine long enough to do it, but she made them as a way to apologize. To atone for what her partners — what *Firelei* — had done. She wanted to help give magic back to everyone, but even after several decades..." Atheris closed her fist around the charms and tucked them back under her shirt. "Not everyone was ready to forgive witches."

"Wait." Saros studied her, but she kept her gaze fixed ahead at the glowing trees. "Those amulets you have..."

She shoved her hands into her coat pockets. "One for each witch. Still one missing, though."

Saros halted. "Those are— Those are real? Those are the original...?"

Atheris marched ahead, sparing only a quick glance back. "Yes."

Saros caught up to her, unable to rein in his interest. "How do you have these? Atheris, that's extraordinary."

"The amber one is mine," she said, "but the other two, yes, are the ones Serefine made. Black for herself, white for Thalia. Firelei's is still missing. No one in my family has ever been able to find it."

Saros's mind was spinning. "Your... family?"

She sighed. "Yes. Listen, I've already said too much. Secret's out, I'm distantly related to Serefine. Just— Don't overthink it, all right?" She shot him an uncharacteristically nervous look.

Saros didn't know what to say. He didn't know how to articulate that if she was truly a witch, like she was implying, that meant she shared something with Saros — a possession of magic that the rest of the world hated. Saros didn't know how much truth was in the stories about connections between witches and necromancy, but at the very least, this meant she would *understand*. He could tell her about his curse, and she would understand.

She eyed him warily, obviously misunderstanding his shock. "Okay, stop looking at me like that. See, I shouldn't have told you that. I could've told the story without— Damn it." She ruffled her hair. "Just say it."

"Are you... Are you a witch?"

She clenched her jaw and nodded once.

Saros felt dizzy with relief. "Atheris, that's— That's extraordinary. I'm—"

"I had a feeling I'd find you here."

Saros froze at the unmistakable prod of a weapon at his back. Atheris's eyes widened and she staggered backward. Zenith leapt off of Saros's shoulders with a yowl; he didn't have time to see where she went before six people cloaked in black surrounded him and Atheris with daggers drawn.

Saros turned his head toward his attacker. His eyes traced up the gloved hand, the black sleeve, and finally settled on a jarringly familiar face.

Shit. He had wanted to be wrong.

Saros swallowed. "You."

Rune LeRouge grinned. "*You*."

CHAPTER 5
WANING CRESCENT VI

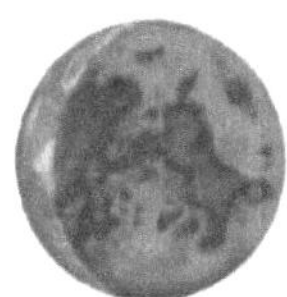

SAROS COULDN'T BREATHE. He stood absolutely frozen, heart pounding as Rune lay the edge of his dagger across Saros's throat. This was impossible; how had Rune even found Saros? How had he known to search *here*, of all places? And what was he doing with this cult?

Rune gripped Saros's arm and bent it behind his back, fingers pressing hard enough to send pins and needles down to his numb hand. "What a coincidence that God should lead me through His realm and directly to you. Although, it seems fitting, doesn't it? These Woods *are* said to be infested with monsters, after all."

"Rune, what— What are you talking about? What do you want?" Saros flicked a glance to Atheris, who stood with her hands raised before a pale-skinned woman with a scarred face. Atheris glared at the cultist with enough fury to set her on fire. If only magic worked like that.

"Oh, it's very simple." Rune drew Saros flush against his body and leaned in close enough to lower his voice to a murmur. "I want atonement. I want peace. I want evil purged from this world. And my mission concludes with you."

Saros's pulse thundered. Rune's answer had clarified absolutely nothing, but Saros had a dreadful feeling about it. He knew Rune had been horrified — traumatized, even — by his contact with necromancy, but was Rune truly so corrupted by this religious fanaticism that he was willing to kill for his god?

"If it's me you want," Saros said, "let Atheris go." He slightly nodded in her direction.

Rune considered. "Fine. The girl isn't important. Go."

The woman holding Atheris at knifepoint lowered her weapon, and Atheris relaxed. She flicked a glance at Saros, and Saros saw what was about to happen but had no chance to stop it. In one fluid move, Atheris drew her own dagger, lunged, and effortlessly disarmed the cultist. She locked the other woman in a tight hold with both blades across the cultist's throat.

"Don't," Atheris warned as the woman tried to struggle. Two more cultists closed in around Atheris, but she glared back at them, challenging them to try it. The cultists hesitated. Atheris turned her gaze to Rune, then Saros. "Someone better explain what the fuck is going on."

Rune's hand tightened on the knife at Saros's throat. Saros probably could have overpowered him if he tried, but he was less interested in fighting Rune than he was in knowing what Rune really wanted. When Rune had rejected Saros seven years ago, Saros had thought Rune was content to never see him again. But now it appeared Rune had been *searching* for him. Yet if he intended to kill Saros, why hadn't he done it already?

"Let her go and get out of here," Rune growled at Atheris. "I won't warn you again."

"Atheris," Saros whispered, "please. Go."

She shook her head and adjusted the knives at the woman's throat. "Let him go first."

"Oh, no," Rune said. He tightened his hold on Saros's arm. Saros could feel his warm breath on his neck. "Not again. I need him, you see, and he is just too special to let run away."

Saros's sense of dread warred with his needling anxiety that he didn't have time for this. Every second he spent with Rune's dagger at his throat stole time off his waning life. He refused to miss the appearance of Jovian's Tomb because Rune LeRouge threatened him.

"Tell me what you want, Rune," Saros growled. "I'm not what you think I am."

"You most certainly are." Rune's voice was velvet against Saros's ear, and he couldn't suppress an involuntary shiver. "I have a duty, a mission from God Himself, and you are the final piece. With your blood, I will have my salvation."

Saros's blood ran cold as he pieced together the implications of Rune's words. "How... How many have you killed?"

"Like I said," Rune murmured, "you are the last one."

Saros understood. Rune wasn't just hunting Saros; he was hunting necromancers. But how many others could possibly exist? Was it really so common to be cursed with this magic? Perhaps not, if Rune had successfully found and murdered everyone except Saros.

He swallowed, wincing as the blade nicked his skin. "What's happened to you, Rune?"

Rune pressed closer. "You did."

Saros clenched his jaw. "You still don't understand. I *saved* you."

"God is the only one who can save me, monster."

"Remember," Saros pleaded. "You— It doesn't have to be like this. You must remember."

Saros had spent the past seven years running over every possible reunion between him and Rune, but none of those rehearsed encounters was anything close to the scene before him now. It was like the moment he'd restored Rune's life all over again; then, he had expected Rune to be upset and confused. But the last thing he'd anticipated was for Rune to wake up hating him.

"What I remember," Rune growled, "is being torn out of God's arms and dragged back to a world I didn't know. What I *remember* is the cold, agonizing touch of dark magic taking over my body and scarring my soul. Of this I am certain, *necromancer*." He spat the word. "You are the one to blame."

Saros didn't know what else to say to make him understand. He hadn't known that Rune wouldn't retain his memories when Saros had saved him. He hadn't thought of *any* repercussions; he hadn't even known it was magic saving Rune's life until the power sprang to life within Saros and acted for him. It was love and love alone that had guided him.

"Saros." Atheris's hushed voice was laced with horror. When Saros glanced at her, he found something worse on her face. Betrayal.

Whatever trust she'd had in him, it was broken now.

"Oh?" Rune's voice lilted with amusement. "So you haven't told your new friend what you really are? I suppose I can't blame you. I can't imagine necromancers retain many friends. Your own family tossed you away, didn't they? We can't blame them, either, can—"

"*Enough*," Saros snapped. Rune didn't get to throw that in his face when he didn't remember being the only one who *hadn't* shunned him. He felt Rune's hold on him loosen slightly, and wrenched his arm out of his grip. The dagger bit into his neck, but he ignored the slight scrape and twisted out of Rune's grasp. Saros drew the dagger he'd taken from the dead cultist and aimed it toward Rune, but Rune saw straight through him.

His silver eyes gleamed; a hint of a smirk curled at the corner of his lips. "Don't waste my time, necromancer. We both know how this will end."

Saros tightened his grip on the knife as the tremor in his hands became obvious. "Isn't that what you want? My blood on your hands?"

"Not like this. These things are delicate." Rune twirled his own dagger in his hand. "This doesn't have to be difficult."

"I'm not going to lie down and let you kill me for your religious delusions."

Rune's gaze darkened. He clenched his jaw, and when he struck again, Saros ducked and scrambled out of his way. He used the trees for cover, but Rune was quick; Saros barely managed to evade his calculated strikes. Rune fought expertly, as though he considered this a dance rather than a fight, and Saros could do nothing more than dodge his attacks.

He knew he was on the losing end of this fight, and Rune knew it too. Saros saw the realization dawn in Rune's eyes that Saros wasn't going to retaliate violently, and when Rune next lunged at him, he didn't hold back. Saros hadn't realized he'd been hesitating before; now,

Rune struck wildly, shredding bark off the trees when his knife hit the trunks rather than Saros's throat.

He didn't know what to do. He couldn't kill Rune. He didn't even want to *hurt* Rune. But Rune clearly possessed none of the same reservations about Saros; the moment Saros lost his footing on a root, Rune seized the collar of his coat and slammed him back against a tree, knife across his throat.

For a heartbeat, both of them froze. Rune's glare bore into Saros. His lip curled back in a scowl, and Saros's pulse kept time with Rune's heavy breathing.

"If you want my life so badly, Rune," Saros breathed, "why do you hesitate?"

Rune narrowed his eyes. He clenched his jaw tighter, adjusting his hand around the hilt of his knife.

Saros dropped his dagger. The foliage at his feet caught it with a rustle of leaves. Rune's gaze flicked down, following the sound, and Saros seized Rune's wrist, twisted his arm, and shoved him away. He grabbed the dagger in the second Rune stumbled, but before he could take another step, Rune gave a sharp whistle. The other cultists abandoned Atheris and surged forward to surround Saros.

"*No!*" Atheris screamed. Saros had a split second to glimpse her dropping to her knees, and then the cultists started swinging at him and it was all he could do to stay on his feet and avoid getting shredded by their knives. But his energy was waning fast, and his aching, fatigued body was no match for a flock of skilled assassins. He couldn't dodge their strikes forever; he needed an out, even the slightest opening that would let him run.

Something crashed through the foliage, and with a deafening yowl, Zenith bowled through the mob of cultists and threw herself in front of Saros. In large panther form, she took out five of Rune's followers with one swipe of her paw; the others shouted and fell back, some disappearing into the trees.

Saros turned in a circle, seeking Rune. Sure enough, he remained, dagger in hand. Blood from his fallen companions spattered his face and his black hair was falling loose of its tie. He glared at Saros with deep fury that was still, after all this time, devastating to see on his face.

Zenith growled, but Saros placed his hand on her side. "Don't," he murmured to her. It would have been smarter to let her go ahead and attack Rune, but Saros did not wish to see such a bloody demise for the man he used to love.

Before Saros could decide what to do, Atheris shouted a spell: *"Ra Aurre.!"* Droplets of water rose up from the soil and foliage and solidified mid-air into deadly spears of ice. Atheris lifted her gaze to Rune.

"No, wait." Saros moved closer to her, but she kept her distance and aimed the ice shards at him instead.

"Stay away."

He froze, lifting both hands. "Atheris..." How could she think he was a threat?

"Don't come any closer." Her gaze was sharp and cold as the ice floating over her hand. "Not until you explain to me who the *fuck* you are."

"Atheris, it's me," he pleaded. "It's me. I've always been— I haven't changed."

She started to reply, but suddenly her eyes went wide and she threw herself at him. He stumbled, but his reflexes were too slow; he didn't have a chance to so much as turn his head before someone slammed into his back and pain exploded through his body.

Saros hit the ground. His vision flipped upside-down. Burning agony clawed through him, blurring his surroundings to hazy oblivion. His heartbeat throbbed at the gushing center of the wound where Rune's dagger had sunk in; blood soaked his shirt and crawled, hot and slick, over his skin. Distantly, shouts rang in his ears. He heaved in a deep breath, gritting his teeth against the nausea rising in his throat, and tried to lift his head. He caught a foggy glimpse of Rune before the shadowy trees swallowed his lithe form, and then Atheris's panicked face filled his narrowing field of vision.

"Saros, stay with me. *Fuck*." Strong hands gripped his shoulders. Atheris spoke again but her words were slurred and garbled in Saros's ears. He tried to shake his head but his muscles refused and his chin dropped to his chest.

"Bitch!" Atheris shook him, which sent fresh agony rolling through him. "*Shit.*" A sharp ringing in his ears drowned out whatever she said next. Darkness sliced across his vision. He blinked, and then he was staring up at the swaying branches crisscrossed over the night sky. The moon, slight as a sliver, winked at him overhead.

"Don't die," Atheris's voice crept into his consciousness again. "Don't fucking die. Okay, this is gonna hurt. I'm sorry."

Saros tried to make an inquisitive noise, but then a worse, stronger, hotter pain sank its teeth into his flesh and swallowed him whole.

*B*UT BEFORE ALL OF THAT *— before he turned on me, before he wrote me out of his life, before he transformed into someone I didn't know — he was kind and beautiful and I loved him.*

I'll never know how or when it started. He had been my best friend since we were children; his grandmother and my mother went way back. I had many fond memories of our families dining together, for holidays as well as regular days for no reason at all. That his family was, in my father's eyes, below us, never stopped us from sharing our lives.

As adolescents we remained inseparable, stumbling together through the struggles and stings of first loves. We shared our sympathies and commiserations, but I think we knew, even then, that no one would mean as much to us as each other.

The stories all insist that true love should be confessed dramatically, in the rain or under the stars or in the throes of danger. But if there is such a thing as true love, it is not a loud thing. For us, it was a quiet, gentle companion on our shoulders.

One day we were as we had always been. The next, it was as if the world had shifted slightly under my feet. My heart felt lighter whenever I saw him. His presence warmed me, made me feel like I was glowing. Floating. I smiled more with him, and him with me.

I had resigned to smother my feelings. He didn't need to know that what I felt for him now was any different from what we had always had. It would only add complication. It would only distance him. I didn't want to change a thing.

It was a normal, dreary autumn day when he confessed to me the very same feelings as I harbored for him.

We were by the river, seated on the old bridge with our legs hanging over the edge. His shoulder was pressed to mine, his hands fidgeting in his lap. I turned my head and studied him, muted in the overcast dusk of autumn's last breath. That crease that only appeared between his brows when he was stressed was present on his face, and though he gazed down at the river, his eyes were distant.

"What's wrong?" I asked him. "You're not yourself." I kept my voice hushed, reluctant to break the gentle tranquility between us.

He swallowed and looked down at his restless hands. "Nothing. Just a lot on my mind."

"Like what?" I leaned into his shoulder. "You know you can tell me anything."

He shook his head, just slightly. "Not this."

I frowned. "What do you mean?"

"It..." He shook his head again, more adamantly. "It doesn't matter. It'll pass."

I didn't think my heart had ever beat so hard. "Rune. You can tell me."

He looked at me, and the expression on his face was nearly enough to explain everything he was hesitant to say. His eyes were pleading, desperate, and he pressed his lips together as if physically restraining himself from speaking. But I reached over and took his hand, and his tension eased. His eyes fluttered, and he glanced briefly down at our hands, then met my gaze once more.

"Saros," he said, but his next words stuck.

"Rune," I replied. Tell me, *I silently begged him,* because I don't think I can say it myself.

He bit his lip, then turned to me, set a hand on my cheek, and quickly and softly pressed his lips to mine.

I kissed him back before he could believe, even for a second, that that one kiss was the end of it.

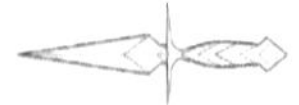

THE DARK RECEDED GRADUALLY, lifting from Saros's mind like night fading into dawn. Everything felt foggy. His bones ached with a familiar cold. He barely felt the steady thrum of his heart. It hurt to take in too much air, and dull, smoldering pain throbbed in his abdomen, but he was alive. There was that, at least.

The air he inhaled was damp and smelled of rot and moss. He was still in the Woods, then, but the ground beneath him was hard and solid rather than loamy earth. He cracked open his eyes and found not a canopy of trees or a starry sky above, but a cobwebbed and rotting roof. Slivers of moonlight seeped through scattered breaks in the old wood. Saros turned his head, wincing at the stiffness in his neck, and found he was in a barn. An old, dilapidated, precariously slouching barn.

Better than a tent in the Woods, he reasoned. Or a cave in a gorge, Atheris would agree.

Wait. *Atheris*. Saros tried to sit up, but a stab of pain shot through him and he canceled that decision immediately. Everything flooded back to him then — Rune, the cult, Atheris taking them down with her magic. Then Rune had stabbed Saros, and everything after that was blank.

Close by, someone cleared their throat. Saros turned his head the other way, and relief flooded him at the sight of Atheris sitting cross-legged on the floor beside him.

She gave him a faint, flat smile.

Saros blinked a few times to make sure she wouldn't disappear. "Are you real?"

Her eyes widened. "No." She deepened her voice and rolled her eyes back so only the whites showed. "I am God incarnate, here to make you pay for your sins. Your free will is an illusion."

Saros stared at her.

She blinked her eyes back to normal, then smirked. "Ha. Anyway." She ruffled her hair. "Yeah, of course I'm real. How much do you remember?"

Saros rubbed his forehead. "Most of it. Rune and his cult. Zenith came to our rescue. And you..." He trailed off.

Atheris's coat rustled as she shrugged. She pushed her glasses up her nose. "I wasn't quick enough. Never am."

"I told you to run," Saros said quietly. Obviously he was glad she hadn't, but if something had happened to her, he wouldn't have been able to forgive himself.

Atheris snorted. "If I had run, you'd be dead. And you should know by now that I don't run from the action, Saros."

"Yeah, you run toward it." He cracked a smile.

"Exactly." She smirked, but the humor was short-lived. Her smile faded, and then she turned her head down. Her frizzy, unkempt hair was free of its usual bun and fell over her eyes. Dried blood was still smeared across her cheek, but if she'd been hurt, it wasn't obvious. At least Rune still possessed a fragment of respect that stopped him from hurting people who weren't his targets, but that didn't come close to excusing anything that had just happened.

"Are you okay, Atheris?" Saros asked.

"Sure, yeah, I just used magic to hurt someone, which I vowed never to do, and then watched you almost die. I'm totally fine."

Saros inched his arm toward her and extended his hand, but couldn't quite reach. "I'm sorry," he mumbled. "I didn't think... I have no idea how Rune found me. I never thought it would be like this."

"Rune? The insane guy with the creepy silver eyes who was enjoying having you at knifepoint *way* too much?" Atheris blew a loose piece of hair out of her eyes. "First name basis, huh? I don't know who he is to you, Saros, but I wish I'd stabbed him a few more times."

Saros's heart seized. "He's not dead, is he?"

Atheris stared at him. "Okay, firstly, I refuse to unpack why you're so clearly distressed at the idea of him being dead, but know that it has been observed and noted. Secondly, no, he's not dead. I got him in the shoulder. Slippery bastard moves too fast. Besides, I had to let him go so I could help you before you bled out."

He sighed. "Thank you." Though whether he meant for saving him or for letting Rune go alive, he wasn't quite sure.

She nodded. "Great. So are you going to tell me who he is? And... is it true?"

Saros knew that question was coming eventually. His hand

instinctively went to his side, seeking the timepiece that lived in his coat pocket, but he realized that his coat wasn't on him. A pang of dread rang through him at the thought that the watch might be lost. Despite it being a piece of the past he should never have kept, he would still mourn its loss if it was truly gone. Yes, it held painful memories, but it was the one remaining tangible reminder that Rune used to be someone else.

Saros made himself meet Atheris's eyes. "His name is Rune LeRouge, and he used to be my best friend."

Atheris blinked a few times. "Best friend, huh?"

"I said *used to be*." Saros opened and closed his stiff hand. "I knew he was different now, but not like this."

"Hm. I guess the history makes sense, given that you carry around a picture of him."

That made Saros bolt upright, entirely forgetting his injury until sharp pain ripped through his side. He bit out through gritted teeth, "What did you say?"

Atheris winced, and with a guilty look, fished into her coat pocket and produced Saros's timepiece.

He snatched it from her without hesitation. "Where did— Wait, you *opened* it?"

"You've been knocked out for six hours! I got bored! And also nosy!" Atheris adjusted her glasses. "I'm sorry, okay? But the photograph inside... That's you with him?"

Saros closed his hand around the watch. Its familiar shape and weight grounded him and eased some of his anxious energy, but he still didn't want to explain all of this to Atheris. Although, there was no point in lying when she already had a bunch of the pieces. He might as well put them together.

"Yes," he told her. He studied the patterned lid of the watch and traced his thumb over it, only barely able to feel the etched design through his glove.

"He must have been pretty special to you," Atheris said softly, "if you've kept it all this time."

Saros eased back against the wall, wincing again at the pain now throbbing all the way across his abdomen. He turned the watch over in his hand, reluctant to continue this conversation. He didn't want to keep *everything* from Atheris — even though he already did that rather a lot — but going into this chapter of his past was too much. It was too deep. And it hurt.

"So, if he was your... friend" — Saros noted the weighted pause — "then why did he try to kill you?"

Saros knew that Atheris knew why, but he was also well aware that he hadn't answered the other part to her earlier question. He looked up at her, trying to read the intention behind her eyes. He'd been absolutely prepared to tell her about his curse earlier after hearing that she was a witch. He had believed, wholeheartedly, that they would understand each other.

But then he'd seen the way she'd looked at him — the way she'd turned a weapon on him with fear in her eyes — after Rune had revealed what Saros was. And now he didn't know what to expect.

He had to tell her. No matter how she reacted, no matter if she decided to walk away and go home right this second, she deserved an answer after everything that had happened earlier tonight.

"Because of what I am," Saros said. "Because of my magic — the curse that was forced upon me as a child."

Atheris watched him steadily. "It's true, then. What he said. What he called you."

Saros swallowed and nodded. "I am a necromancer."

Atheris leaned back on her hands, holding Saros's gaze. "And I'm a witch."

He'd known that, of course, from their earlier conversation. But he could tell it was significant for her to explicitly tell him.

"So you weren't the only one keeping secrets." She bit her lip. "I'm not supposed to reveal that, ever. You know how people are about witches."

"And you know how they are about necromancers."

A hint of a smile touched the corner of Atheris's mouth. "Sounds like we're on the same page, then. I knew there was something that drew me to you, Saros Antarian."

He let the tension out of his muscles. "It... means a lot to me, that you understand. And I'm sorry you had to find out how you did."

She shrugged. "I get why you kept it a secret. It's the same reason why I never told you about my true magic."

"I was going to tell you," Saros said. "When you were talking about the amulets and your family, I asked if you were a witch because if you were, I thought you'd understand me in a way no one else ever has. I was about to tell you when Rune and his cult showed up."

Atheris flickered a smile. "I'm glad to hear you trust me with that."

"Likewise."

Silence hung between them for a moment. Somewhere outside, a wolf — or whatever Illir's Woods' version of a wolf might be — howled a mournful note. Insects trilled, and Saros could hear small critters skittering around in the shadowed corners of the barn. Only then did it occur to him that a barn was an odd thing to find in the middle of a forest. And odder still that Atheris had stumbled upon it precisely when she'd needed shelter.

His thoughts wandered back to Rune. "I think I understand, now, what he wants. The cult, too."

"Obviously they've got something against necromancy."

Saros nodded. "Seven years ago, Rune died. I saved him. That was when my power awakened, when I first understood this curse I have. But I didn't know what I was doing when I brought Rune back to life. I saved him entirely by instinct, and when he woke up..." Saros sighed and looked down at the timepiece. "He didn't know who I was. He remembered nothing, and all he felt was overwhelming fear of the magic that had just saved his life. He thinks it's evil, and he thinks he's been poisoned by dark magic. And it sounds like he also believes that if he eliminates every living necromancer — especially me, the one he thinks cursed him — he'll be cleansed."

"Sounds like a whole crock of shit."

Saros had to agree. Rune clearly didn't understand anything about Saros's power, and didn't wish to learn. As far as Saros knew, necromancy could only be bestowed by witches who possessed dark magic. It wasn't some kind of disease that could be spread from a necromancer to someone else. The only one it harmed was the necromancer themself — a slow, painful punishment for daring to play god.

As if Saros had asked for this. As if he had chased this power out of greed like Jovian had.

"But how did he find you?" Atheris asked. "If you haven't seen him in seven years and he had no idea where you were, why was he in the Woods at all?"

"I don't know." Saros had a bad feeling about it.

"Do you think he's also looking for Jovian's Tomb?"

"I would be more surprised if he wasn't." Saros looked up at the patch of sky visible through the holes in the roof. The stars were fading, the sky brightening. Dawn was soon. They couldn't stay here much longer.

"But why?" Atheris prodded. "You said the lake is magic. Why would Rune be searching for it if he's so afraid of magic?"

"It's not magic he hates," Saros said. "It's necromancy specifically." He looked at Atheris again. Perhaps it was time to tell her the whole truth. "Jovian's Tomb isn't just a potent source of magic, Atheris. It's said to be the source of necromantic power. Jovian was allegedly the first necromancer."

She raised her eyebrows, but barely looked shocked. "Okay, now everything makes sense." Her eyes darted around the room, and Saros could practically see her racing thoughts. "Okay. Okay. So you want to find the lake because you think it'll, what, strengthen the power you already have?"

"I think it'll stop my power from killing me," Saros said. "Or it'll take it away entirely."

"I see. But Rune..." Atheris frowned. "Why would someone so terrified of necromancy want to find a necromancer's tomb?"

Saros could only think of one plausible answer. It was delusional, but after what he'd seen from Rune tonight, no possibility was too irrational. He met Atheris's eyes just as she put it together, too.

Her eyes widened. "To destroy it? But—"

"Obviously that's not possible," Saros said. "Honestly, I do not care about Rune's crusade. Whatever he's plotting, he will fail. But I won't let him get in the way of our search for the lake. I won't let him be the death of me."

"He very much does not agree with that."

Saros leaned his head back on the wall behind him. "I don't know how he's navigating his way to the lake, and I don't know how much he knows. But we have to get there before him, Atheris. Before it's too late for me, and before he does anything stupid. Even I don't know all the powers that tomb holds."

"Right, so, I love the enthusiasm," Atheris said, "but one problem with that." She gestured at his midsection, namely the blood staining his shirt. "I am *not* a medic, so the magic I used to close your wound isn't going to hold forever, especially if you keep moving abruptly. It was enough to keep you from bleeding out, but the minute we continue walking, the wound's going to open again. It hasn't been long enough for your body to start healing naturally. You have to see an actual medic, but the issue with that—"

"There's no time," Saros said. "We're in *Illir's Woods*. Going out of our way to find a hospital would take too long. How much time have we lost already?"

"Only a few hours," Atheris said. "You can afford to rest a little longer."

Saros was tempted to take off his gloves and show her the fading just to prove a point. "I really can't."

"That wasn't a suggestion. Also, I'm tired." She got up and brushed off her hands on her pants, then went over to her own bedroll that she had spread out against the opposite wall. "Try not to die in your sleep."

Saros grumbled, but he knew there was no point in arguing. He sighed and closed his eyes, and within minutes, sleep claimed him.

CHAPTER 6
WANING CRESCENT VII

TRAVEL BECAME DIFFICULT AND AGONIZING. Saros had not realized how strenuous it was to hike through dense foliage and wild forest until every one of his core muscles hurt. Just two hours after leaving the abandoned barn behind, Saros thought he might pass out. The stab wound on his back, positioned just over his hip, throbbed and burned with every step. He paused to check on it frequently, fearing it had reopened, torn wider, or become infected, but Atheris assured him the magic she'd used should hold *if* he was careful.

But there was only so much care he could take when the land meandered up and down hills and the ground beneath his feet was rocky and uneven. Each time he tripped on a root or stepped in a hole, his muscles seized and the stab wound screamed.

As the day crawled by, waning toward evening, Saros's awareness dwindled until all he could feel was the pain in his side and his magic's pull toward the lake. Everything else was a blur. If Atheris had sought his attention or spoken to him, he didn't know it. He was barely aware of her presence at all.

But he couldn't stop, not even for this. It was already the third day. He had only two remaining until the new moon, and if he wasn't at the site of Jovian's Tomb by then, he was dead.

Then again, if he kept pressing on like this, what would kill him faster? The fading, or his injury?

"*Saros.*" Atheris suddenly grabbed his arm and wrenched him backward. He hissed in pain, but realized why she'd stopped him: a river ran in front of him, nearly hidden beneath the dense flora. If Saros had taken another step he would have toppled right in.

He let out a breath as his head stopped spinning. "Thanks."

"Yeah, no problem." Atheris let go of his sleeve. "Weird spot for a river."

"It's Illir's Woods." Saros's voice sounded distant in his own head. He focused on the sound of rushing water in an effort to ground himself in reality. But he must be closer to passing out than he thought, because he swore he heard whispers in that river. It wasn't just white noise, it was *speaking.*

Saros's senses battled his logic as he tried to figure out if he was hallucinating or if Illir's Woods was really so strange and extraordinary as to have a river that could speak. But he *swore* he heard it: *This way, this way, this way, thiswaythiswaythisway...*

Saros traced the river's path around the trees, but at a distance it became nearly invisible again. He glanced once at Atheris, then turned and followed the river.

"Um— Okay." Atheris hurried to catch up with him, trudging along at his side. "Did you see something? Can you feel the tomb's magic?"

"No, it's different." Saros walked as fast as his pain-ridden body would carry him. Within minutes, the trees thinned and Saros and Atheris drew up short at the edge of the forest. Ahead, a rocky beach sloped down toward a gleaming turquoise lake.

Saros's heart pounded. For a second he questioned whether it was real, because it— It couldn't be. He didn't feel...

"Wait, why doesn't it feel weird?" Atheris said.

"It's not Jovian's Tomb," Saros said. The scarce spirits that had just lifted plummeted back down. "It's just a lake."

"Well, shit. I guess that would've been too easy." Atheris set her hands on her hips and blew hair out of her face. "Hey, uh, are you okay? You look..."

"No." Now his vision was flecked with tiny white stars.

"Shit," Atheris hissed. She dropped her bag and reached out to him, but paused. "Can I— Okay, let's get closer to that lake. The ground is flat, and there's some rocks where you can sit down. I'll try applying the healing spell again, but..."

Saros nodded. He hardly felt it as she wrapped an arm around him and carefully led him down the slope toward the water. At this point, he didn't care what she did to him as long as it cleared his head and took away the pain.

"Okay." Atheris took his arm and wrapped it around her shoulders, supporting Saros's body with her own. He had to keep much of his weight on his own feet; she was too much shorter than him to be any real help, but it was better than no help at all.

They stumbled onto pure black sand scattered with smooth, glassy pebbles. Obsidian boulders sat in heaps on the beach, some poking out of the water as if ready to pounce. Atheris settled Saros by one of the rocks, and the relief he felt merely from sitting down was almost enough to heal him. Atheris then retreated to the Woods, likely to find something medicinal, and Saros laid his head back on the stone to catch his breath. He really hoped Rune hadn't hit anything critical. Though, if he had, Saros would probably be dead by now. And that was curious, wasn't it? If Rune had meant to kill him — if he was truly as murderous as the venom in his words and fire in his eyes suggested — he would have. He could have easily snatched Saros's life.

What do you really want, Rune? Is it to take my life, or only toy with it? And did that hesitation mean there was a flicker of recognition in Rune's mind? Did part of him still remember who Saros had been to him before the fear and hatred had taken over?

Saros watched Atheris poke around in the bushes, and the reality of this new obstacle settled heavily on his shoulders. He could *not* let Rune slow him down. There was never supposed to be an obstacle like this; navigating Illir's Woods was challenging enough without a cult on his tail.

This was Saros's one chance to survive. If Rune of all people screwed it up for him, he swore he'd haunt that man for the rest of his life.

Saros shifted his position against the boulders. The dull ache he'd tried to ignore all day was sharpening with a vengeance; whatever Atheris came back with, he hoped it would kill the pain as well as heal him.

A warm trickle slid down the small of his back.

Fuck. When had it started bleeding again? Saros tried to sit up, but his core muscles protested fiercely. His heart started to race. "Atheris!" His voice sounded distant in his own ears. "Atheris, come back!"

"What, I'm right here! What's— Oh, *shit.*" Atheris dropped to her knees in front of him, eyes wide with horror. Saros looked down and saw that his blood had soaked all the way around to the front of his shirt.

"Shit. *Shit.* Okay, give me your canteen." Atheris snapped her fingers.

Her words made no sense in Saros's head. "Huh?"

She grumbled something and then snatched his bag and rifled through it until she found the container of water. She unscrewed the cap and held it in her teeth, then poured water onto each of her hands. She scrubbed them together a few times before flicking off the excess water — mostly onto Saros. "Okay, turn around. I need to see."

Saros shook his head. Even breathing hurt; there was no way he could twist his whole body around. "I can't."

"You can, and you *will*, if you want to stop bleeding." Atheris gripped his arm. "I'll steady you. Come on."

Saros took a few deep breaths, then gritted his teeth and slowly turned his back to Atheris. Burning pain clawed its way up his back; the coarse boulder before him was the only thing keeping him upright.

Atheris wrenched his shirt up and Saros gasped as the fabric unstuck from the blood congealing around the stab wound. Cold water rushed over his skin, relieving some of his discomfort even as it stung. Saros leaned his forehead against the rock and waited for whatever Atheris would inflict upon him next, but seconds dragged by and she did nothing.

He peeked over his shoulder and found her pale-faced and frozen with her hands hovering over his back.

"Atheris?"

She blinked a few times and dragged a hand through her hair. "Shit, Saros. I can't..."

"Don't tell me you can't do anything."

"I— I can apply the spell again, but if it didn't hold before..." She bit her lip and met his eyes. "Saros, I'm not a medic. I don't know what else to do."

"What are you saying? I can't *die*, Atheris!"

"You're not going to *die*," she snapped. Saros could hear the panic edging her voice. "But you need serious medical attention that I can't give you."

Saros shook his head. "You have to do *something*!"

"I know! Let me think!" She shoved to her feet and paced back and forth a few times, then fished into her pockets and drew out the herbs she'd collected from the Woods. "Okay. There is other magic that can help you, but I don't think you're going to like it."

"I don't like slowly bleeding to death, either," Saros snapped. "I don't care. Do it. Whatever it is, just... make it stop."

Atheris bit her lip and nodded, then held up one of the herbs. "Option one: I can make a salve from this plant that will gradually heal you, but it won't do much for the pain. There's still a risk of the wound reopening if you don't take it easy for the next few days, but this remedy is stronger than the other spell I used."

"So slow healing and I'm still in pain. What's option two?"

She grimaced. "The other option is using magic to cauterize the wound so it—"

"No!" Saros cut her off, shaking his head. "No, absolutely not."

"Okay, heard and understood, but listen." Atheris raised her eyebrows. "You want to be back on your feet with minimal pain hindering you from getting to this lake? You want to make it to the tomb before your murderous little friend does? You want to be *absolutely sure* this injury doesn't get worse?"

"Atheris, *melting my skin together* is going to create more problems."

"But it will also solve at least three of them."

He clenched his jaw. "How long will the salve take to heal the wound?"

She shrugged. "At least a week to close completely."

"Are you saying that because it's true or because you *want* to melt my skin closed?"

"Saros, I don't *want* to hurt you. I want you to look at this logically."

"Oh, my apologies for being hesitant to be in more pain!"

"You want me to be real?" Atheris waved her hand with the leaf. "This is going to put you in more pain than cauterizing the wound. I won't try to convince you that that *won't* hurt like a motherfucker, but if we do this, I can actually give you something that will numb the pain while the burns settle and heal."

"Why can't you numb the pain with the salve?"

"Because the plant I know that will numb the pain reacts poorly with the plant that creates the salve, and you'll end up with a horrible, burning rash."

Saros sighed and dragged his hands through his hair. He could not believe he was about to agree to this. "Okay."

Atheris eyed him skeptically. "Are you sure?"

"Don't make me think about this any more than I have to. I trust you," he said. "You're telling me this is my best option. Fine. Do it."

Atheris nodded. "All right. Um. I'm sorry in advance."

He clenched his jaw. "Just get it over with, Atheris."

She fished her amulets out of her shirt and lifted the cord over her head, then clutched the amber stone in her hand. She spoke the spell for fire, and the stone burst alive with a bright orange flame.

Saros eyed it with a deep, sickening pit of dread sinking in his gut.

Atheris cupped her free hand around the amulet until the flame died down and left the stone smoldering red-hot. Then she met Saros's eyes. "I, uh, would advise you not to watch."

Saros didn't object. He wrenched off one of his gloves and wadded it between his teeth, then pressed his forehead to the rock again and closed his eyes.

The pain was immediate and ruthless. Every one of Saros's senses got smothered under the scalding explosion of agony. He felt a scream scrape his throat but couldn't hear it; he felt a steady hand on his shoulder, holding him up, but even that hurt. Everything hurt. Every nerve in his body was aflame. Shudders ran through him, and when the sharp, brilliant pain returned, he blacked out.

It was only a short second before he blinked back to vague consciousness, but now the worst of the agony had lifted. In the wake of the burning he was freezing even as sweat ran down his face. His vision swam. He couldn't stop shaking. Hot pain crawled under his skin, pooling around his injury. He was glad he lacked the focus to look at the wounds.

As his senses crept back one by one, his surroundings came back to him and he heard hurried footsteps approaching him. Atheris dropped to her knees at his side again — had she left? When? Why? — and then he felt blessedly cool water run over his skin.

He dropped the glove from his mouth and gasped in a deep breath. The tension bled from his muscles and he slumped against the rocks. Some of the fog muffling his head cleared, and he heard Atheris's voice.

"You're okay, Saros, you're okay. It's over. I'm sorry. Illir's balls, I'm fucking sorry." Her voice was strained with... Fear? Guilt? Something like that, Saros thought.

He managed to turn his head and focus on her face. He blinked a few times and realized her cheeks were streaked with tears. Frowning, he set his gloved hand on her shoulder. "Atheris." His voice was scraped raw. "It's okay."

She sank back in the sand, shoved her glasses up into her hair, and dragged her hands across her face.

Saros closed his eyes. The cool water from the lake had eased the lingering burn from Atheris's magic, and the pain was receding surprisingly quickly.

In fact, within minutes, Saros couldn't feel a hint of what he'd just endured.

He managed to sit up a little straighter and eyed Atheris curiously. "What did you do?"

She looked up. "Huh?"

"The pain is gone. Completely. It's as though you *didn't* just melt my skin together."

She stared at him. "How is that possible? Are you about to pass out? Is it just so bad that your body is saying, 'No, actually, I don't want to feel this?'"

"No, I feel fine." Saros tugged his shirt up only to find that Atheris had bandaged the wound. "Oh. Where did you get the bandages?"

"Brought them with me in case of disaster," she said. "Good thing I did. But this is weird, that you're in absolutely no pain. I did, in fact, just melt your skin together."

"Mrrow."

Saros and Atheris turned their heads. Zenith stood by the edge of the lake, ears perked and tail standing up. She dipped one paw into the water and drew it across her face.

"Okay, I don't speak cat," Atheris said. "What's that supposed to mean?"

"I think…" Saros snapped his fingers to summon her and she trotted over, purring. He ran his hand over her head and scratched her ears. "I think she means the lake somehow helped. Its water must have some sort of healing properties?"

Zenith made a soft, affirmative noise.

"Yeah?" Saros stroked his hand down her back. "Is that right?"

She let out a slightly more impatient meow.

"How is this cat literally talking to you right now?" Atheris said. She opened her coat and lifted her white snake off her shoulders, holding it up to look it in the eyes. "Can you do that? Can you talk to me?"

The snake stared back at her and flicked its tongue.

"No? Nothing in there? Figures." She placed it around her shoulders again. "Magic lake, huh? I guess that adds up, for Illir's Woods. Too bad it's not the magic lake we *want*."

"Speak for yourself. I for one am rather grateful for this particular magic lake. Let's hope there's no secret side effects." Saros carefully got to his feet, expecting the newly healed wounds to hurt, but he still felt nothing. Not that he *wanted* to be in pain, but it was a weird dissonance, knowing he'd been badly injured but unable to feel it.

"Okay, hang on." Atheris got up and brushed sand off her pants. "I know you feel right as rain, but that doesn't reverse anything that just happened. I'm still ordering you to take it easy. Can Zenith change into the panther on command?"

Saros looked at Zenith. She blinked up at him, whiskers twitching. "I... have no idea. I'd never seen her do that before the other night. But let's see."

He knelt in the sand in front of her. "Zenith, uh... change?"

She blinked again and licked her nose. For a second, she didn't look keen to do anything at all. Then she turned around and walked away from him.

He glanced at Atheris, who pursed her lips.

Saros looked at Zenith again, ready to try a different command, but now she was pacing in a circle. Gradually, she quickened to a trot, then a sprint, increasing speed in a tightening circle until she was a black blur against the black sand. When she finally slowed, she was once again a giant panther.

Zenith shook out her velvety coat, then turned to Saros and made a deep, rumbling purr. She padded over to him and butted his head with her own, which would've concussed him if she'd done it any harder. He grinned, still mystified by this extraordinary animal, and ran his hands over her soft fur.

"Perfect! I don't understand this even a little, but it's fine!" Atheris approached Zenith and held up her hand, to which Zenith pressed her pink nose. "Do you mind if we catch a ride, girl?"

Saros frowned. "Wait, what?"

Zenith drew back and made another low noise that was more of a growl than a purr. But she didn't sound angry, just... exasperated. She huffed through her nose, then crouched down to put her back at a more convenient height for Saros and Atheris to climb on.

"You're kidding," Saros said. "She's not a horse! This seems unfair."

"Hey, I asked, and she's clearly agreeing," Atheris said. "This is consensual riding."

Saros shot her a dry look. "Don't talk about my cat like that."

She snorted and climbed onto Zenith's back. "Come on, Saros. Unless you'd like to walk?"

Zenith eyed him expectantly, as if pleading with him to take advantage of this offering while he had it. He gave in, mostly because the idea of hiking in the wake of having his skin melted closed made him want to drown himself in that lake.

Saros grabbed a fistful of Zenith's scruff and, gritting his teeth against the ache in his bones, hauled himself onto her back. He settled behind her shoulders, in front of Atheris, and turned back to look at her.

"What?" she said.

"Atheris." He met her eyes. "If those snakes get *anywhere* near me, I *will* throw you off of this cat and leave you for the wolves and fucked-up monsters."

She looked surprised for half a second, then cackled. "No promises."

"I am dead serious. I won't hesitate."

"Such a way to treat your dear friend after I saved your life." She tutted and shook her head.

Saros rolled his eyes and nudged his heel against Zenith's side. She stood up and took a few steps forward up the beach. Now that Saros wasn't dizzy with pain, he could feel the lake's pull more clearly. This natural lake felt like a barrier, like if they went around it in any direction, they'd be going away from Jovian's Tomb.

"Okay, Zenith," he said. "Take us back the way we came."

He thought he'd have to nudge her again, but she made an affirmative noise and then leapt forward, crossing the beach in two giant bounds. Saros scrambled to hold on and Atheris grabbed onto him, sending a jolt of pain through his side. He hissed through his teeth, pulling hard on Zenith's scruff. "Easy, Zenith! Easy!"

She halted and turned her head over her shoulder, whiskers twitching.

"Don't look at me like that. You can't go that fast. We'll fall off." He eased his hold on her fur. "Come on, now. *Walk*. No running, no leaping, or— I don't know, prancing."

"*Prancing?*"

"What?" Saros glanced back at Atheris. "Do *you* know what to expect from a highly intelligent feline who can shapeshift at will?"

"She doesn't seem like the prancing type." Atheris shrugged.

Zenith snorted, twitching her ears, then continued forward into the trees at an easier pace. Saros sat back with a sigh, and Atheris let go of him.

Zenith carried them swiftly through the Woods, expertly weaving around the trees and navigating the uneven ground with much more grace than Saros and Atheris would on their two feet. In minutes they'd covered more ground than they otherwise would have in half an hour.

"All right, I'll say it," Saros said, "you were right. This is better than walking."

"Sometimes the renowned Atheris Fay has good ideas."

Saros went to turn to her when a deafening cacophony of screeches filled the air. He looked up just in time to see a massive flock of enormous birds soar over the treetops. Long tail feathers streamed behind them, and their wing beats rustled the trees. They sounded to each other in shrieks of various pitches that echoed across the sky and through the woods. Within the trees, other creatures called out in reply, and the trees themselves turned their round, rolling eyeballs skyward. Their branches swayed as if waving at the feathered creatures overhead.

"You know, maybe this place isn't so bad," Atheris said.

Saros eyed her curiously. "No?"

"Just because the creatures are fucked up doesn't mean they're going to kill us," she said with a shrug. "Besides, I think the Woods are helping us."

"What?" Saros had suspected something similar, but he'd chalked it up to his imagination.

"What made you follow that river to the lake?" Atheris asked.

"Most likely a hallucination," Saros said, even as he doubted it.

And Atheris knew that. "You heard something, didn't you?"

He hesitated, but nodded. "The river. It sounded like... I mean, this is crazy. But it sounded like the water was saying 'This way.' Like it wanted us to follow it."

"And the lake's water ended up healing your injury," Atheris said. "The river wanted you to find the lake so you could be healed. And the Woods showed me the correct plant to use for the salve. The bushes and plants *moved* to let me find what I needed." She gazed up at the trees; they gazed back. "I dunno, Saros, I don't think this forest is out to get us — or anyone. I think it's just misunderstood."

"I wouldn't be surprised," Saros said. He supposed that just because a place was hostile to humans didn't mean it was any less of a home to other creatures. To the odd animals that dwelled here, Illir's Woods was perfectly inhabitable. Perhaps humans weren't meant to belong here. Saros could see the beauty in that.

He glanced over his shoulder at Atheris. "So, what, you think it's Illir Himself who doesn't want us to die?"

"You're really asking the resident witch about a god?" Atheris snorted. "Why don't you ask your devout little friend?"

"Stop calling him little," Saros muttered.

"Oh? Is he not? Because to me it seemed he was overcompensating with that dagger."

"Illir's teeth, Atheris, shut up."

She cackled.

If there was any sort of god in these Woods, Saros prayed to them for patience. It was going to be a long day.

CHAPTER 7
NEW MOON I

THEY TRAVELED UNTIL NIGHTFALL. Saros's eyes drooped, he'd been suffering a persistent headache for a while now, and a sharp twinge in his lower back was acting up after many hours on Zenith's back. As the feline plodded along, Saros searched their surroundings for a place to make camp. He tried not to be too picky; nowhere was ideal in Illir's Woods, but there had to be a glade or some boulders or *something* to provide a little shelter...

Zenith suddenly drew up short, and Saros looked ahead. "What is it?"

She purred and crept forward a few more steps. Saros peered into the dark, but whatever she saw was invisible to him.

Then something shifted within the trees, drawing Saros's attention upward. He watched, and when the wind settled a little, he saw a steady plume of white smoke rising toward the sky.

Zenith made an approving noise and continued forward. Saros was too baffled to stop her. How was there smoke in the middle of Illir's Woods? Who else would be camping out here? It couldn't be Rune's cult; Zenith wouldn't be taking them in that direction if she sensed danger.

He thought of what Atheris had suggested earlier, that the Woods might be helping them. If that was true, was it now granting Saros's wish of a safe haven for the night? The idea was less comforting than it ought to have been; Saros didn't like the idea of the Woods listening to his thoughts.

Because if the Woods heard and granted travelers' wishes, was that the reason Rune was so easily led to Saros? Was Illir's Woods helping him as much as it was helping Saros?

Zenith stopped walking and meowed, drawing Saros out of his thoughts. He looked up, and the scene in front of him made even less sense than everything else about this damned forest. A squat building hewn from dark lumber sat tucked among the trees, crowned with a splintered wooden sign that was too faded to read. The doors were open, the light inside was bright and warm, and smoke steadily rose from the chimney. Saros could hear a murmur of voices from within, and the mouthwatering smell of food was almost enough to reel him right in.

But he nudged his heel against Zenith's side, halting her before she had taken more than another step forward. She gave an indignant growl that vibrated through her whole body. "Can't fault me for being cautious," Saros said. "This place shouldn't be here. This is impossible."

Impossible was a relative term in Illir's Woods, and though Saros was beginning to understand what that truly meant, he still hesitated to trust any kindness these Woods placed before him.

He turned his head over his shoulder and found Atheris sound asleep. He'd figured, since she hadn't said a word in hours, but sitting upright on the back of a giant panther could not be the most comfortable way to sleep.

"Atheris," he said gently, poking her arm. "Hey. Wake up."

She gasped and jerked her head up. "I'm here!"

"How were you asleep like that?"

"Huh?" She rubbed her neck. "Ow. Where are we?" Then she sniffed and her eyes widened. "Whoa. What is that *smell*?"

Saros nodded toward the tavern. "What do you think? Genuine respite for travelers, or a blatant trap?"

"We're in Illir's Woods, Saros. Everything's a trap."

"So we definitely shouldn't stop there."

"Obviously not." Atheris pursed her lips.

Saros glanced at the building, then back at Atheris, and then they both scrambled off Zenith's back and strode ahead toward the tavern. Zenith padded alongside Saros, purring, then bounded ahead and changed back to her normal size.

Atheris hurried her pace, but Saros couldn't bring himself to walk any faster. Nearly every part of him was stiff or hurt or both, but the promise of actual food that wasn't nuts and dried fruit *plus* the possibility of somewhere to sleep other than a bedroll in a tent, kept him trudging forward until he caught up with Atheris at the tavern's front steps.

She looked like she might actually drool. "I don't think I care if we die here as long as I can eat whatever's cooking."

"Ideally we don't die here," Saros reminded her. He bent down to grab Zenith and let her climb onto his shoulders, then with one last glance back at the Woods, he followed Atheris inside.

Warmth and jovial noise enveloped him at once. The place was packed, every table crowded with people dressed in everything from plain everyday overcoats to fancy suits and dresses fit for a royal party. Their only consistency was, oddly, their hair: every one of the patrons in the building had the same long, shiny black hair.

Saros couldn't make sense of it. Where had all these people come from? Were they even real?

"O...kay," Atheris mumbled. "So, uh, this is weird, but I don't feel threatened, so... food?" She raised her eyebrows and turned on her heel, sauntering toward the bar, where a tall, muscular woman with purple-streaked hair was pouring drinks for the flock of guests gathered at one corner.

Saros, having nowhere else to go, followed Atheris and quietly took a seat at the opposite corner from the others. He was content to wait for the barkeep to notice him, but Atheris marched directly toward her and took a seat in front of her. She leaned her elbows on the bar and placed her chin on her interlaced hands, and Saros watched the barkeep do a double take when she glanced Atheris's way.

He resisted the immediate urge to flee the scene as he understood her goal. Illir's teeth, if he had to watch her flounder her way through flirting with this woman for the foreseeable future, he might have to leave her here and hightail it to Jovian's Tomb on his own.

But a minute went by and Atheris didn't make a fool of herself. Saros watched in mild fascination as she struck up and maintained a conversation with the barkeep, who visibly warmed up to her within seconds. The tall woman laughed and waved her hand at something Atheris had said, and he swore Atheris's freckled cheeks turned a shade redder. The barkeep grabbed a glass from the shelf behind her, plucked a bottle of amber liquor from beneath the bar, and slid the glass to Atheris. She leaned an elbow on the bar and met Atheris's eyes with a smirk as she poured the drink.

Saros couldn't believe his eyes. He wasn't sure if he was impressed, or...

Okay, he was a little impressed.

Atheris made an obvious point to brush her hand against the barkeep's as she took the glass and raised it to her lips. She gave an approving nod, then got up and flicked her hand in a salute before joining Saros in his secluded corner.

"Precisely what I needed," she said as she perched on a stool beside him. "Want one? I'm sure I can talk Bex into it." She waggled her eyebrows.

"I'm fine," he muttered. He never had mixed well with alcohol. He glanced at the barkeep, who had definitely looked this way more than once since Atheris had sat down. "Did you flirt with her just to get a free drink?"

"No way! That wasn't even my goal. She's just pretty, I'm an opportunist, and to be honest I'm surprised she talked to me at all, let alone flirted back *and* gave me a free drink." She sipped the liquor. "Think she'd let me buy one for her?"

Saros shrugged. This wasn't exactly his area of expertise. But he didn't see why Atheris shouldn't ask, given how the barkeep had responded to what Saros was still convinced was very cringey flirting.

"Oh, come on." Atheris nudged his shoulder. "Be my wingman."

"Clearly you don't need one." Saros turned his attention to the chalkboard mounted on the wall behind the bar. Underneath a dozen beverage options — of the alcoholic variety and otherwise — was a short food menu of five items. His eye caught on the one dish without any meat in it — vegetable stew with "exotic" spices, whatever that meant — but part of him was still hesitant to eat anything from this place. There were too many myths about malicious creatures luring in unsuspecting victims with enchanted food. Illir's Woods was the last place on earth to let his guard down.

"I know that look," Atheris said. "No way in hell are we leaving now. I'm starving, I still wanna talk to Bex, and I'm also tipsy. I'll be *insufferable* if we leave now, Saros. You think I don't shut up normally? Wait till you see drunk Atheris. You'll—"

"I get it," he muttered, rubbing his forehead. "Why don't you tell your barkeep friend all about it?"

"Excellent idea." Atheris downed the rest of her drink and waved her hand in the air to grab the woman's attention. "Bex! Hey! Got a second?"

Saros wanted to disappear.

Bex sauntered over and leaned forward on the bar. "Hey, darling. Ready for another already? I can make you somethin' special." Her blue eyes glinted.

Atheris grinned, biting her lip. For a blink Saros swore she looked *shy*, and the bashful expression was totally out of place on her face. "Sounds perfect to me. Show me what you got." She actually, literally batted her eyes, and Saros resisted the urge to roll his own.

He sat in awkward silence for another minute before gently clearing his throat. Atheris startled like she'd forgotten he was there — *Thanks, Atheris* — and visibly scrambled to put her thoughts in order. "Oh! And we'd like to order some food. What do you recommend?"

Bex rubbed her chin. "Anything but the meat pies, really. Cook tends to get... *creative* with those."

Yeah, Saros didn't want to know what was in those.

"I'll have your favorite, then," Atheris said. "Saros?"

"The stew, if you would," he said.

"Oh, good choice." Bex grinned, then knocked a knuckle on the counter next to Atheris's glass. "Comin' right up, along with a surprise drink for you, darling. And anything to drink for you, sir?"

Saros shook his head. "Nah. Thanks."

"Sure." She went off to check on the rowdy group on the other corner of the bar, laughing along with them for a minute, then disappeared into a back room.

Saros looked at Atheris. "That was mortifying, just so you know."

"Yeah, well, so was watching your not-little not-friend take you from behind with that dagger of his."

Saros put his face in his hands. "Illir's teeth, I really do hate you."

Atheris cackled. "Nah, you love me. Hey, and speaking of which, tell me *more* about Rune."

"Absolutely not."

"Can I ask you questions, though?"

"No."

"Okaaay, but what if I told you about *my* terrible ex?"

"Be my guest. You're still not getting a word about Rune." He disliked her implication that Rune was terrible, but after watching him stab Saros in the back, he supposed it was a fair observation.

He finally surfaced from his hands and looked at her. "I never said he was my ex."

She gave him a look.

Saros frowned and turned away from her, focusing his attention on his gloved hands on the counter. She could needle him all she wanted; she was not getting this story out of him.

Across the tavern, raucous laughter burst into the air. Saros glanced over his shoulder at the clustered guests and felt something tug in his chest. He'd gotten used to being a loner these past seven years, but he missed having close friends like this. He missed the easy and carefree connections with people who looked at him like a *person*, not like a curse he didn't ask for.

"Not that I'm assuming anything," Atheris said, swiveling side to side on the stool, "but you *do* carry around a photograph of him."

Saros ignored her.

"Hey, look, I'm not judging you." She was undeterred. "Obviously I wouldn't judge you. I'm just making an *observation*. You still love him, don't you?"

Saros looked up at her sharply, but bit his tongue. He refused to entertain even a vague answer to that question. It wasn't simple, anyway. It wasn't a yes or no. The Rune that he loved was not the man who had tried to take his life. He was the Rune from before, who had been Saros's dearest friend, who had never stopped caring for Saros even after the fear of his curse had ostracized him from everyone else in his life. He was the Rune who had loved Saros in return, and had been afraid to tell him lest he unsettle the deep bond they already had.

"Okay, point taken." Atheris drew her knee up to her chest. "So *my* disaster ex was my second girlfriend, who — I'll be honest — I really thought would be the last one. You know, like, I thought she was *the* one. Ugh. But we'd been friends for years before we were anything more, and it took both of us an *embarrassingly* long time to realize that we wanted to be more than friends. She kissed me for the first time in the *rain*, Saros. The *rain*." She let out a dramatic fake sob.

"Anyway, after we got that sorted out, nothing was awkward or anything. We just clicked." She lowered her voice to a murmur. "She even knew that I'm a witch and it didn't matter."

The hint of melancholy that had shadowed her eyes instantly vanished as Bex returned with Atheris's drink and both of their meals. Atheris's eyes lit up at the drink, which was a pale pink color with an orange slice balanced on the rim of the glass. "You're a wonder, Bex. This looks delicious."

"A perfect match, then." Bex left with a wink.

Atheris stared after her, mouth hanging open. "Oh, I wanna kiss her so bad." She took a sip of the drink and her eyes widened. "Oh, shit, this is good. But yeah, disaster ex *claimed* she didn't mind my magic, but then I heard rumors." She set her glass down and sighed, toying with the orange garnish. "I don't know how long it had been going on, but she had spread all these stories about me. Shit like, I'd enchanted her to be friends with me, and then tricked her into falling in love with me. Then of course all our mutual friends came up with similar stories, saying they'd suspected all along that there was something *tricky* about me." She scoffed. "As if I needed to become more of an outcast than I already was."

Saros studied her as his dinner cooled in front of him, fascinated by the way she peeled back and then covered up the layers that made up her life. One second she bore her heart and her miseries to him, the pain still resonant in her eyes, and the next, her bubbly spark outshone everything else. He couldn't help but wonder if she could see his layers as well as he could see hers.

Atheris downed a quarter of her drink in one go, then turned to her food. Bex had brought her a massive piece of breaded fish drizzled in something creamy and surrounded by browned slices of potato. Atheris plucked one of the potato slices and dragged it through the sauce, then took an experimental bite. Her eyes lit up again. "Oh! Okay, that's good too. So far, nothing but praise for this place. Good food, good drinks, hot barkeep. Five stars."

Saros eyed his own food. A warm, pleasant smell wafted off the stew, and he moved it around to cool it. He took a hesitant sip, still convinced that the food in this place would land him with an additional curse, but the worry instantly fled his mind when he tasted it. It *was* good; hot and hearty and ablaze with spices Saros couldn't even name.

Atheris grinned. "See? Sometimes it's worth it to investigate taverns in Illir's Woods that by all logic shouldn't be here."

"Guess so." Saros kept eating, giving Atheris space to continue her story if she wished. But her mood had shifted back to its usual lightness, and Saros didn't want to pressure her to relive what must be distressing memories. But he did want her to know that he sympathized.

"Hey." He looked up at her. "That was rotten, what that girl did to you. Especially after you were friends for so long already. I'm sorry."

She blinked, obviously surprised at his words, and started to shrug it off but then just nodded. "Yeah."

"You don't have to talk about it." Saros stirred the stew. "Just wanted to say that."

Atheris fell quiet, and Saros thought that was the end of the conversation, but then she slid her hand toward him and touched his wrist. "Thanks. That means a lot." She glanced up at him. "And look, I won't pry about your history with Rune. But I can recognize that it's painful for you, and I'm sorry about... whatever happened there, too."

Saros nodded. "Does that mean you won't tell any more inappropriate jokes?"

A devilish grin split her face. "No. Not even a little."

"Yeah, I didn't think so."

Atheris turned her attention to her food then, but Saros searched for something else to say, something *more* that would offer a piece of himself that showed her he understood. But he came up empty. The whole story behind his curse was too much, and his history with Rune was too fragile. He didn't know how to tell a little without spilling all of it.

"Can I ask you something?" Atheris chewed on a potato slice. "It's not about Rune, I promise."

Saros nodded.

But before she could voice her question, the gaggle of noisy guests burst out of their chairs and moved in an oscillating mob toward the doors. They laughed and howled and cackled in a way that almost sounded birdlike, and when they shuffled past the bar Saros caught glimpses of distinctly inhuman eyes and sharp fangs in their mouths.

He barely tried not to stare.

As they neared the door, one by one they spun on their heels and swept outside in a flurry of... feathers? Saros was sure he must be seeing things, but no — they transformed from humanoid to fully birdlike in a blink. They rushed outside, leaving black feathers scattered in their wake.

Behind the bar, Bex tsked. "Told 'em time after time not to transform till they get outside. Always leavin' a mess of feathers."

Saros exchanged a bewildered look with Atheris.

"What?" Bex chuckled as she approached their corner of the bar. "Didya think you'd stumbled into a dreadfully normal tavern? In the middle of Illir's Woods?"

"Saros thought we were going to die here," Atheris mumbled around a mouthful of food.

"You're the one who said you didn't *care* if we died here as long as you got to eat," he pointed out.

"And I stand by that."

Bex collected the empty glasses left by the other guests. "Now I'm no *expert* in readin' folks, but I do meet all kindsa people here. So I've got a sense for when folks aren't all they seem to be." She turned to

Saros and Atheris. "What's the story with you two, then? Where you from? Where you *going*?"

Saros set his hand on Atheris's arm, stopping her before she had even taken a breath. She looked at him, and he hoped his glare translated correctly through her intoxication. To his relief, she shut her mouth, thought for a second, then turned to Bex again.

"Don't suppose you get many folks saying they're just passing through, huh?"

Bex smiled, and Atheris visibly swooned. "Every time someone says that to me," she reached under the bar and brought up a jar packed with coins and notes, "I take the tip they leave and put it in here. Someday it'll buy me a ticket south."

Saros had about a thousand questions for someone who ran a tavern and presumably lived in Illir's Woods, but while he was content to finish his dinner and silently wonder about Bex's life, Atheris launched into a series of increasingly personal questions for the barkeep.

While they chatted, Saros tuned them out and returned his attention to his food. His thoughts wandered idly between the Woods, Jovian's Tomb, his next steps, his curse... but he adamantly refused to think about Rune. That inkling of a suspicion that the Woods were listening to him lurked at the back of his mind.

Behind him, the tavern door groaned open and Bex abruptly looked up. She frowned and stood straighter, and her instant mood shift made Saros turn around to look.

Oh, no. A man dressed in a long black cloak stood in the doorway, face shadowed by the cloak's hood. For a heartbeat Saros feared it was Rune, but no, the man's build was broader and taller than Rune. Yet the black cloak unmistakably matched the cult, and the man openly carried a dagger at his hip.

Bex gave the man a once-over. "Can I help ya?"

He silently scanned the room for a moment, and Saros tried not to react when his gaze landed on him, but then the man shrugged and trudged toward the back of the tavern.

Saros looked at Atheris, who returned his wary expression.

It *could* be a coincidence that the man happened to have a black cloak and long dagger similar to Rune's cultists, but this wasn't the place to give people the benefit of the doubt. They should go. This man's presence was clearly a threat, a hint that Rune knew where Saros was and they had not seen the last of each other.

This whole situation was probably a trap, now that Saros considered it. Rune wouldn't burst in here with his whole cult, knives out, and make a scene. Instead, he sent in one man as a warning, and to lure Saros out.

If Saros was a little smarter, he would not step directly into this trap. But he wanted an end to this.

He stood up from the bar, stopping Atheris when she did the same. "No. Stay here. This is between me and him."

He strode outside before she could argue.

The night was a blanket of solid darkness over the Woods. Overhead, the moon was barely a sliver, and everything outside of the glow from the tavern's windows was utterly invisible to Saros. He sensed a presence beyond the light's reach, a threat lying in wait for him to move closer.

He stepped farther away from the tavern, but stopped before the edge of the pool of light. "I know you're here," he called. His voice sounded too loud amid the silence. "It doesn't have to be like this, Rune. I just want to talk."

Somewhere within the trees, a branch snapped. Foliage rustled. Saros waited, heart pounding, but the noises quieted and no one approached.

"Rune," Saros called again. "Show yourself. Enough with the games. I know you think you've been hurt or corrupted or whatever, but that's not how this magic works. The only one it's hurting is me."

He moved to the very edge of the light's reach, peering ahead into the shadows. But with his eyes used to the brightness within the tavern, he couldn't see a thing out here.

"Damn it, Rune," he muttered, and stepped into the darkness.

The forest's eerie silence frayed his nerves, and even his own footsteps startled him each time he snapped a twig. He walked in uneasy solitude for several minutes until someone stepped into his path.

Saros stopped and his breath caught. Seeing Rune again was no less of a shock than last time, an odd mix of relief and dread. Saros's instincts battled each other, the one desperate to retain his closest friend warring against the one desperate to stay alive.

"You're back on your feet rather fast, aren't you?" Rune steadily rotated the dagger in his hand, a casual fidget, but Saros had seen his skill with the weapon. He couldn't let it come down to a fight again.

"No thanks to you," he said. He studied Rune closely, still unable to reconcile the man he remembered with the man before him now. "What will it take for you to understand that I am not a threat to you?"

"And what will it take for you to understand that my duty goes far beyond you and me?" Rune moved a step closer, holding Saros's gaze. "This is bigger than us. We're so small, so foolish and juvenile in the grand scheme of God's universe. We don't matter, Saros. Only God does."

Saros couldn't stop himself from cringing. "If we don't matter," he said, "then why are you following me? What do you want with Jovian's Tomb?"

"The tomb?" Rune smiled. "The tomb will be my ultimate triumph, of course. The necromantic curse began with Jovian, and it will end with him. Adds a little poetry that it will be your end, as well. What a satisfying story this will make."

Saros didn't know what to do. Rune wasn't going to listen, wasn't going to change his mind. But maybe Saros could at least shake the foundation of Rune's belief. The opposite of faith was doubt, was it not?

Saros glanced around at the trees, then back at Rune. "You're right about one thing, at least."

Rune arched an eyebrow.

"Necromancy is unnatural," Saros went on. "It is a curse. It ruined my life probably as much as it ruined yours."

"Don't mock me," Rune snarled. "You thrive on that power."

"Do I?" Saros tugged off one of his gloves and held up his hand. It was dark, but he saw Rune's eyes widen. "It's killing me, Rune. This is the price I pay for—"

"For playing God." Rune curled his lip.

"Yes," Saros said, "for playing god. But I did not ask for this. We both agree that this power is a curse. It was given to me against my knowledge and against my will. That's a mystery I've never been able to solve. And I'll resent it forever, not for slowly killing me, but for taking away the most important person in my life."

Rune's eyes softened, just a little. He slightly let his guard down. "Don't you want to be free of it?"

"More than anything," Saros said. His heart pounded harder, but he made a conscious effort to remain calm so he didn't lose Rune. Maybe, just maybe, this would work. "I am a victim of this power just as much as you are."

"If that's true," Rune said softly, "why did you curse me with it? If it is truly harmful to you, why would you force that upon someone else the same way it had been forced upon you?"

"I didn't mean to," Saros said. "I never meant to hurt you. All I wanted was to save you. All I knew was that I couldn't let you die."

Rune frowned, blinking a few times, and his eyes darted around as he chased a hint of memory. Saros waited, silently begging him to remember *something*. When he sought Saros's gaze again, there was finally a faint hint of doubt in his eyes. "Who was it that you lost when this curse claimed you?"

Saros drifted a little closer to Rune. "Someone I loved. The one and only person I loved."

Rune held Saros's gaze. "Who were they?"

Moment of truth. Saros lowered his voice to a murmur. "You."

Rune's eyes widened, and for a heartbeat Saros thought that did the trick. But then Rune's expression twisted into fury once more and he flung himself at Saros, screaming, "*Liar!*"

Saros just barely stumbled out of the way. He used the trees as cover as he dodged Rune's wild strikes, tripping over roots and bushes as he made his way back toward the tavern.

He was stupid to think that might've worked. Even pandering to Rune's beliefs wasn't enough to jog memories he didn't have. But Saros, in all his foolishness, had held onto the faint hope that the Rune he used to know was still in there somewhere. How could he not hope?

How could he give up so easily on someone who had never given up on him?

Saros flinched as a small knife *thunked* into a tree inches from his head. He turned around, tripped, and in the seconds it took his body to hit the forest floor, everything happened all at once.

Rune leapt at him, dagger drawn, eyes ablaze. A furious roar rang through the woods, and something soared over Saros's head. He had just enough of a second to glimpse a familiar massive panther leaping at Rune before he hit the ground and time sped back to normal.

Zenith collided with Rune and brought him down hard. She growled and Rune shrieked, and Saros scrambled to his feet and bolted toward them before he knew what he was doing.

"Zenith! Stop!" He grabbed Rune's discarded dagger from the ground and rushed to Zenith, who had Rune pinned under one of her massive paws. She loomed over him, growling, bared teeth inches from his throat. Rune stared at Zenith with raw terror in his eyes. His hands gripped her leg, trying to pry her paw off his chest, but she didn't budge. He writhed under her weight, kicking and struggling, and this sight of him facing the real possibility of his death and being *terrified* of it sent a strange shiver down Saros's spine.

He liked seeing Rune like this. He liked it rather a lot.

But he still couldn't let Zenith kill him. He grabbed a handful of fur on her side to try to pull her back; she didn't even flinch, and Saros's hand came away wet and sticky.

Only then did he realize that Zenith reeked of blood. "Zenith? What...?"

She turned her head and growled at him, flattening her ears to her head. Her yellow eyes darted between him and somewhere over his shoulder. She growled again, and when Saros didn't move, she batted at him with her paw.

"Okay, okay, you want me to go, but..." His stomach sank as he put it together. Zenith had stayed back at the tavern, with Atheris and...

Oh no.

Saros whirled on Rune. "What have you done?"

Rune's chest heaved as he struggled for breath beneath Zenith's hold. He grinned, eyes wild. "I can't keep letting you get away, can I?

Consider it collateral damage, necromancer. And know that it's all your fault."

Saros's heart pitched. *No.*

Fuck, he'd left Atheris back there alone, with—

"You son of a bitch," Saros snarled, and sprinted back toward the tavern. "Show me the way!" he commanded the Woods, and he would've been more amazed that the Woods listened if he wasn't on the verge of panic. The trees bent and groaned and leaned out of the way. Plants and shrubs stood up on their roots and scurried out of his path. The tavern's glowing windows appeared ahead and Saros pushed himself faster.

Don't be dead, he begged. *Please don't be dead.*

He burst through the tavern doors and froze in his tracks.

At first all he saw was blood — everywhere, too much of it, splattered and pooled in dark puddles on the wood floor. The sickly metallic smell of it filled his nose. It took every effort to take a single step farther into the tavern, and with every following step he wished he hadn't.

He found Bex the barkeep first, facedown and still. He didn't need to check her pulse. Her life had bled out in a puddle around her body.

Saros held his breath as he made his way around the bar. His heartbeat throbbed at the back of his throat. The floor creaked under his boots, each sound a firecracker in the still, deathly silence.

Maybe Atheris had gotten away. Maybe she'd chased out the cultist. Maybe— Maybe— Maybe—

Saros heard a crunch underfoot and looked down. Atheris's glasses lay broken and blood-spattered at his feet.

No.

Saros froze. The stale air in the tavern choked him. His vision blurred until all he could see were spots of red. *Find her*, urged a voice at the back of his mind. *She's already gone*, argued another voice. *Run.*

But Saros couldn't do that. He brought his surroundings back into sharp focus with a deep breath. Reluctantly, he followed the spatters and smears of blood on the floor until he glimpsed a hand lying limp on the ground, visible around the corner of the bar. The skin was tan and freckled, the fingers decorated with familiar rings. Saros closed his eyes and swallowed his nausea, then stepped around the back of the bar and forced himself to look.

She had fallen just a few feet away from Bex, who perhaps had tried to protect her. She lay twisted on her side, as if she'd fallen and tried to get back up only to slump back to the floor. Her blood smeared the floorboards surrounding her and leaked steadily from a wound across her throat. Her ginger hair stuck in pieces and clumps to her cheeks and forehead.

A glimpse of her face drained the strength out of Saros. He crumpled to his knees beside her and pressed his gloved hand to her shoulder, gripping it until his numb fingers ached. "Atheris." His voice stuck in his throat. "No...No, no, no, no, no, *no*. Not you. Not... *Fuck*."

Saros broke down. This was his fault. He had brought Atheris into this, he had let her come with him into Illir's Woods, he had gotten her involved with his search for the lake, and he had left her in danger. Her life had been in his hands and she had trusted him.

And he had let this happen. He had let her die.

A sob broke out of him. He gripped her shoulders and begged her to come back. *Wake up.* He was a *fucking necromancer* and his magic had burst alive before; why wasn't it working now? *Wake up, damn it.* Why couldn't he do anything when it mattered?

He bowed his head until his forehead was pressed to her shoulder. The sharp scent of blood strangled his senses. "*I'm sorry*," he told her again. *I'm sorry I'm sorry I'm sorry.*

Saros didn't know what to do. He couldn't leave her here. She was supposed to be with him through this entire ordeal. She was supposed to see the lake and then go back to Evyrmyre and thrive. She was supposed to *live*.

He could save her. He had to. And if he did it soon enough, maybe she wouldn't forget everything like Rune had.

Saros took a shaky breath. If he tried to save Atheris, it would kill him. He was already faded enough that another moon cycle would drain his life; actually using his power would kill him instantly.

He gazed at her, his odd and unlikely friend. Was he willing to let his own life slip away to save hers when he was less than two days away from having this curse lifted? He had come so far, had spent all those sleepless nights obsessively tracking the moon and stars, all for this one last chance to save himself. He had sworn time after time that this curse would not be the end of him, that there was a life waiting for him beyond this magic and the exile that came with it.

But between him and her, Saros already knew which one of them deserved their life more.

He sat back on his heels and dragged his hands through his hair, forgetting about the blood slicking his gloves until he felt it on his scalp. A needling sense of urgency sent his heart sprinting; *you're running out of time.*

There was only a brief window for his power to work properly; he couldn't revive anything that had been dead for more than an hour. He'd never tried, of course, but the few writings he'd found had strongly advised against using necromancy on long-dead things. But even if this worked, what if it was already too late for Atheris to retain her memories? What if she, too, woke up and hated him?

Though if the magic killed him like he fully expected it to, Atheris's opinion of him hardly mattered.

Saros gently turned Atheris's body so she lay on her back, and moved her head so her face was turned upward. Her hair fell back, and Saros's throat tightened at the sight of her open, blank, lifeless eyes.

"God damn it, Atheris, I'm so sorry." Saros pulled off his gloves and stuffed them into his coat pocket, then pressed his skeletal hands to her heart, one on top of the other.

Please work. Please don't let it be too late. Please bring her back.

Before, Saros's magic had awakened in a flurry of panic, of desperation. Now, after nearly a decade of suppression, perhaps it needed focus. He closed his eyes and reached for the power that dwelled within him. At once, his blood turned to ice and cold seeped into his veins. His head swam, upsetting his concentration, but he blinked the dizzy spell away and focused. A few more blinks, and his surroundings faded as if behind a veil.

Bright and clear against the otherwise desaturated space, Atheris's spirit hovered around her body. She still appeared vaguely humanoid, a blurry outline of a human shape. She bent over her body as if confused to find herself outside of it.

"There you are," Saros murmured, and reached out to her with his magic. He felt her life force respond to the pull at once; her soul was as strong and stubborn as she was, clinging to her mortal body just like Rune's had all those years ago. She didn't want to go. She didn't want to die.

I know, Saros thought to her. *I won't let you. Come back.*

He reached for her spirit and pulled it close, and felt his own soul lose its energy. The jolt was akin to getting stabbed, but instead of physical pain he felt a slow, involuntary pull toward sleep. He was washed in cold all over again; everything went numb from his fingertips to his shoulders. The cold seizing his heart stole his breath. Blackness crept into the edges of his vision and he started to lose his focus on the other side, but he kept a tight hold on Atheris's soul and fixed his gaze on her body — her round face, her faint freckles, her messy hair, the blood smeared on her skin — and he willed her life back into her with every ounce of affection he felt for her.

Atheris, come back, he demanded. *You're not done yet.*

The cold eased as her soul settled back into her body. Saros gasped as the magic ran its course through him, wracking him with shudders as it restored the life that had been stolen from Atheris and healed the wounds that had killed her.

That part had been a surprise the first time Saros had used his power. He had not expected something as unnatural as necromancy to heal. He'd have sooner expected the curse to restore a person's life under the exact conditions of their final moment, injuries and all.

He chose not to question it. It was thanks to that small kindness that Atheris was safe.

He watched the color return to her face as her heart started beating again. Her eyes had slid shut, and the pain had smoothed from her features. She gasped in a breath, and Saros let go.

He released a shuddering sigh, then the dark claimed him and he collapsed to the floor.

INTERLUDE
NEW MOON II

SAFYRE SHOULD HAVE BEEN ASLEEP, but it was only because they weren't that they heard the trees speak.

He's here.

They looked up abruptly from the spell they'd been poring over all night, and held their breath so as to be absolutely sure they heard the trees' whisper correctly.

Heartbeats later, the trees spoke again. *He's here.*

"Illir's *teeth*," Saf muttered. They nearly displaced everything on the table — flickering candles and all — in their haste to get across the room. *He's here.* How many years had Saf waited to hear those words? Yet here they were, utterly unprepared both emotionally and practically; they spared barely a second to kick off their house slippers in favor of boots and grab a cloak to throw over their shoulders. Their last scrap of rationality reminded them to toss a spell over their shoulder on the way out the door so all those candles didn't burn down their cluttered cottage while they were gone.

"Show me," Saf commanded the Woods. They strode into the trees, cloak billowing behind them. "Bring me to him."

Creaking and groaning, the trees raised their branches and leaned out of Saf's path. Roots burst from the soil and crawled over the loamy forest floor, dragging the tree trunks with them. The branches' eyes flicked wildly from side to side, agitated with palpable excitement. Saf reckoned they probably felt the same burst of magic — very *specific* magic — that Saf's spell had detected. The Woods had likely known the moment he had stepped within its reaches.

Trees, shrubs, bushes, and animals shuffled and leapt out of Saf's path. The Woods opened before them, creating a clear path beneath crooked branches that rustled with activity. Bioluminescent leaves whispered to each other and to Saf, eager to spread the news.

He's here.

Gods. After all these years, he was here. He had returned. But Saf had to wonder; was it on purpose? Did he know? A foolish part of them dared to hope that he remembered. That he was finally coming home.

But their logic knew better. He had been too young, and it had been too many years. Saf knew how the world was outside these Woods; that world would not have let him remember.

It was a fate that had met far too many people that Saf had once known and loved. So far, none of those who had been taken had ever returned — until now.

He's here. He was the first. Saf quickened their pace.

The Woods led them to a clearing where a quaint little tavern backed up to the treeline. Absently, Saf realized they hadn't seen Rusty Root in a long time; they'd assumed Bex had walked her shape-shifting abode out of the Woods like she'd always promised she would. But apparently the place's roots went too deep, and just as well.

So you found your way here, Saf mused as they approached the tavern. Or rather, it was more likely the Woods had led him here. Saf wondered what an outsider would make of it; did he even notice that the Woods were leading him, or was he oblivious to the forest's sentience? Saf couldn't wait to pick his brain.

They pushed open the tavern's door, expecting a lively scene. What they got instead made them freeze.

Saf clapped a hand over their mouth and nose. The stench of blood choked them. Red splotches edged their vision as they took in the deserted room. Chairs and tables lay overturned, some splintered, and shards of glass scattered across the floor. Yet despite the apparently violent scuffle, Saf saw no victims.

Not yet, anyway. They clenched their teeth and carefully made their way across the room, holding up the edge of their cloak so it didn't drag through the smears of blood or rain of broken glass. They approached the bar, and just as they glimpsed a body on the ground, they heard a sob.

Despite themself, Saf jumped. Their pulse quickened and they darted around the back of the bar, where they found too many things to take in at once.

Two unmoving bodies lay on the floor. One of them was a silver-haired man that Saf did not recognize. The other was Bex, and if not for the presence of exactly one living person in front of them, Saf would have gotten stuck. Even still, it was not until the young woman scrambled unsteadily to her feet that they were able to tear their gaze away from their old friend's body.

"Wh-Who are you? What do— Where did you come from?"

Saf took a deep breath and turned to the woman. Bloodstained and visibly shaking, she backed as far away from Saf as the space allowed. Her hands searched and fumbled around her waist, seeking a weapon she'd clearly lost, but then she betrayed herself by grasping for something around her neck — only briefly; she dropped her hand abruptly, but Saf had already noticed.

"You're a magician." Saf tried to keep their voice calm, but given the scene, they couldn't keep a slight wobble out of it.

"I'm a witch," the girl snapped. "And I'll ask again, who the fuck are you and why are you here?"

Saf held up their hands placatingly. "You've no reason to worry. My name is Safyre. I live nearby. A spell I had set led me here. Coincidentally, I am also a witch, though it's not often I hear outsiders declare themselves so freely."

"I've been through a lot of shit in the past twenty-four hours." Her hands clenched at her sides. "I don't care anymore."

Saf considered her. She couldn't be far from her early twenties, yet her sharp edges and strong spirit suggested a harsh life. Someone unaccustomed to misfortune would not still be on the defense in a situation like this.

"What is your name?" Saf queried.

"Atheris." Her green eyes flicked to the man lying at her feet, and finally her stony expression crumbled. She gasped in a breath and then looked up at Saf again with glassy eyes. "Can you help him?"

Truthfully, Saf didn't know. "What happened here?"

"I don't— I don't know." The girl, Atheris, pressed the back of her hand to her mouth. "We were here to rest, and then this guy showed up and Saros went outside chasing that fucking cultist even though I told him not to, and then t-the other guy attacked us and— I c-couldn't... I couldn't do enough."

She slumped back against the shelves on the wall behind her and dragged a bloodstained hand through her disheveled hair. Her gaze wandered to Bex and her eyes glazed over. "I tried to protect her. But he got to me first. He..." She lifted a hand to her neck, where Saf glimpsed a fresh scar that curved like a gruesome smile across her olive skin. Confusion creased her features, and then she once again looked down at the man. "Oh, you fucking *moron*."

Saf tilted their head to the side. They had a number of questions, but opted to shelve them for now and instead sank to one knee on a relatively clean spot on the floor. They reached toward the silver-haired man, but paused with a start when the obsidian ring on their middle finger suddenly flared hot.

The air rushed from their lungs. *It's him?* Oh gods, Saf hoped he wasn't dead. They pressed their fingers to his pale throat and waited, their own heart pounding, to feel something.

Too many seconds passed. Then, faintly, there it was. Weak, but there.

Saf let out the breath they'd been holding and bowed their head over his body. He was here. Saf would've preferred it wasn't like this, but he was alive and he was here and he would be the first to return.

Saf had so much to tell him. But they had to deal with this mess first.

They looked up at the young woman, who stared back at them with confusion barely masking her exhaustion. "So you were attacked. You were hurt. I can help both of you. We just need to..." They glanced at Bex and their stomach twisted.

"Not be here? Sounds good to me." Atheris shuffled closer to Saf. "I... I don't know what happened after I got hurt. It's... blurry. I think — I don't know. But he... saved me. And if it's in the way I'm afraid it is, based on what he's told me, I'm surprised he's alive." She paused. "He *is* alive, right?"

"He's alive," Saf confirmed. "But yes, we need to get out of here. Er..." They considered the man — Saros, was it? Saf recalled a different name, but they weren't entirely surprised to find him with a new one. No matter; the current problem was that even with two people, it would be a struggle to drag him back to the cottage. Saf ran through a list of spells in their mind that could help, but before they could settle on one, Atheris stepped past them and went to the tavern door.

Saf turned their head. "Where are—"

For some reason, she whistled.

Moments later, heavy footsteps — too many to be human — rapidly approached the tavern. Saf rose to their feet, ready for whatever chose to show itself, but they dropped their guard when Atheris alone stepped back into the tavern.

"Come on," she said. "I'll help you get him outside."

"We can't carry him to my cottage. It's not far, but as you can see, brute strength is not a trait I possess."

Atheris gave them a once-over, squinting a little. "Yeah, gathered that. Lucky for both of us, we have easy transportation." She went back to her friend and squatted beside him.

Saf couldn't guess what she possibly meant by *transportation*, but they supposed they would find out soon enough. They went to Saros's other side and helped Atheris lift him halfway up, and then together they heaved him to his feet. He *was* lighter than Saf had expected, but he was at least five inches taller than Saf, with far more inches on Atheris, and he dragged like dead weight between the two of them.

"Wait," Atheris said as they neared the door. She turned her head over her shoulder. "What about Bex? Er, the—"

"The barkeep, yes. I know her," Saf murmured. "There's nothing we can do."

Atheris looked like she meant to say more, but she only gazed silently back at the room for a moment before continuing forward. Saf didn't know the extent of her connection with the tavern's owner, but they sympathized. They didn't wish to leave her here any more than Atheris did, but what choice did they have?

Outside, Saf was perplexed to find a giant black panther waiting for them. It sat with its tail neatly curled around its paws, ears perked and yellow eyes wide. When it spotted Atheris, its pupils narrowed and it released a low purr, then sank down into a crouch.

Saf put the pieces together and turned to Atheris. "*This* is our transportation?"

"Do you have a better idea?" She adjusted her grip around Saros's ribs. "This is Zenith. She's Saros's familiar... kind of. Point is, she's friendly, she's saved our asses numerous times, and she can move quick. Any questions?"

Saf opened their mouth.

"No? Great. Climb aboard." Atheris surged ahead and Saf had no choice but to follow. Together they slumped Saros's body against the panther, who then turned its head and gently grabbed Saros's coat in its teeth and dragged him fully onto its back. Atheris climbed up next, seating herself behind its shoulders, and then Saf reluctantly took a seat behind Saros. He looked like a dead fish, laid horizontally across the panther's back with limp limbs; Saf placed their hands on him to keep him in place as the panther rose to its feet and strode forward.

"Wait — Zenith, hold on." Atheris patted her side, then turned in her seat and gazed back at the tavern again. "*Ra Ascien*," she said, and a small fire burst to life at the tavern's door.

Atheris looked back and briefly caught Saf's eye. They nodded once, understanding, and then Atheris urged the panther forward.

The ride was smoother than they expected. The Woods shifted and parted for the feline just as they'd bent to Saf's command; they asked the trees to lead them home, and in minutes their cottage appeared at the end of the path the Woods had created.

"So it does listen," Atheris mumbled, likely to herself, but Saf jumped in.

"It does. If the Woods senses likeness within you, it will do as you ask. Is it safe to guess you have inexplicably been led in the right direction since you've been here?"

"Yeah. It's helping us." She looked back at Saf as the panther came to a stop by the cottage's door. "But I didn't expect to see the trees and stuff literally *step* out of my way."

Saf smiled. "Everything is one of a kind here. Now, let's get our friend comfortable and I will see what I can do for him. And for you, too. You need only ask."

With some difficulty, Saf and Atheris dragged themselves and Saros off the panther's back and made their way into the house. Saf directed Atheris toward their singular extra bedroom, silently thanking their past self for leaving it as a bedroom rather than converting it into an extension of their library. The idea had gripped them many times, yet something had told them to leave the extra room as it was. It would come in handy someday.

And indeed it had.

Saf and Atheris lay Saros's unconscious body on the bed as gently as possible, then Saf straightened and blew out a sigh. "Right. Well, seeing as how I'm not covered in blood after carrying him, I'd wager that he's not physically injured. Which begs the question..." They turned to Atheris. "What *is* wrong with him?"

They could see Atheris's hesitation in her green eyes, but it was thankfully short-lived. "He's a necromancer," she said. "If he used his power, it— I don't know. He said something about his power draining him. Like, if he used it too much it would kill him."

Saf frowned. That didn't add up. Such magic *strengthened* its user; it was not supposed to weaken them, and certainly not kill them. "Have you seen him use this power?"

"No. Unless..." She winced and absently rubbed the scar on her neck.

Saf understood. "He saved you, didn't he? You died, and he brought you back."

Now she fully flinched. She pressed her palm over her throat. "I don't know. I— Like I said, everything is weird and blurry and I have no idea what happened to me." Her voice broke and she gasped, then slumped heavily onto the edge of the bed.

"Okay, okay." Saf took a seat on the opposite side of the mattress. "I'm sorry. You've a lot to process. What you've told me will be sufficient for me to help him. Mostly what he needs is rest. His strength and his power will recharge, and in a few days he should wake. Until then—"

"A few *days?*" Atheris abruptly looked up. "No! He doesn't *have* a few days. We need— After all this, we can't miss it."

Oh. Saf narrowed their eyes. "Miss what?"

Atheris's hands curled into fists on her lap. "Jovian's Tomb."

There it is. Saf couldn't help a smile. "I see. Of course... that's what brought him here." They turned to him. "But why wait so long to come back?" they murmured. "Did it not call you sooner?"

For years, they had tried to convince their fellow witches of the Woods to keep the tomb close. But they had run out of excuses as to why it should always remain within or near the Woods, and the witches had begun to grumble about it being too easy to follow if it was always in the same general area. Saf had lost the argument, and for the past five years, the coven had called the lake to places far outside the Woods.

Until this month, when they had casually pointed out that it had been rather a long time since they had all been able to gather close to home. And finally, in just two more nights, Jovian would return to the Woods.

And the lost one would return to his true family.

"Do you... know him?" Atheris asked softly.

Saf glanced at her. "I used to. A very long time ago."

She shook her head. "How is that possible?"

Curious. Saf had assumed these two to be close friends, if not more. "What do you know of his past?"

"Admittedly not much," Atheris grumbled. "He's secretive, but in fairness so am I. We have to be."

"Hmm." Saf twisted the obsidian ring around their finger. "Such is the hardship of witches beyond these Woods. You clearly care about him, though, and you know of his magic — which, given what I have seen, is likely his closest-kept secret. Yet you don't know of his past."

"I know a few things," Atheris said, a touch defensively. "But how far back are we talking?"

"Far." Saf stood and moved toward Saros's upper body. They placed their hands over his heart and murmured a spell for strength. Magic warmed their palms, though oddly the warmth did not transfer to Saros's body. He remained still, and strangely cold.

"You knew him as a child?" Atheris asked. Saf could feel her curious gaze bearing into them as they moved their hands to a different spell position. "What was he like? Grumpy and pouty as he is now?"

Saf flickered a smile when they'd completed a healing spell. "Not that I remember. He was quiet, but full of curiosity. He liked to explore and unravel things, and I was right there with him. The answers to all of his questions." They sighed and let their eyes slide out of focus. Instead of the pale, deathly man in front of them, they saw the boy they remembered: bright, mismatched eyes, a joyful round face, a brilliant grin, an ever-present wrinkle of thought between his brows. He loved the Woods and just like every child here, he was raised by a community of parents and relatives. The witches here cared for their own.

At least until it wasn't enough.

"You were close, then?" Atheris spoke softer now. Saf could hear the exhaustion weighing on her voice; the night was catching up with her.

"We were." Saf placed two fingers crossed over each other on Saros's forehead and whispered another strengthening spell. "But I doubt he remembers me. I doubt he remembers being here at all."

"When you say 'here,' you mean... Illir's Woods?"

Saf glanced at her and nodded. "You don't know of the witches who dwell here, even as a witch yourself?"

"I'm... a little out of touch." Atheris shrugged and toyed with the leather cord around her neck, sliding her fingers along it until the strung amulets slid to meet her hand. She fiddled with the stones, and Saf wouldn't have glanced twice at the talismans if they hadn't caught a glimpse of a familiar, impossible, undeniably recognizable artifact.

Amulets were typically the blended colors of natural stone. In rare cases, they were fashioned from precious gemstones like emeralds and rubies — Saf had opinions about that — to flaunt a flash of wealth. But Saf only knew of one purely white amulet with a solid black companion.

They could hardly stop themself from gawking. Those were the amulets of Serefine and Thalia, arguably the most famous and most powerful witches who had ever lived.

How the *hell* did this girl have those amulets?

Saf had to bite their tongue against the questions that wanted to flood out of their mouth. They tore their gaze away from the amulets and focused on the unconscious man in front of them. The color was slowly crawling back to his face, and he didn't look quite so dead anymore. *Good*. One more strengthening spell would be enough for now. Rest would ultimately heal him more than Saf could.

They glanced again at Atheris and straightened, resting their hands on their hips. "We're a community here, in the Woods. A very old, very honorable coven. They are my family and my protectors. We look out for each other." They glanced at Saros. "As well as we can, anyway."

Atheris followed their gaze. "What happened? To him, I mean."

"Stolen," Saf murmured. The memory surfaced with a familiar dull ache. It still felt surreal to have the friend they had lost here in front of them once again — though with a lifetime between them now. The ache in their chest worsened with the knowledge that this man would not remember the boy he'd been, nor would he remember Saf.

"Stolen?" Atheris's voice brought Saf out of their thoughts. "Like, he was kidnapped? Why?"

"His father did not want him to be raised by witches." Saf curled their lip. "His mother had brought him here so both of them would be safe, and he would grow up among people like him. But his father found them, and he took him." Saf met Atheris's eyes. "And I imagine he wiped everything about us from Saros's mind."

Atheris nodded slowly. Clearly stories like this were not foreign to her; she might be out of touch with witches but she had not always been. Saf wondered what had drawn her away from them — or what had *forced* her away.

"I'm sorry that happened." Atheris stood up and rolled her shoulders. Saf noticed for the first time that she had two snakes draped around her neck; their little heads peeked out from beneath her coat. "It sounds like you... really cared for him."

Saf lifted a shoulder. "In the all-consuming way that children love each other."

"Mhm." Atheris rubbed her eye. "He'll be okay, right? Be real with me."

"I will do everything I can," Saf assured her. They reached out and offered their hand; Atheris hesitated, then took it. Saf squeezed. "I promise you. Rest, my friend. You can use my bedroom, just across the hall. Let me know if there's anything you need. You are safe here."

She nodded and let go of Saf's hand. With a final glance at Saros, she shuffled out of the room. Saf heard the door softly close across the hall.

They looked down at Saros and touched his shoulder. While he had appeared close to death before, he now merely seemed to be sleeping. Saf watched the steady rise and fall of his chest, listening to his gentle breathing.

He's here. The Woods had led him here, and Saf knew they had to do everything in their power to keep him here. They had so much to tell him.

They spread their hand across his shoulder, and then drifted away. "You're home now," they murmured to him. "I'll see you soon."

CHAPTER 8
NEW MOON III

I ACTED ON PURE INSTINCT. I saw Rune falter, I saw the moment his strength left him and the river's strength won. I didn't think. I didn't consider what might be hidden beneath the churning surface. I launched myself into the water with one thought alone: Save him.

What was he thinking? He wasn't a strong swimmer. The day was hot and dry; even an hour under that midsummer sun was enough to leech the energy right out of us. We'd been outside too long. He shouldn't have jumped into such a rough stretch of river.

The water was murky, the sandy floor disturbed by the current. Silt stung my eyes as I fought my way toward the shadow of his body. The river tossed and rolled him as he sank, and already he'd stopped struggling. Blood clouded the water in a dark plume around his head.

Something overtook me in that moment, at the sight of him unmoving and limp. Something gripped me from the inside, and every note of fatigue lifted from my limbs.

The next moments are a blur in my memory. Somehow I reached him, dragged him to the surface, heaved both our bodies onto the riverbank. I must have begged the universe itself to bring him back to me.

I remember my panic. I remember taking his cold face in my hands and pressing my shaking fingers to his throat, desperate to feel a pulse that I knew was already gone. But how? How had his life slipped away so quickly? How could he be gone?

I will never forget the jolt I felt upon realizing that I could feel his life force — his spirit, his soul — there with me. And then I saw *it: his spirit hovered around his body, still clinging to the physical form he'd always known. I felt his confusion at finding himself outside his body, and I knew intrinsically that he didn't want to leave. He wasn't ready.*

And good, because god damn it, I wasn't ready either.

That same rush of adrenaline that had pushed me toward him in the water gripped me again, drenching me in ice. I pulled him close to me and begged for his life, and this time, something answered.

He gasped awake.

It was the first time I had cried in many, many years. I didn't know what had happened, I didn't know how this was possible, but he was alive and he was safe and the overwhelming relief I felt chased away the exhaustion I would later feel from the magic.

Rune looked at me like I was the miracle. But then the shock bled from his face and soured into something dark. Something hateful.

He scrambled back from me, visibly shaking, and gasped out the same words over and over: What have you done? What have you done? What have you done?

"Rune," I said, as calmly as my shaking voice would allow, "it's all right. You're okay."

He replied, "How do you know who I am?"

I was too stunned to answer.

His eyes narrowed. "Who are you?"

"Rune, it's me," I stammered. "Saros. Y-Your friend. Your—"

"No." He staggered to his feet and put yet more distance between us. His eyes were wide with terror, and he was visibly trembling. But there was no mistaking the hatred in his gaze.

"You can't be. You are no friend of mine," he said, and I will never forget the venom in his voice as he snarled, "necromancer."

SAROS SURFACED FROM A HEAVY, near-death unconsciousness and found that everything hurt. His head. His bones. Breathing. He was sure that if he moved at all, his bones would shatter like brittle glass.

But he'd heard a voice, and he swore it was familiar. He made himself turn his head, waited for the throbbing in his skull to ease, and slowly opened his eyes. A woman's face came into focus, carrying a flicker of recognition. Smooth, rosy porcelain skin. A freckle on her chin. Long, thick brown hair. Her eyes were like his — one dark brown, the other a muddy green. A memory called her *Mother*, but that didn't make sense. He remembered his mother; a quiet, withdrawn, emotionless husk of a stronger person Saros had never known.

The woman before him was not her. She spoke a name, and it tickled another memory, long buried. Saros squinted, trying to bring her face into sharper focus, but when he blinked the face before him changed.

A younger woman hovered before him now, her tan skin scattered with freckles, ginger hair framing her round face. Her eyes were both bright green, and a black snake rested on her shoulders.

Atheris? Saros blinked, but the mirage didn't disappear. Guilt turned his stomach over. "No... You're dead." She was a ghost, nothing more. "I'm sorry. I'm sorry I let you die."

"Saros, I'm not dead." Her voice rang sharply in his ears. So real. So familiar. He wanted this ghost to keep talking forever. "Look, I'm right here. You're looking right at me and saying I'm not real?" She snapped her fingers in front of his eyes, making him flinch.

She's dead. Maybe if he repeated the truth enough times, his mind would stop playing tricks on him. He blinked again, then closed his eyes. *When I look again, she'll be gone.*

But there she was, sitting cross-legged in a wooden chair with her elbows on her knees and chin in her hand.

Saros blinked a few more times. His throat tightened. "You're real?"

"I'm real," she said.

His yet unfocused eyes drifted around the hazy space. "Where is... Where did she go?" Saros tried to sit up, but he had no strength to hold him and he crumpled back down onto the bed with a groan.

Wait. He was on a bed? An actual bed, not a thin mat on the forest floor, nor on the forest floor itself. The room surrounding him was warm, illuminated by dim oil lamps, and smelled faintly of sage. The walls were bare but for a few bundles of herbs and dried flowers, and the few pieces of basic furniture were plain. Saros spotted his and Atheris's coats and traveling bags heaped on a chair in the far corner.

"Where did who go?" Atheris said. "It's just me." Her voice softened. "I'm not going anywhere. Don't think you can get rid of me that easily."

Saros looked at Atheris again, and part of him had expected her to have disappeared. "Am *I* dead?"

"Nope. But you have been out cold for over an entire day."

Saros bolted upright. "An entire *day*? Atheris, did we miss it?"

"No. Also, lie down. You need to take it easy."

He compromised by settling back against the headboard. Across the room, the heap of coats on the chair moved, and Zenith's head popped up. Saros felt a rush of relief that she was okay, and clearly the feeling was mutual; she let out a loud meow and bolted across the room, launching herself onto the bed and directly onto Saros's stomach.

"*Ow*," he wheezed, but gladly indulged her with pets and scratches. She settled on his chest, purring hard enough to vibrate her whole body. It was only when he stroked his hand down her back that he realized his gloves were missing, and out of habit, he quickly tucked his hands out of sight.

"The new moon is tonight," Atheris said. To her credit, she didn't comment on his hands even though she had most likely seen them. "I double checked the notes against the sky, and we're as close as we can get. Can you feel it?"

He closed his eyes and felt for the tug toward Jovian's Tomb, but it wasn't there. He felt *hollow*, like a ghost rather than a living man. Curiosity got the better of him; shoving aside his self-consciousness, he pushed up his sleeves. He hissed through his teeth.

"Fuck." His hands were completely transparent, all bone and no flesh, and the fading reached as far up his arms as he could see. If he had to guess, it went at least to his elbows.

"Saros..." Atheris failed to hide the edge of shock in her voice. "I...
I saw your hands, but what is this?"

He pulled his sleeves back down and crossed his arms again,
tucking Zenith against his chest. The room's warmth and the thick
blankets on his lap did little to actually warm him. No wonder he felt
so fragile. He was surprised the fading hadn't spread farther, and he
was even more surprised that it hadn't killed him.

"This is why I need to find Jovian's Tomb," he said quietly. "This is
what I mean when I say this magic is killing me. Each time I use the
power, my soul and my body literally fade away. And even if I don't use
the magic, the fading worsens slightly with each moon cycle."

He glanced up at Atheris, and the shock in her eyes made him
realize that she was only just now putting the pieces together. Her
hand went to the fresh scar across her throat.

Saros had to look away as his mind's eye vividly remembered her
blood-smeared skin and her dull, dead eyes. He swore he could still
smell all that blood even though both of them wore clean clothes.

"You did save me," Atheris murmured. "I was— I was dead,
wasn't I?"

Saros met her gaze and nodded once. His heart gave a nervous thud
as he watched the truth settle in her eyes, and it was several agonizing
seconds before she finally sighed and stood up.

"Atheris, please..." He wasn't sure what, exactly, he was asking of
her, but if she turned on him the same way Rune had, he didn't know
what he'd do. He could not bear to love and then lose a friend twice.

Atheris might have accepted him as a necromancer, but now that
she'd actually been touched by the power, would she feel differently?
Would she react like Rune had, with fear and denial and a rabid
desperation to cleanse herself of it?

She dragged her hand through her choppy hair and turned away
from him, pacing a lap toward the far wall and back. She stopped
beside the bed again, sighed, and just when Saros thought she'd flee the
room, she instead threw her arms around him.

He froze.

Wait, but...

"I was dead," she mumbled into his shoulder. "And you knew you might die if you saved me, but you did it anyway. You crazy bastard." Her arms tightened around him. "You didn't have to do that. Why would you do that? You fucking idiot, why would you do that?"

His surprise fled and relief washed over him instead. He hugged her back as tightly as he dared without hurting her and closed his eyes, silently thanking whatever higher power was out there. Maybe Illir, but maybe also Jovian. The magic had *worked*, Atheris was alive, and she hadn't forgotten everything she knew. She hadn't forgotten him.

"I couldn't let you die, my friend."

What sort of monster would it have made him to let her die when he had, at his fingertips, the power to defy death? Was that what everyone truly feared about necromancers — not their magic itself, but their ability to choose?

Saros felt something cold and smooth touch his arm, and opened his eyes only to find himself nose-to-nose with Atheris's black snake.

"God damn it!" He shoved back from her and rubbed his arms, as if that would erase the feeling of those awful scales on his skin. "Ugh."

Atheris snorted. "Sorry. I forgot she was there. Not my fault she wanted to say thanks, too." She reached up and stroked her finger down the serpent's body. It raised its head and flicked its tongue against her cheek.

Saros shuddered. "Well. For your sake, I'm glad it survived. What about the other one?"

"Oh, she's fine." Atheris jerked her head toward the chair in the far corner of the room, where Saros could just see the very end of a white snake's tail poking out from the sleeve of his coat.

He slumped back against the headboard. They were all okay. Somehow, they were all okay.

Atheris plopped down on the edge of the bed and picked at a pull in one of the blankets. Looking closer at her now, Saros saw how exhausted she was. She'd said Saros had been unconscious for over a day; had she slept at all in that time? Had she had time to recover from the trauma of dying and coming back, or had she spent all that time worrying about him?

"I'm sorry," he murmured, "for what happened in the tavern. It was a trap, and I should have known it. I was stupid to have underestimated Rune. I guess..." He sighed and looked down at his hands, absently flexing his stiff fingers. "I wanted to trust him. I wanted to turn him back into the person I remember. But I see now that he's too far gone."

Saros clenched and unclenched his hands, then looked up at Atheris. "This was the last straw. He doesn't get to hurt you and get away with it. And that means you can't come with me to the lake."

"*What?*" Atheris jerked back. "No! Saros, come on. I'm not a child. The deal was that I help you make the map and then I get to see the lake for myself."

"I know what the deal was," Saros said. "That was before there was a threat. Atheris, I saved you once and I'd do it again, but it was a stroke of luck that both of us survived. I don't know what would happen if I had to use the magic again."

"But—"

"Please." Saros reached over and set his hand on her arm. "Please, stay here. Promise me you'll stay here. I wouldn't forgive myself if something happened to you again."

"That sounds like a you problem," she said. "I can take care of myself."

"I never said you couldn't."

"I'm a fucking witch, Saros." She crossed her arms. "The magic you've seen me use is only a fraction of what I can do. I can't just pace around these rooms while you go to the lake. I *have* to get there. Did you really think I'm *only* here to prove my own sanity?" Her hand went to the string of amulets around her neck.

It dawned on Saros, then. "Oh."

Atheris at least had the courtesy to look a little guilty. "I think Firelei's talisman is in Jovian's Tomb."

Saros narrowed his eyes. "So that's why you're here?"

She hesitated, then nodded.

"So you weren't really helping me. You used my work — my calculations, my charts, *my* failures, *my* hours and hours of study — so you wouldn't have to do it yourself." Anger burned hot and sharp under Saros's skin. "How convenient for you."

"No!" Atheris shook her head. "No, Saros, I— Look, it's not that I *didn't* want to help you. I did. I recognized how important this was to you. But I also realized that helping you could help me too. It *is* true that I want to see the lake again to prove to myself that it's real. That wasn't made up. And when we met, or even a few days ago before we left, I didn't know that I could tell you the whole truth. I thought you understood that."

Of course he did. But that didn't make him feel any less used.

"When you introduced yourself to me and asked for my story, and then asked for my help, I saw an opportunity," Atheris went on. "I saw a way to achieve something that no one in my family has ever been able to do. I..." She ruffled her hair.

"What?" Saros prompted, unable to soften the sharp edge in his tone.

"I thought it would make them welcome me home!"

For a minute, her words hung in silence. Saros didn't know what to say, so he leaned forward and placed his hand on her shoulder. She flinched a little, then finally looked at him.

"I'm sorry," Saros said.

She shrugged and turned away. "'S fine."

"No." He shook his head. "I shouldn't have jumped to conclusions without knowing your whole story. Makes me quite the hypocrite, doesn't it? I kept my biggest secrets from you until they quite literally smacked us in the face." He flickered a smile and got a faint one in return. "I understand why you couldn't tell me about the amulet. I don't blame you for it."

Atheris nodded and toyed with the rings on her fingers. "I didn't leave home just to go to Evyrmyre. I mean— That's why I went to Artunia specifically. But I left because... I wasn't given a choice."

Saros waited, giving her space to say more if she wanted to. But he already knew he would understand this, too, on a deeper level than perhaps anyone else.

"They said I was..." Her mouth twisted. "A pathetic waste of powerful magic. I was never good enough, never unique enough, never clever enough. 'Go learn something useful,' they said. 'Go earn your place in this family.' And they told me not to come back until I deserved it."

Saros's heart broke for her. How could anyone look at what she had done and accomplished and say it wasn't enough?

"Even inventing new magic wouldn't be good enough," she continued. Her voice was heavy and a little unsteady. "I have to find that talisman." She turned to him. "*I have to*. I can't just wait around here for you to get your shit together. The lake's got stuff to tell me, too."

"How do you know the talisman is there?" Saros asked. When she shot him a glare, he added, "I'm not doubting you. I'm just curious. You said the lake felt like it had something you wanted, right? And you think it's Firelei's amulet?"

"I'm positive of it." Atheris toyed with the other two stones around her neck. "After I saw the lake, I kept having these dreams about it. Eventually they all connected together into one long dream that showed me..." She trailed off.

"Showed you... where the amulet is?" Saros prompted.

"Yeah." Atheris turned her head. Her fingers fiddled anxiously with the talismans around her neck. The gentle clacking filled the heavy silence that hung between them. "It showed *me* offering the amulet to Jovian's Tomb, I assume for safe keeping. It was like *I* was Serefine, or seeing things through her eyes, but there's a part of the dream where I can see my reflection in the lake's surface. And I'm not Serefine. I'm myself. The amulet is in my hands, and my hands are in the water." Atheris blinked a few times. "It's there, Saros. I can feel it. And I have to go get it."

Saros sighed. After everything she'd just told him, how could he force her to stay here? She was right, anyway; she was powerful and could take care of herself. But that didn't stop him from worrying.

"All right," he grumbled. "Just be careful. When the tomb appears, Rune and the cult will be there."

Atheris abruptly turned back to him. "*He's still not dead?*"

Saros gazed down at his skeletal hands. "I stopped Zenith from killing him."

"Why the *fuck*—"

He didn't have a good answer. He remembered the strange, satisfying thrill he'd felt seeing Rune pinned down and struggling for his life; did some twisted part of him *want* to see Rune suffer? Saros couldn't fathom where that desire would have come from. This whole mess was because he'd *saved* Rune, not hurt him. But now he couldn't make up his mind.

"Well, if you won't beat his ass, I will," Atheris said.

That got a faint smile out of Saros. "Sure you will."

She nudged him, grinning. "Watch me."

"Alternatively, you could stay out of it and leave him to me."

"Which would inevitably require me to save *your* ass." She raised her eyebrows. "I could teach you some magic while we're here. We have at least fourteen hours until the tomb will appear. We both need to rest, yeah, but if Rune's gonna play dirty, so should you."

She was right, and Saros was admittedly interested in whatever magic she wished to teach him. But he had a more pressing question first. "By the way, where exactly *are* we?"

"Oh, right." Atheris gave a nervous laugh, which did not inspire confidence. "So we are still in the Woods, and we are very close to the site where the tomb will appear. You can thank the Woods itself for that — and the witch who lives here."

Saros's interest grew. "A witch lives here?"

Atheris nodded. "They've been nothing but kind and accommodating to us, but I can tell there's a lot more to them than they're letting on. You... You'll definitely want to talk to them."

A flicker of hope ignited in Saros's chest. "About the tomb?"

An odd expression crossed Atheris's face. "Among other things."

"Mrr," Zenith purred. Saros stroked his hand down her back. "What did they tell you?"

"Nothing that is mine to tell." Atheris unfolded herself from the chair and rolled her shoulders. "Get some rest. Safyre said you'd be out for a few days, and you woke up after barely one. You'll need more of your strength back so you can beat Rune's ass."

She left the room, smirking.

Saros rubbed his forehead. He didn't know what to make of any of this, but at the very least he was thankful for three things: that he was alive, that Atheris was alive, and that they were close to Jovian's Tomb. The rest would sort itself out in time.

Zenith purred again, and Saros absently scratched the soft fur under her chin. "You've done a lot for us, haven't you? If any of us deserve to sleep for a week, it's you."

She gave a quiet, affirmative meow.

"Can you do one more thing for me?" He gently poked at her white whiskers and she twitched her nose. "Fetch, Zenith."

She climbed off his lap and shook out her fur, then jumped down from the bed with a solid *thunk*. On quiet steps she hurried across the room to the chair where she'd been sleeping, then nosed around in Saros's coat. He didn't have to tell her what to look for; she knew. Familiars understood unspoken intentions just as well as they heard verbal commands.

But this time, Zenith came up with nothing. She looked back at him over her shoulder, tail swishing, and made an inquisitive noise.

Saros's heart sank like a stone. "It's gone?" No, no, it couldn't be gone. Saros shoved back the blankets on his lap and slid his legs off the bed, but when he tried to stand up his strength fled and he sank back down. "Zenith, are you sure? Bring my coat here, please." He held out his hands, and Zenith grabbed a sleeve in her teeth and dragged his coat off the chair, then dropped it at his feet. Atheris's white snake emerged from the folds of fabric and flicked its tongue at Saros before freeing itself from his coat.

Saros gathered the garment into his lap and searched the pockets even as he knew he would not find the timepiece. If it was here, Zenith would have found it. Still, he grasped and shook every inch of the well-worn wool coat until there was no place left for it to be.

He dropped the coat onto his lap and set his head in his hands. The brass timepiece was gone, and the photograph of himself and Rune along with it. If he asked, would the Woods lead him back to it?

Did Saros really want it to?

He longed for the familiar object and the memories it held, but he also knew that he was better off without it. The timepiece was a token of a past Saros would never get back, and the photograph inside was from another lifetime that was no longer his. Holding onto it, even for its sentimental comfort, held him back from moving forward.

If there was ever a time for Saros to finally move forward, it was now, on the eve of Jovian's appearance. The Woods could have his past and his wishes.

Whatever awaited him tonight, he hoped, would be better than everything behind him.

CHAPTER 9
NEW MOON IV

THE WITCH'S house was filled with bones. Once Saros had rested enough that he could get out of bed for more than two minutes, he had stepped out of a plain but normal bedroom into a space that would blend in better with a museum than a house. Shelves on the walls displayed skulls of every shape, size, and species — some Saros recognized, others that were definitely not found outside of Illir's Woods — and every cluttered antique table bore at least one fully intact animal skeleton.

Saros had taken no more than three steps into the room and he was already overwhelmed, unsure where to step or which direction to move. He scanned the room for some kind of pattern or obvious direction of movement, but any logic here was unknown to him. There was so *much*: glass and metal trinkets, sculptures made of wood and stone, jars filled with strange colored liquids, massive jugs with faded warning labels, dozens of vases of flowers in various stages of life, and just a truly disturbing quantity of bones.

A door creaked somewhere down the hall behind Saros, and he turned as Atheris walked into the room. She looked less tired than earlier, and her hair was pulled back in its usual half-up, half-down style. She was still missing her glasses, and noticeably squinted as she took in the room. "It's, uh..."

"Chilling," Saros offered.

"Pretty awesome," Atheris concluded.

That wasn't how Saros would've described it, but to each their own. He took another hesitant step into the room, unable to stave his curiosity despite the macabre décor. What sorts of secrets and lost knowledge lurked in this witch's home? Witches were powerful and ancient beings, with bloodlines that went back millennia. Saros had always been fascinated by their history — and their power. He felt a sort of kinship with them, one social outcast to another.

There was also a strong connection between witches and necromancy that was of particular interest to Saros. If it was true that necromancy was a curse witches could bestow, Saros had some questions for this witch who had welcomed him and Atheris into their home without hesitation.

Saros drifted around the room, absently examining the witch's collections. He hovered over a corkboard bearing the intact corpses of a variety of beetles, pinned there by their legs and wings. One of them was nearly the size of his hand, with twelve legs and two sets of wings. It was a beautiful shiny green, but that was about the only positive opinion Saros had of the insect.

He curled his lip and looked away, searching for Atheris. "Do you know where they are?" he called across the room.

Atheris looked up from inspecting a feline skeleton. "Who, the witch?" She moved on to another table, this one cluttered with bell jars and clear vases. Saros went closer and saw that each one housed dead animals suspended in preserving fluids. His stomach turned over.

"Yes, the witch. Have you seen them today?"

Atheris turned away from the jars and looked around, then perked up and darted over to a bookcase. Waist-high and cluttered with yet more trinkets, the dark wood shelves were almost invisible among everything else. Saros hesitated, though he itched to go dig through those books. But it was perhaps not the best show of courtesy to nose his way into their host's belongings.

"Whoa, Saros!" Atheris spun around. "Get over here and look at this."

"I really don't wish to see any more dead animals."

"It's not! Look." She bounced on her toes as he made his way toward her. He stopped beside her and found her with a massive book in her arms, open to a pair of black pages covered in white chalky sketches of the moon's phases.

Saros frowned. "What is this?"

"It's gotta be something about the lake, right?" Atheris lifted the book a little higher. "It's also very heavy. But look, whoever wrote these notes was clearly tracking the moon as obsessively as you did. Do you think there's more in here about Jovian's Tomb that this person knew that we don't?"

Saros shrugged absently as he studied the page. That was entirely possible, but so far it looked like normal astronomy to him — observations of the moon, its orbit, its phases, its gravity, and its position in the sky. He turned the page, finding it filled with scattered, nearly illegible notes, but his eyes caught on exactly the words he wanted.

Jovian's Tomb.

He leaned closer to the book and read faster. It was a frustrating challenge to decipher the messy scrawl, but whoever had written this had followed the same logic that had brought Saros out here searching for the lake. This scholar's star charts looked nearly identical to Saros's; they had even made their search in the same season. At the bottom of the page, beneath a sketch of the new moon, the scholar had drawn the lake itself: a dark, glassy body of water tucked in a basin surrounded by mountains. Beneath the drawing, heavy strokes of white chalk wrote out, *FROM OUR GOD WE DESCEND SO SHALL WE RISE: IN DUST, IN BLOOD, IN BONE.*

Saros frowned. If this scholar was a necromancer or even a witch, surely they weren't referring to Illir when they said *god.* So did they mean *Jovian?* But he wasn't a god. Not actually. He was just a mortal who had gained godlike power.

Unless there *were* some who considered him a god? An antithesis to Illir, his divine opposite, worthy of devotion because he'd rebelled.

But what necromancer in their right mind would consider their cursed magic something deserving of worship? Saros had never heard of anyone believing necromancy to be anything less than evil. It was a curse, that was the undisputed truth, and according to the ones who made the rules and told everyone else what to believe, a person cursed with necromancy was hardly a person at all. Magic that ate away at your soul, by extension, also chipped away your humanity.

It was a solitary curse to bear, but Saros had mostly made his peace with his isolation. He didn't miss the carefully-curated norms of society that he'd barely learned how to navigate. But he *did* miss the few close connections he'd had. He missed having friends. He missed having community. And so this intrigued him — this suggestion of others, may they be necromancers or witches or something else, who looked up to Jovian as their god and defied everything the world said about them.

If what this book suggested was true, it meant Saros did not have to be isolated. He could find others like him, and they would understand each other on a deeper level than even he and Atheris did.

He could barely wrap his head around this. Never in his life had he thought to seek other necromancers. He would not have even known how to start. He'd always been treated like his existence was a singular misfortune, that he alone was cursed and hated by Illir. This was so ingrained in him that he had never questioned it, never *thought* to question it.

Of course, what killed one's hope and spirit quicker than making them believe they were alone in the world?

"Saros." Atheris's voice barged into his thoughts. "I admire your ability to concentrate so deeply, and I desperately envy it, but my arms are getting tired. I'm not a book stand. Either take the thing or let me set it down."

He blinked back to reality and took the tome from her arms, finding it heavier than he expected. He cleared a spot on top of the bookcase and set the book down. But a stab of anxiety stopped him from investigating deeper. What if he was wrong about all of this? What if the lake couldn't take back what it gave? Truths often got twisted in myths, and if the lake was only a source, then what did that mean for Saros's magic — and his life? For so many years, he'd been hell bent on finding this lake and returning the curse to its grave so he could take his life back, and now when the time was mere hours away, he realized he didn't know what kind of life he wished to take back.

He didn't know what he'd do if the lake couldn't relieve him of his power. But he also didn't know what he'd do if it *did*. Should he even try to return to his hometown and reconnect with his family? Was it worth it after they'd shown their true colors by exiling him? Did he even want them to welcome him back?

No, he realized. No, he didn't.

So what else was there? The bright city of Artunia, Evyrmyre Academy, a bustling hive of magic and innovation. Surely he could find a place there if he wanted, and he could veer back onto the path he'd always planned for his life. But did he still want that?

What *did* he want?

Rune, said a voice in the back of his mind. *Rune, Rune, Rune.*

Saros silenced the thought. Though part of him still desperately wanted Rune in his life, he knew that that was impossible. It was always going to be impossible. The Rune he had known and loved was gone.

Saros let the book come back into focus. He flipped back to the page with the illustration of Jovian's Tomb and lingered on the words beneath the drawing. *SO SHALL WE RISE.*

There were more living necromancers out there. There *must* be. So maybe this was his choice, no matter what happened tonight. Maybe he just wanted to be seen and known.

Saros glanced up, searching for Atheris, who had slipped away to another part of the room while Saros had been buried in his thoughts. "You never did say if you've seen our witch host today. Where are—"

"Oh, looking for me?"

Saros turned.

Every story he had ever heard about witches suggested that they were hideously inhuman. Obviously Atheris was proof that those stories were wrong. But a part of him still expected that someone so in tune with such powerful magic would look at least a little... *off*. After all, Saros himself was a living example that dark, hungry power ate away at the body.

So he did not expect this witch to be so enchantingly beautiful.

They were tall and slim, roughly Saros's height, with warm russet skin and waves of black hair that reached past their waist. A single white streak interrupted the black pigment, running from roots to ends along the right side of their head. They had braided delicate beads and bells into their curls, and wore magic amulets around their neck even though, as a witch, they didn't need them. Their wrists bore shining gold bracelets, their ears were laden with dangling blue gems and silver rings, and a tiny ruby pierced their left eyebrow, winking in the light as they turned a suspicious yet amused look upon Saros and Atheris.

"Oh, hey, Safyre," Atheris set a marble orb back on the table in front of her and then tucked her hands into her pockets, rocking back on her heels. "Fancy seeing you here."

"Yes, it's clearly the most unusual thing in the world to find me in my own home." Their voice was smooth like honey, dangerously hypnotic and perfect for persuading nature's powers to bend to their will. "I told you not to touch anything. This stuff is fragile."

"For what it's worth," Atheris said, "we didn't *break* anything."

Saros nodded in Safyre's direction. "Apologies for being nosy. We don't mean to be rude after you've welcomed us into your home. But I can't help being curious about your..." His eyes darted toward a canine skeleton on a nearby table. "Er... collection."

Safyre's expression softened. They drifted a step forward, heeled boots clicking on the wood floor. This witch was dressed like they had just come from a nobleman's party; a dark indigo waistcoat hugged their slender frame and complemented the bluish-silver shirt neatly tucked into their dark violet breeches.

"Our friend Atheris told me about you while you were recovering," they said to Saros. "I know a thing or two about your situation, so I have to say I'm a little surprised to see you back on your feet so soon. Restoring a life takes the average necromancer out for at least two days when they're out of practice." They made their way around the maze of shelves and tables and then stopped before

Saros, dark eyes alight with interest. "Clearly you're above average, then."

"That sets expectations rather high, doesn't it?" Saros smiled faintly. "Our friend Atheris told me a little about you, as well. Am I right to presume, based on everything here, that you are somewhat of an expert on magic? Namely necromancy?"

Safyre hummed. "An expert? You flatter me, friend. Though if you insist as much, I'll tell you what I can." They tipped their head to the side; the charms and bells woven in their hair delicately clinked together. "Answer me this, first: why do you seek Jovian's Tomb, Saros?"

He was reluctant to say, simply out of fear of hearing an answer he didn't want. What if Safyre laughed at his foolishness and told him he was stupid to think the lake would lift his curse? What if this whole effort was pointless, and one way or another, Saros was just going to die? What if the lake made his power *worse*, and leeched the last of his humanity right out of him?

He tried to silence the doubts. He was so close. This was not the time to second guess everything he'd worked for. But faced with someone who likely knew the answer to his one deepest hope, he couldn't put it into words.

"It's easier to show you," he said, and slipped off one of his gloves. Safyre's eyes widened.

"God," they murmured, lifting a hand. "May I?"

Saros nodded. He shoved down the instinct that desperately wanted to hide his hands; he'd never intentionally shown anyone before. But his interest to hear what Safyre had to say about the fading won over his discomfort. It was telling already that Saf seemed shocked at the sight of it. Saros had always thought that the fading would affect anyone afflicted with a necromantic curse; if Saf knew so much about necromancy, surely they would have seen this before.

They gently touched his hand, and Saros couldn't stifle a gasp. Their skin was *warm* — vividly, blessedly warm against his otherwise numb and cold hand. Saros hadn't felt anything close to this, even from a fire, in years.

Safyre glanced up to his face. "Does it hurt?"

"No," Saros breathed. "Just aches, usually. But I didn't expect to be able to feel your touch."

"Completely numb, then?" Safyre turned his hand over and pressed it between both of their own.

"Mostly," Saros corrected. "I can feel enough that I can still use my hands. But I couldn't tell you the last time I felt warmth."

He was positive Safyre could feel his pulse through his palm. Were they using magic to return the life to his hand, or was this just the effect of Saros's power interacting with Safyre's? If a witch's magic could heal him, did that mean Jovian's Tomb could, too? But if that was the case, why didn't Saros feel this when Atheris touched his hands?

Because she never has, he realized. He always had the gloves on around her, and even earlier when he'd taken them off, he'd touched her arm, not her hand.

Safyre continued their study of Saros's hand, gently tapping each translucent finger. "Do you know what caused this?"

"Necromancy." Was that not obvious? "It worsens when I use my power, but even if I don't, the fade spreads each month. I set out to find Jovian's Tomb earlier this week because I did not think I would survive another month. I am quite surprised I survived restoring Atheris's life."

Saros realized then that Atheris hadn't said a word in a while, and looked around for her only to find himself alone with Safyre. He didn't think Atheris was capable of doing anything quietly, but she'd slipped away without a sound.

"Is it?" Safyre questioned, bringing Saros's attention back to them. "You've proven for certain that this is a result of your power?"

"The correlation is clear," Saros said. "The fading began soon after I first used my power. Since then, it has only worsened. Besides, why *wouldn't* this curse slowly kill me?" He tugged his hand out of Safyre's grip and slipped his glove back on. "You asked why I seek Jovian's Tomb. This is why. I've heard the stories, I've studied the cycles. I think — I hope — the lake can reverse the fading before it kills me."

Safyre tipped their head to the side. "An informed theory. But there is more to the story, if you are willing to listen."

"Anything you can tell me will likely be more accurate than what I've heard all my life."

"*Most* of your life," Safyre mused. They traced their painted thumbnail across their bottom lip. "But not all. You don't remember, do you?"

Saros frowned. "What?"

Safyre's expression turned oddly sad. Their dark eyes glistened, doe-like, beneath softly creased brows. "It must seem like another lifetime to you. I suppose I shouldn't be surprised that you don't remember. I can't imagine what your childhood was like with... him. With all of them."

Saros drifted a step backwards and crossed his arms. "What are you talking about?"

"I know you, Saros," Safyre said. "And you know me. Or you did, once."

Saros had been on board with everything this witch had said until now. "I don't understand. I've never— How could we know each other?"

"Didn't Atheris tell you how I found you?" Saf asked.

"Luck, I assumed."

"Indeed, but that's not all. Come, let's settle somewhere more comfortable." They gestured toward the hallway. "You've quite a lot of history to catch up on."

Saros had no idea what to expect, but he followed the witch nonetheless. They led him past the room where he'd woken up and stopped at a closed door at the end of the hallway. There they paused, glanced over their shoulder at Saros, and pushed open the door to invite him in first.

He stepped into another room similar to the main one, though with much less senseless clutter. There was logic to the objects and furniture occupying this space; one corner of the room was all towering bookshelves packed to capacity, with a small table and a scatter of cushions in front of the shelves. Larger tables occupied most of the floor space, bearing stacks of books, open scrolls, and half-empty oil lamps. Statues and sculptures draped in white sheets stood like sentinels overseeing the room, and bronze-framed oil paintings decorated the walls.

"So you've got a thing for magic, bones, and... art," Saros commented.

"My interests are eclectic," Safyre replied. They headed straight for the bookshelves, but Saros took his time following them. He studied the paintings on the walls, glanced over the papers and open books on the tables as he passed. He found maps, mostly. Books on astronomy and stars and the earth's movement lay open. He spotted several charts and diagrams detailing various plants and their uses in magic. Another book was open to a page on the canid family and their typical magical abilities. Saros itched to find a section on felines and learn what other powers Zenith might be hiding.

He sensed Safyre's eyes on him as he meandered his way across the room, but when he joined them by the bookshelves, they didn't look annoyed. Only amused. "Sorry," Saros said. "I don't want to waste your time."

"Nonsense." They waved a hand. "Time spent with interesting people is never wasted." They smiled — a sleek, sly thing — and leaned back against the shelves.

"I didn't realize I was so interesting," Saros said. He kept his tone light, not quite teasing but undoubtedly nudging open that door. He glanced up and down the bookshelves, but most of the spines were blank leather, free of any distinguishing titles. His gaze circled back to Safyre.

At least they didn't seem to mind his frequent glances in their direction.

"Your interest in Jovian's Tomb interests me," Safyre said, turning to the shelves. "You said you think the tomb can save you. But what does that mean to you? What is your salvation, Saros?"

He looked down at the colorful plush cushions scattered on the floor. He still didn't want to admit the truth for fear of it being impossible. But wouldn't it be better to know now and avoid getting his hopes up any higher?

Also, if there were other necromancers, maybe Saros could live with his power as long as it stopped actively killing him. Maybe he could be part of a community — a family — *and* retain his power. Maybe he didn't have to choose.

"I want..." He sighed. "I thought I wanted the curse to be taken from me. But I saw something that could change everything, assuming the fading doesn't kill me."

Safyre turned to him with a thick book cradled in their arms. "You are not the first necromancer I've met who has chased after that lake hoping it'll solve all their problems. But you are the first I've heard say that you wish to be rid of your power. Why? Because you think it's killing you?"

Saros shrugged. "And because it took everything from me."

Safyre nodded, understanding. "And you believe that if you give up this power, your life will return to normal? You can get back everything you had before?"

"Well, not everything," Saros mumbled. "But I'm tired of being othered. I don't want to hide. I don't want to be feared."

"No?" Safyre raised an eyebrow. "On the contrary, I prefer it this way."

Saros frowned. "Why?"

They traced their fingers along the edge of the book. "Look at how magicians treat animals — and the rest of the natural world. These creatures and life forms are appreciated and protected only for their magical value. They are taken from the places in which they are meant to live and they are placed in stuffy homes instead, kept alive as long as possible because these magicians are so addicted to the power these creatures lend. Even animals that would otherwise be threatening to humans — bears, wolves, tigers, snakes — are treated as harmless, spoiled pets rather than the predators they are. They've all been reduced to ornaments, expressions of wealth and power. But you don't see anyone hiring witches as entertainers, do you?"

Saros admitted they had a point. He remembered his neighbors treating their cats, dogs, birds, and other pets with great care and love, but the animals were less like family members and more like... trophies. He remembered his friends bragging to each other about what animals their families kept and how one was better or more powerful than another.

Safyre was right. They weren't friends or companions. They were only ornaments.

"So you'd rather be feared than loved?" Saros asked Safyre. "You'd rather be shunned than welcomed?"

"If the choice is between being the free hawk or being the caged bird, what would you rather be?" Safyre said. "Why cower and be the prey when I could be the predator? I could do without the violent discrimination, of course, but I don't wish to be exploited. I know I'm pretty, but that doesn't make me a decoration."

Saros hummed. Fair enough.

"But who needs *them*, when we have our own?" Safyre drifted a step closer to Saros, meeting his gaze. "Do you know what the most remarkable thing about necromancy is, Saros? Do you know what makes you and I one and the same?"

"We're connected by this magic, aren't we? Necromancy is bestowed by witches."

"Hmm, so say some myths," said Safyre. "Unsurprisingly, the truth has been buried. It's true that witches and necromancers are intertwined, but it's because we are the only types of magicians whose power is ours alone." They placed a hand on their chest. "It's in our blood. We are born with these powers, Saros. We do not borrow magic from the world, and it is certainly no bestowed curse."

Saros stared at them as their words settled in. An anxious warmth spread through him; he almost felt sick — lightheaded, dizzy, as if the floor had dropped out from under him. "But necromancy... Necromancy isn't *natural*. Why does it— Why is it killing me, then, if it's part of me? Why can I remember a time when I *wasn't* like this? It *must* have been given to me. They told me..."

"What, that you were the victim of a cruel and unfortunate curse, but oh, you must have done something to deserve it, because Illir doesn't punish innocents?" Safyre quirked their pierced eyebrow. "Yes, those devout worshippers of Illir do like to spin it that way. But I wouldn't lie to you about this, Saros, not after all you've ever been told are lies. Necromancy and true magic trace back eons, to a time when humans *did* enjoy natural affinities for magic before it was taken from us. We're a rare breed, and we are dwindling.

"You say you recall a time before your power was known to you." Safyre drifted another step closer to him. They searched his eyes, and Saros saw something like hope in theirs. "And you said that this fading effect began after you used your power for the first time. There is a reason for both of these things, Saros, and the truth is in your past. In *our* past."

And they'd lost him again. "You keep saying that, but we *can't* have met before. I know my life, and you aren't part of it." He studied them, trying to find a flicker of memory, without luck. "I'd remember if you were."

Safyre sighed and turned their head. Whatever hope Saros had glimpsed in their eyes was gone now, overwritten by a long-suffering sadness that ran deep. Saros did not quite believe that he was the person Safyre had lost, but whoever they were, Safyre clearly missed them terribly.

"I'm sorry," Saros said softly. "But I don't think I'm—"

"You are." Safyre left the book in their hands on the table and strode across the room to a shelf on the wall above one of the long tables. They stood on their toes to reach a small, dusty volume, then brought it back to Saros and set it reverently on the table. "I don't know how else to show you. It is up to you whether you wish to believe me, but I would not lie about this. Have a look."

Saros hesitated. A sharp curiosity compelled him to hear what Safyre had to say, but fear of that very same revelation held him in place. He'd barely swallowed the fact that this power that had been killing him for seven years was *part* of him; what other foundation of his life was this witch about to rattle? His entire childhood? Everything he'd ever known? Did Saros even want to know?

I do, he realized. If there were years of his life that had been erased from his memory, he deserved to know. He might never regain those memories, but they were still his.

He briefly met Safyre's gaze, then carefully opened the black leather cover of the book.

The first page was wrinkled around a faded wax seal that depicted a pair of hands with the thumbs and forefingers touching. A slim crescent moon floated in the spade-shaped space between the fingers.

Saros waited for Safyre to turn the page; it was a long minute before they finally did.

The following two pages were filled, margin to margin, with names. A careful, elegant hand had listed each one in perfectly neat columns. Safyre turned the page again, and again, and again, and Saros was met with the same sight. The handwriting grew smaller, fitting three columns on each page instead of two, and with each turned page the penmanship grew sloppier until Saros could hardly recognize letters. After ten pages, Safyre finally turned to a blank one and spread their hand flat on the paper.

Saros met their gaze. "What... is this?"

"Almost sixty years of everyone we have lost."

It was a minute before Saros could conjure a reply. "Lost... how?"

"We rarely know the details, and that is very much for the best." Safyre traced their fingers along the edges of the book. "All we know is that they disappear, or are taken, or otherwise never come back." They turned back two pages and smoothed out the paper, then slid the book closer to Saros.

He scanned the rows of names, pulse quickening with each second. Somehow, he knew that he would find his name here. He stopped seeing the names as full words and saw only the first letters, searching for a sweeping capital S. But then a flicker of something like a memory made him pause. He frowned. "I wasn't called Saros."

He heard Safyre's quick intake of breath. "You remember?"

"No, I..." He blinked a few times, chasing the flicker. "When I woke up here, I saw someone. She knew me. She called me a different name. But..."

"What did she look like?" Safyre prompted.

"Like me," Saros murmured. His eyes remained fixed on the book but the names were blurs of ink before his unfocused gaze. "She looked kind. There was strength in her eyes. She had brown hair, like I used to..." He trailed off and blinked back to the present, then turned to Safyre. "What does this mean?"

They shifted closer to him, their shoulder nearly touching his, and flipped a few pages in the book until they came to an illustration that took up the entire length of the page, oriented sideways for more space. Safyre rotated the book to better view the drawing; Saros felt their eyes on him as he leaned closer to study it.

Against a dark background of trees, a group of roughly fifty people stood proudly together. Some were smiling, others not, but their closeness with each other was evident; many of them had their arms around each other or hands on one another's shoulders. Children stood before their parents, a few holding infant siblings in their arms. The graphite had smeared and faded with age, but Saros could still make out the lovingly rendered details of each person's face. Whoever had drawn this portrait had done so with great care, and it was only thanks to that attention that Saros recognized the woman he had glimpsed when he'd woken.

"That's her." He grabbed a pencil from the table and touched the point of it to the drawing so as not to disturb the graphite with his glove. He glanced at Safyre. "Who is she?"

Safyre smiled and placed their hand on top of Saros's, guiding the pencil tip to hover over a child standing in front of the woman. "Who is *that*?"

Saros looked closer. The woman had her hands on a little boy's shoulders, perhaps to help him stand still for the duration of the portrait. He couldn't have been more than four years old. His face was round like hers, and the artist had given him a messy head of dark, growing-out hair. The boy could've been anyone, but what made Saros pause was the tiny detail the artist had given to his eyes — one was visibly, intentionally lighter than the other. Just like those of the woman behind him.

Saros placed both his hands flat on the table and leaned his weight onto them. "Am I only seeing what you're suggesting I should see?"

"You tell me. You recognized her." Saf touched the flat end of the pencil to the woman in the illustration. Then they moved it to point at another child, this one a bit taller and skinnier than the first. Short, curly hair framed a narrow face with wide, dark eyes. Only a hint of a smile warmed the child's face as they gripped the hand of the adult standing behind them.

Saros looked up at Safyre and met those same wide, dark eyes. "That's you?"

They nodded.

"And…" Saros glanced at the other child again. There was really no denying it, but he still found it hard to get the words out. A tight lump in his throat constricted his voice. "And that's… me, isn't it?"

Safyre placed their hand on top of Saros's. "I can't make you believe me, and I can't restore memories that were forced out of you. But you are of these Woods, Saros. You were part of a tight-knit family that has not forgotten you. Though some of us are more stubborn than others."

Saros didn't know how to react to this. It didn't feel real. Safyre might as well have been telling him about someone else's life. Part of him *didn't* believe them, but he wanted to. He wanted to believe that, once, he had lived among people who had truly, deeply cared for him.

The family he had known — his moody father and his withdrawn mother — had never been outright *cruel* to him. He had grown up with food on the table, clothes on his back, and a roof over his head. His parents had not harmed him or berated him or told him they didn't want him.

But they also weren't warm. They kept him alive and content but not quite happy. They weren't loving or soft or comforting. And then he'd discovered his magic and they had finally kicked him out of their house to live in shameful isolation. That spoke louder than any words they might've snarled or bruises they might've left.

Saros looked at the drawing again. All those smiling faces and loving touches. The protective hands on his shoulders and calm expression on his face. He'd been happy here; he knew it in his bones even if he didn't consciously remember it.

This had been his family; these people had loved him, and he had been taken away from them. The man he'd called Father had deprived him of a childhood of comfort and safety and had instead thrown him into a world that hated him.

"Why?" Saros turned to Safyre again. "Why was I taken away from this?"

"So that you'd grow up miserable," Safyre said. They seemed to realize just then that their hand was still touching Saros's and they quickly moved. Their decorated fingers fiddled with the book's pages instead. "Most people don't know that witches have inherent magic.

They think we have to use amulets and talismans from nature just like everyone else. Therefore they conclude that if a child is kept from learning about magic, they won't become a witch."

Saros nodded. "I was forbidden from reading about it. I wasn't allowed to be friends with or even speak to anyone who showed an interest in magic. I knew it existed, of course, and I never had any hatred toward it. But I was taught to fear it."

"Mhmm," Safyre hummed. "Your father thought you'd be raised to be a witch if you stayed here with us and your mother. She thought you were both safe, that your father would never step so far into the Woods that he'd find us." Safyre met his eyes again. "She was wrong."

It wasn't fair. Where would Saros be if his life had been here in the Woods instead of in that secluded, stubborn little town? *Who* would he be if he had been surrounded by people like him rather than people who shunned him?

"Do you understand now?" Safyre asked. "You were never cursed, Saros. Only deprived of the truth. And that deprivation — that suppression of your inherent magic — is what has caused this effect on your body."

"The fading is because I *didn't* use my power?"

"I believe so." Safyre turned their back to the table and leaned against it, crossing their arms over their chest. "Our magic is meant to grow with us, to be strengthened and exercised. But you neglected it for so many years, I doubt you recognized its presence at all. I'm not surprised that you were oblivious to it until you were... what, sixteen? Eighteen?"

"Twenty," Saros murmured. He was not surprised, either, that he had never felt a hint of it. If not for Rune, Saros might not have ever known his power at all.

He still struggled to wrap his head around all of this. His history here. His magic. The lie that was his entire life. He was surprised he wasn't more shaken by all these revelations, and perhaps when the shock wore off he would sink into an existential crisis, but despite everything, this newfound knowledge of his past was comforting. He wasn't cursed. He hadn't done something to *deserve* to be cursed. He simply was as he was, and it was no fault of his that he had been cast out by his own family.

"So does this mean anyone can be born a necromancer?" Saros asked.

"Technically, yes, but it's incredibly rare. To be born a witch is uncommon enough; when people of a certain lineage are consistently hunted and murdered like beasts, it's hard to find a partner at all — let alone someone who isn't already distantly related to you. But I'd say you're about as likely to be born a necromancer as you are to have... say, heterochromia." Saf met Saros's eyes.

He flickered a smile. "Guess I got exceedingly lucky, then."

"Above average, indeed." Safyre's eyes softened. "This is a lot to take in, I understand. It's surreal to me, too, to see you again. The others never forgot you, but I never stopped missing you, my friend."

Saros wished he shared the same memories. He sensed a closeness with Safyre that suggested there was a part of him that had always known them, and he knew even without those memories that they would have been as important to him as Rune had been.

Something occurred to him then. "*We're* not related, are we?"

Safyre snorted. "No. But as children we were the only two of our age, so we were inseparable." A gentle smile smoothed that decades-deep sadness from their face. "I've had spells set all over these Woods for years. I didn't know what sort of magic to expect, so I set them to detect a variety, including necromancy. The moment there was a surge of such magic in the Woods, I would know. Last night, it finally happened." They studied Saros as if they could will the memories out of the far reaches of his mind. "You're not going to die, Saros."

He flexed his gloved hands. "I might."

"No." Safyre set their hand on his arm, and even through his sleeve, Saros could feel a hint of their warmth. "Not if you play your cards carefully. Jovian will speak to you tonight, Saros. Listen."

He fixed his gaze on their hand where it rested just above his wrist. Their fingers were long and slim, like a musician's, and decorated with bronze and copper rings of varying sizes. One on their middle finger was sculpted in the shape of a crow's skull.

Safyre noticed. "Beautiful work of art, isn't it?" They lifted their hand and spread their fingers. "A gift from the coven Elder."

"You really are into bones, huh?"

"Well, if that's what's on your mind…" Safyre flashed a wicked smile, and Saros shut his mouth. They laughed. "But really, can you blame me for finding life and death fascinating? You of all people should understand. You…" Safyre leaned into his side and met his eyes more closely than before. "You have a unique, beautiful, powerful connection to a force of nature the rest of us can only wonder about. That, Saros, is the farthest possible thing from a curse."

Saros held their gaze. Their words alighted something in his chest that kicked his pulse up a notch. He felt the same heady rush of adrenaline as when he'd found the possibility of more necromancers — the terrifying yet soul-fulfilling ordeal of being seen.

Safyre set their hand on Saros's arm again, then gently skimmed their fingers down his wrist to the edge of his glove. They glanced up and met his gaze, and when he nodded once they tugged his glove off, set it aside, and did the same with the other one. They gathered Saros's hands in both of theirs, and the sudden, sharp warmth made him gasp.

"Safyre…"

"Oh, do call me Saf," they murmured. "We needn't be so formal. How does that feel?"

Saros nodded, barely daring to breathe lest Saf let go and deprive him of this warmth that he'd gone so long without. "Can anything reverse this?"

"I don't know," Saf murmured. "I've never seen anything like it. Is it just your hands?"

"Not anymore." Saros drew away from them and pushed his sleeves up to his elbows. He cringed at the unsettling sight of his bones through his skin; it never got less jarring. "What about the others you said are here? Other witches. Would they know?"

"Perhaps."

Saros waited for them to say more, but they didn't. "And Jovian's Tomb? Will it help me? Will it *heal* me?"

Saf studied him a moment longer, then reached across the table — leaning markedly closer to Saros in the process — and presented him with a white envelope sealed with black wax. "This will tell you everything you wish to know."

Incredulously, Saros took the envelope and snapped the seal. "This *one* paper will answer— Oh."

The paper unfolded to reveal an invitation, which was perhaps the last thing Saros wished to see.

Lunar Ball
Herein celebrating the New Moon
A night of mystery, secrets, and indulgence
Dusk in the Grove, we await our God

"A party?" He flicked an unimpressed glance at Saf. "How is this going to do anything for me other than make me miserable?"

"I believe it will do quite a lot for you," Saf said. "This is when Jovian's Tomb will appear. Conveniently nearby, thanks to yours truly." They smirked. "It is nice when these things work out, isn't it?"

Saros blinked. "*You* control where the lake shows up?"

"Well, not *me* personally." Saf flipped their hair over their shoulder with a delicate clatter of beads and bells. "Could you imagine if I had that much power? I'd be insufferable. No, I'm lucky if the others take my logic into consideration. I *have* been trying to keep the tomb close, hoping you would someday come find it."

"Hold on." Saros set the invitation down and rubbed his temples. "Your coven controls the tomb?"

"Yes." Saf smirked. "What, you thought it was random?"

"Why wouldn't I?" This was somehow more surprising than anything else Saros had just learned. Or maybe his mind had reached its limit of acceptable life-changing revelations and *now* the shock was hitting him. "It took me almost a decade to track this lake. It had no pattern to its appearances other than being associated with the new moon. I tracked the weather, the constellations, the exact time of each confirmed appearance..." He shook his head. "So none of that mattered, and it was just— What, *luck* that I happened to go looking for the lake in the month it *happened* to be close enough that I could find it?"

"Perhaps luck, if that's what you wish to call it," Saf said. "But I think it was something stronger than luck that made all of these pieces align. You were meant to come back to us, Saros. It was fated. And it will be my honor tonight to reintroduce you to your true family, if you are willing." They met his gaze and softened their voice. "I hope you are."

Saros read the invitation again. *Dusk in the Grove, we await our God.* He didn't have to ask who that *god* was. It was not Illir.

So if this was his chance, not only to stand before Jovian's Tomb like he had longed to do for years, but also to meet other witches — perhaps other necromancers — he would be a fool to say no. He could handle one social gathering for the sake of literally everything he had wanted for nearly his entire life.

"Before I say yes," he said, "there's something you should know." He set the invitation on the table and went to reach for the timepiece in his pocket only to remember it was gone. His heart missed a beat at its unfamiliar absence. "I don't know how much Atheris told you about what happened back at the tavern where you found us, but there's someone following me, and he's got a cult behind him. He's dangerous, he's delusional, and he will most likely be there tonight when the lake appears."

Saros sought Saf's eyes and mentally begged them to understand. "I don't want to bring harm to the community you have here. Rune is after me alone. When he shows up, I will deal with him. I can't put you or the others in danger."

Saf crossed their arms and leaned their hip against the table. "We have procedures in place in the event our corner of the Woods is compromised. Don't worry about us. Witches don't cower and hide, Saros. If this man is after your life, we'll give him hell."

Saros had been afraid Saf would say something like that. "No. I can't let you do that. You don't owe me protection."

"Yes, we do." Saf gripped his arm. "How long have you gone without anyone taking care of you, Saros? You were taken from your family and raised in a world that was against you from the very start.

They erased your memory of us and they took your name. And then, what, cast you out when they were tired of dealing with you? When they decided you were a *stain* on the family?" They searched his eyes. "Saros. We lost you once. We won't let it happen again."

"You don't even know me." Saros meant the words to come out sharper than they did, but he couldn't conjure any heat behind them. He *wanted* Saf and the other witches to know him now just as they had known him long ago, but he could not let that selfish desire put all of these people in the path of Rune's vengeance. He could not let them all become names in that book.

"I may not know you now," Saf said softly, "but I did once. And the person I remember was worth protecting. You don't have to be alone anymore, Saros."

He hardly wanted to get his hopes up over this, but clearly Saf was not going to take no for an answer. Saros sighed and met their eyes with a nod. "Okay. I'll go. I want to know what I've been missing."

Saf's smile could have thawed the winter. Saros didn't know what made them look at him like this, but he wasn't about to question it. It was quite the nice change of pace to see admiration — perhaps also a hint of desire — in someone's eyes rather than fear or hatred. Saros could let himself get used to this.

"You'll need proper attire, of course," Saf said. "I probably have something that will suit you. And Atheris, as well."

"This invitation is also extended to her, then?" Saros was sure she'd be genuinely thrilled.

"But of course. Jovian's Tomb has something for everyone, you know." Saf winked.

Saros found Atheris back in the main room, tucked in a far corner with her nose buried so deep in a book that if not for her bright hair, she would've blended in with the clutter. He let the creaky floor announce his presence, and she did a double take when she glanced up.

"Oh. Where have *you* been?" She eyed him suspiciously. "You look weird."

Saros raised an eyebrow. "Thank you?"

"No, like... What's wrong?" Atheris laid the book in her hands across her lap. "What did Safyre tell you?"

"Noth—" He stopped himself even before he saw the incredulous look on Atheris's face. At this point, there was no reason to keep anything from her. "A lot," he said instead. "They told me a lot. Did you know there's a coven that lives in Illir's Woods?"

"Not before Safyre suggested it, no." Atheris rubbed her eye. "But that's not what's got you rattled."

Saros glanced over the random objects and dusty books cluttering the shelves and tables around him. He didn't know what made him hesitate to confide in Atheris; perhaps a lifetime of conditioning to keep everything about himself *to* himself. He had not realized how much he adhered to that unbreakable rule.

But there was no longer a reason for it to be unbreakable. He met Atheris's curious gaze. "I was born into that coven. I was part of it."

He expected her to look shocked, to react with the dramatic gusto he'd come to expect from her. At the very least, he'd expected her to leap out of her seat with an exclamation of *Holy shit*. But she just nodded. Her face remained solemn.

"You knew?" He couldn't fathom how she would.

"Safyre told me," she explained. "They didn't give me the whole story, but they said they knew you. I... I figured that if you knew you'd been part of a coven, you would have told me when we talked about magic before."

Saros nodded slowly. "I had no idea. I... don't know what to make of it. But..." He presented the invitation. "Saf offered us both a chance to learn more."

Atheris snatched the envelope. "What is this?"

"Something you will be far more thrilled about than I am."

She unfolded the parchment, and her eyes widened with delight. "Oh my *god*."

"Thought so." Saros smiled to himself.

"A *ball*?" Atheris beamed. "Holy shit, this is the best thing I've seen all week. Okay, okay, wait, what do we wear? We can't go like *this*." She gestured at her baggy sweater and Saros's plain clothes.

"Saf said they would lend us some proper outfits if we need them," Saros said, folding his hands behind his back. He realized only then that he hadn't put his gloves back on. "I told them we certainly would."

Atheris jumped to her feet and dropped the still-open book on the vacated chair. "Oh, hell yes. *Hell* yes. Let's see what they've got. I'm going to look my goddamned best tonight, and that's a *threat*."

Saros laughed softly. "Only a few hours until dusk. We'd better hurry."

Atheris shoved past him and darted out of the room as if she'd miss out on Saf's wardrobe if she wasn't fast enough. Saros was in no such rush; he picked up the book Atheris had been reading and meant to replace it on a nearby shelf, but the page she'd left open made him freeze.

Bold strokes of charcoal crowned the paper with an ominous heading:

TO BESTOW THE HANDS OF GODS

Beneath the title were two short stanzas of text in a language Saros didn't recognize. But he didn't need to know what it said to understand that this was a spell.

A spell for *what*, he couldn't be sure without translating the verses. But if necromancy was inherent, if the power was not something bestowed but something born, then what the hell was this?

Saros glanced over his shoulder to make sure he was alone in the room, then he quickly tore the page out of the book and tucked it in his back pocket.

Yet another question for Saf.

CHAPTER 10

NEW MOON V

SAROS STOOD before an ornate mirror at the end of the hall and saw a version of himself that he'd thought was gone. It had been many, many years since he'd found an occasion for which to dress up, and seeing himself like this again brought an unexpected wave of nostalgia that choked him up. This self-indulgence and the pride that came with it was something he hadn't bothered to seek in a long time.

He traced his hands down the coils of embroidery along the front of his coat. It was deep black, lined with dark red silk, and had silver decorations swirling down the front and cuffing the sleeves. The buttons were polished to a shine, and despite Saf claiming they hadn't worn this coat in ages, it didn't look any worse for wear. Saros was more surprised that it fit him so nicely when Saf was thinner and narrower in the shoulders than he was, but both the coat and the black linen shirt he wore beneath it fit as if they were made for him.

He stopped fussing with the coat and instead turned his attention to his hair, which was still a little damp from the bath he'd enjoyed earlier. He ran his hands through the straight silver strands until it was free of tangles, then pinned back a section to keep it out of his face. He let the rest fall free, the ends brushing the embroidery running along the tops of his shoulders.

Finally, he met his eyes in the glass. He hadn't let himself dwell on his own appearance in a long time, but if there was ever a time to do so, it was now. Saf had said that witches were generally hard to impress, but given his apparent history with these people, he doubted they would judge him based on appearances alone.

Still, looking at himself now, all he saw was a ghost. The fading made him look deathly, worse now that he'd used his power again. His cheekbones stood out too harshly, his face was too pale, the skin beneath his eyes was perpetually dark purple. At least his eyes themselves looked a little brighter than they had recently. Hopefully, after tonight, his restless magic would release its vise grip on him and he would start to come back to life.

Behind him, someone cleared their throat.

Saros turned, expecting to see Saf, but it was Atheris instead. She'd traded her oversized coat and baggy sweater for an elegant multi-piece suit made of dark green fabrics that complemented her ginger hair and brightened her eyes. Delicate gold beads sewn in leafy patterns swirled down the front of the waist-length coat, circling around two columns of brass buttons. She wore her amulets on proud display, strung on fine ribbons beneath the black cravat closing the collar of her white shirt. Her normally wild hair was curled in perfect ringlets that bounced each time she moved.

The ensemble suited her well, but Saros could hardly match the woman standing in front of him with the one he'd known for the past year. "You look nice," he told her earnestly.

She grinned. "Thanks. You clean up pretty well yourself. Trying to impress a certain homicidal ex?"

Saros shot her a glare. Coincidentally, Rune had hardly crossed his mind tonight. "No."

"Then perhaps a charming witch?" Atheris slid past him and fussed with her hair in the mirror.

That, Saros could not deny. But who could blame him? Saf was ethereal, and Saros was not immune to it.

"Your hair looks fine," he said as Atheris continued fretting and had nearly ruined all her curls. "Let's go so we can get this over with."

She spun around on her heel. "I thought you'd be excited for this."

"What part of literally anything about me suggests that I would enjoy a ball?"

"Oh, it's not the party you're looking forward to." Atheris smirked.

Saros turned away from her and retreated down the hall. "I certainly don't know what you mean."

Her heeled boots clicked on the floor as she caught up with him. "Do you think I'm totally oblivious? I saw the way Safyre looked at you earlier. *And* the way you so smoothly flirted with them."

Saros rolled his eyes. "I did not flirt with them."

"Sure you didn't. By the way, since when do you call them *Saf?*"

He glanced at her. "What?"

"Earlier when you showed me the invitation, you called them Saf instead of Safyre." Atheris raised her eyebrows.

"Yes, and?" Saros slid his hands into the pockets of his coat, and only realized he'd subconsciously been reaching for the timepiece when he found it missing. He closed his hand around his gloves instead. "So they told me to call them a nickname. Why do you care so much?"

"I'm just *curious*, that's all."

"Well, that's not my problem."

Atheris sighed. "Worth a try, I guess. Such a stick in the mud. Well, *I'm* going to have a grand time, dance with every beautiful lady witch at this party, and I am going to be extremely vindicated when that lake appears and I can go back to Evyrmyre and rub it in everyone's faces that it is *real* and I saw it *twice*, and *then*—"

"Okay, no one ever said *you* couldn't have fun," Saros grumbled. "But I don't have that luxury."

Atheris fell quiet. "Right. I'm sorry." She stopped walking and touched Saros's arm so he stopped, too. "How... um, how are you feeling?"

"I'm fine," he said, glancing at her once before stepping into the main room.

"Okay, but can I get the real answer? Saros." She jumped in front of him. "You can tell me."

No, it would only ruin her excitement, and he didn't want to weigh her down with his own doubts and worries. The truth was, he was terrified. Even the promise of an indulgent night at Saf's side wasn't enough to chase away the frigid terror that everything would go wrong tonight.

"Hey." Atheris set her hand on his arm. "You don't have to talk about it, but you know that I'd listen, right? You know that I'm your friend, right?"

Saros glanced down at her hand, then met her eyes. "I know."

A smile touched the corner of her mouth. "Okay. Good. Now let's go dance with some witches."

THEY FOUND SAF OUTSIDE, waiting by the front steps of their cabin. Saf stood with their arms crossed and their pierced eyebrow raised, but Saros was too immediately distracted by their beauty to care that they looked exasperated. He tried not to stare; truly, he did, but he couldn't help himself. Saf wore a long, deep indigo gown that kissed the ground and dipped in a V down their chest. Thousands of tiny beads formed constellations on the bodice that sparkled in the lantern light. Braids threaded with silver tinsel swept their hair out of their face and let it cascade down their back. Gold and silver rings decorated their ears and their hands, and their head was crowned with a silver circlet studded with little starbursts. As a final touch, they'd painted their lips and shadowed their eyes.

Their gaze flicked to Saros and he looked away, heat rising to his face. Despite his own formal attire, he suddenly felt plain and underdressed next to them, and had a feeling he'd only continue to feel out of place as the night went on.

But then Saf approached him and touched his wrist, smiling when he met their eyes. "Well, *hello*. I'm glad to see everything fits. How dare you leave me unprepared for how well you dress up?"

Saros laughed softly, mostly out of surprise at Saf's compliment. "I am certainly not the best dressed at this gathering."

"Are you quite sure of that?"

"Have you looked in a mirror?"

Saf grinned. "You flatter me, my friend. By all means, don't stop. Shall we be on our way? The new moon waits for no one. Why don't you walk with me, Saros, if Atheris wouldn't feel too excluded?"

Atheris looked like she'd just witnessed a miracle from the gods themselves. But it took only a moment for a wicked smirk to erase the blank shock on her face. "Not at all. You take *all* the alone time you need." She raised her eyebrows pointedly at Saros, then strode ahead toward a visible path through the trees.

"Stay on the lit path," Saf called to her. "The grove isn't far. You can't miss it."

She raised a thumbs-up, throwing her shoulders back as she marched on.

Saf wrapped their arm around Saros's. "She seems like a good friend. Undoubtedly cares about you. Ironically, I assumed the two of you were an item when I found you, given how distraught she was when she thought you might not make it."

Saros snorted at the idea of him and Atheris being a couple. Romantic preferences aside, they couldn't be more different. If he was at all interested in her, he'd probably strangle her — and she'd probably stab him — after a week of being together. "I assure you, it's for the best that we're outside each other's interests."

Saf laughed softly. "Maybe so. How did you meet her?"

"A mutual interest in Jovian's Tomb," Saros said. "I was looking for eyewitness accounts of the lake, and Atheris's story found its way to me. I just... had a good feeling about her. She wasn't afraid of what she'd seen; she wanted to understand it. So I approached her and asked if she would be willing to help me find it and figure out its pattern."

"And how could she refuse?"

"You would have thought I had handed her a crown and told her she was queen of the universe." Saros smiled and looked up at Atheris, who walked several feet in front of him and Saf. "We started meeting every week to gather and organize our notes and piece together a pattern. Eventually we had a theory, and then a definitive map right to Jovian's Tomb. I wouldn't be here if not for her."

Saf was quiet for a moment, lost in thought. Shadows waxed and waned across their face as the two of them passed beneath each paper lantern strung overhead among the branches. The light caught Saf's jewelry and made the beads on their dress sparkle, giving them an ethereal glow.

"Then I'm very glad you have her in your life," Saf said quietly.

Saros looked up and realized they'd reached the end of the path. The trees opened into a wide, grassy clearing painted with wildflowers that glowed against the dark. Lanterns and ribbons hung from the lower branches of the trees surrounding the edge of the clearing, and dozens of witches had set up tents and tables loaded with food, drinks, and wares. Music filled the air. Voices murmured and laughter blended with the airy melodies. Savory smells wafted across the space, making Saros's mouth water. From a distance it seemed... *sort of* fun, even if his instincts were screaming at the idea of milling about with so many people.

He scanned the clearing until he caught a glimpse of Atheris's orange hair; already she had a goblet in hand and was chatting with a woman wearing a blue knee-length gown. Saros smiled to himself and left her to her fun.

"Can I get you anything?" Saf asked softly. Their silvery voice nearly got lost under the hum of noise, compelling Saros to lean closer to them. He wondered if that was precisely their intention.

Regardless, he was happy to oblige. But it was all too easy to think this was a normal party that Saros could enjoy with Saf on his arm and a drink in his hand. Part of him wished this night could be that easy, but he could not forget why he was really here.

"No," he murmured in reply to Saf's question. "That's all right. Look, this isn't exactly my scene. Don't let me hold you back from enjoying your own party."

"Saros, please, have I not been clear enough about wanting your company?" Saf tightened their grip around his arm. "This is a night of celebration for both of us — for *all* of us. Come on, I'll introduce you first to our family and then to our wine."

They tugged him toward the festivities, and Saros gave up the last of his resistance.

Arm in arm, they wove among the tables and tents, submerging themselves into the scents and sounds. Laughter and singing filled Saros's ears, overwhelming in volume and cacophony. He could not take a step without bumping shoulders with another person, many of whom obliviously shoved their way past him. He stepped on Saf's foot more than once in his attempt to stay out of other people's paths; they didn't seem to mind, but wherever they were taking him, Saros prayed it was away from all of this.

How were there so many people here? Saros had been expecting a small gathering of the coven Saf called family, and perhaps a few others. Was this typical of their new moon gatherings, or was this one somehow special?

Saros would have voiced his questions if he thought Saf could hear him over the noise. He could barely hear his own thoughts.

And, amid this chaotic throng of bodies, how would he know when Rune showed up? Would he find him at all before it was too late?

Saros scanned the faces surrounding him, but there were dozens, all turning and moving and disappearing behind each other like cards shuffled through a deck. Each time he thought he glimpsed Rune's wavy black hair or his silver eyes or black cloak, the details vanished into the sea and he started to see those traits everywhere. Another pair of silver eyes. Another person with black hair. Another long, hooded cloak. Rune was everywhere and nowhere.

"Saros?"

He snapped out of his head with a gasp. He hadn't realized how hard his heart was pounding until it started to slow. Saf came back into focus at his side.

"Are you okay?" They tightened their arm around his.

"Yeah," he sighed. "Just..."

"Overwhelmed?"

That sounded better than *scared shitless*, so Saros nodded. "I did tell you that I hate parties. This isn't what I expected when you said 'ball.'"

"No? What *did* your mind conjure, I wonder?"

"Something more... formal." The balls and dinner parties Saros's father had hosted when Saros was a child were never this lively or chaotic. They were formal events, business transactions, and there had been no room for fun. To Saros, the events were a life-or-death test of etiquette. Even now he found himself standing up straighter out of stress-induced habit.

"*Formal?* Never." Saf laughed softly. "Not to worry. I won't torment you much longer. There's someone I'd like you to meet before we indulge ourselves." Saf tugged his arm and they finally made their way out of the crowd and toward a quieter edge of the clearing. Despite the wide open space, only a fraction of it was occupied by the festival. The rest, Saros reasoned, was reserved for Jovian's Tomb.

Saf kept their arm loosely linked through Saros's as they made their way across a pristine expanse of snow. Though the music and voices followed the two of them away from the festival, Saros let his guard down out here. It was far easier to enjoy the night and all the possibilities it would bring when he didn't have to fight a crowd.

At the very edge of the trees, a white tent glowed from within. A small campfire crackled in front of it.

Saf paused before the tent and turned to Saros. "You're not the only one who doesn't enjoy parties. Our Elder rarely joins the festivities. She'll find her way over there once it's time to summon Jovian, but it's better if you meet her this way."

Saros was not particularly prepared to meet the leader of this witch coven, but he followed Saf into the tent anyway.

Inside, an older woman with white hair and rich brown skin sat cross-legged on a plush cushion. She balanced a smoldering pipe between her fingers and greeted Saf and Saros with a kind smile.

"I was wondering when you'd pay me a visit this evening, Safyre." Her voice was deep and smooth, untouched by her apparent age. "And to whom do I owe the pleasure? Another of your paramours, Safyre? He must be a special one if you're bringing him to me."

Saf cleared their throat and pointedly did not catch Saros's eye when he shot them a look. "Elder, this is Saros. He is — was — one of the lost."

The woman's eyes widened. She leaned forward and reached a hand toward Saros; he shifted a step closer to her. "Come here, young man, my vision isn't what it used to be. Are you really...?"

Saros glanced once at Saf, then knelt on the floor before the woman. She laid a soft hand on his cheek. He didn't know what to say to her; had she known him before? Would she believe Saf when they said he used to be part of this coven? Would she welcome him back when he knew nothing of their ways?

But when he looked into her eyes, he found no suspicion there, only hesitantly hopeful surprise. Her dark eyes welled with tears. "You were one of ours? What is your blessing, young man?"

"My—? Um, what... What do you mean, er— madam? Elder?"

Great. He was doing great.

She laughed softly. "Don't worry yourself over formalities with me, dear. I simply mean to ask after your gift. Your magic."

Saros relaxed a bit. "Oh. I'm... I'm a necromancer." It felt strange to say it aloud after so many years of burying the word beneath six feet of shame. But he knew he would not be shunned here. This was perhaps the only place on earth where he *would* be accepted.

The woman gasped. "Jovian's own power... Blessed, indeed. It is my honor to meet you." She glanced at Saf. "Did you show him the book?"

"I did. He's in it." Saf knelt beside Saros and let the length of their gown fan out around their legs. "He's Kirsi's son, Elder."

Kirsi. That was her name, the woman in the picture, the mother he'd never known. Saros wished he remembered her. She likely had never forgotten him.

The Elder gazed at Saros with barely-concealed awe. "Truly? Well, Safyre, it seems we all owe you an apology for every time we told you to give it up. Your spells worked, and your wish came true."

Saros turned to Saf curiously, finding an oddly sheepish expression on their face. "I was taught, Elder, that we never give up on each other. Even against the odds."

"And your devotion is honorable." She bowed her head toward them, then looked at Saros once more. "I regret to share that your mother, Kirsi, has long since left us. She rests with our god and all the others who came before us. But it is a miracle that you are here. No one else has ever lived to return."

"I'm honored to be here," he said. Her words swam in his mind along with everything Saf had told him. He had a book of questions for her, but the one that made it out of his mouth first was, "You mean Jovian, don't you, when you refer to god?"

"Well, certainly not Illir," Saf muttered.

"I didn't think so," Saros said. "But I have never heard Jovian described as a god."

"We pay our respects to Jovian because he was not afraid to bend the laws of nature," Saf said. They reached over to a clay pot of smoldering leaves and lifted out a long straw, tapping the ashes off the end of it. They brought the other end to their lips, inhaled, and blew out a puff of fragrant smoke. "What is the point of magic if it does not take risks? You know Jovian as the first necromancer, but that is likely untrue. He was just the first to be proud of his power and use it to its full capacity."

"Didn't he nearly destroy all life on earth?" Saros questioned. He wasn't trying to disrespect these witches, but how far did they go to excuse Jovian's actions?

The Elder chuckled softly. "Is that what the stories say these days? Ah, they make up something new every few years. Never gets old. Listen, young man, when you hear only the wider world's version of our tales, the truth gets skewed."

Saf hummed in agreement, exhaling another plume of smoke. "Do you truly think the society that shunned you and made you believe you were cursed was interested in telling the correct history of witches and necromancers?"

No, that wouldn't make much sense, would it? Saros was slowly beginning to understand just how much of what he'd been taught about witches and necromancy and Illir and Jovian was a lie. Of course it had all been twisted by time and intention. Saros would not be surprised in the slightest to learn that the truth about witches had been purposely buried in order to keep them in their place. To keep them ostracized. To turn Jovian and his fate into a bedtime story meant to plant fear of necromancy, and to paint Illir as the hero and savior — the gracious and merciful god.

"You seem to harbor a conflicting fear of Jovian," said the Elder. "Considering where you grew up — that is, outside of our coven —

that is expected. But I wish to bring an end to your miseducation, Saros. I wish to welcome you home to us."

He stared at her. *Just like that?* He'd exchanged a handful of words with this woman — a coven Elder — and she was offering him a place here?

Saros resented the corner of his mind that suspected this was a trick.

"It is merely an offer, not a requirement," Saf said quietly. "If you have a life and a home elsewhere, you are not obligated to stay with us. But we'd be honored to have you."

"I... don't know what to say." Saros met the Elder's eyes, then turned to Saf. "You barely know me, and yet...?"

Saf nodded. "You are the only one who has ever made it back to us. You deserve a place here. Besides..." A smirk curled at the corner of their lips. "I can't let you get away from me that easily."

"Insufferable flirt," the Elder muttered.

Saf pretended not to hear her. They held Saros's gaze. "Well?"

Saros didn't know how to decide. Of course he wanted this. Of course he didn't want to return to his isolated corner of Kasvalta. He had nothing there; no present and no future. Only a bleak past that had so far governed every aspect of his life. Still it stalked him — Rune was living proof — but that would all be over soon. And what came next?

That was the piece Saros had yet to answer. What would follow this night?

It could be this. All he had to do was say yes.

He didn't quite know what he was getting into, but he had nothing to lose. He turned to the Elder once again. "It would be my honor, Elder, to call myself part of this coven."

Her grin rivaled the sun's luminance. She reached for his hands, and Saros entirely forgot about his lack of gloves until the Elder noticeably flinched at his touch. But before Saros could react, she grabbed his wrist and took a closer look.

Saros couldn't read what might've gone through her head, but he felt somewhat like an insect under a magnifying glass. He cleared his throat. "Saf tells me this is a result of suppressing my magic for most of my life. Would you agree?"

"Oh, doubting my judgment, are you?" Saf muttered, but when Saros glanced at them, they were smiling.

"I sought Jovian's Tomb because I thought it would fix this," Saros continued to the Elder. She met his eyes curiously. "I also thought it would take this power away from me so I would no longer have to suffer from it."

The Elder nodded slowly. "Do you still wish for your power to be gone?"

Strange, Saros thought, how his deepest hope could change so abruptly in just a few days' time. "No," he said. "I don't know what will happen when I approach the lake, but I know I will be better than I am now."

The Elder smiled and released Saros's hand. "In that case, I wish you luck. And I look forward to seeing you — both of you — at the ritual."

Saros stopped himself from inquiring about this ritual; he'd learned to recognize a dismissal when he heard one. He nodded in thanks to the Elder, then stood and stepped out of the tent. Saf followed moments later, bringing a waft of sweet herbs with them.

"Shall we?" They offered their arm.

Saros flickered a smile and accepted, but for the first stretch of their walk back to the festival, only the light crunch of ice beneath their boots filled the air. The past few minutes were still catching up to him. He was part of a *coven* now, but what the hell did that actually mean? What would he be expected to do? Saros faintly knew that this was his anxiety speaking, but what if life with this coven was worse than his life before?

What had he just said yes to?

"I can practically hear your thoughts spiraling," Saf commented, effectively breaking said spiral. "In my experience, worries kept confined to the mind only grow bigger." They stopped and turned to Saros, still far enough from the festival that the noise didn't overwhelm their voice. "What's troubling you?"

He shook his head. Saf had spent their whole life with these people. They wouldn't understand his worries. Worse, Saros might offend them. "Nothing," he said. "I don't want to dampen your fun any more than I already have. You should—"

Saf cut him off by pressing a finger to his lips. He froze. They stepped closer to him. "None of that. Remember what I said about enjoying your company?" They drew back with a wry smile. "If we had more time, I could tell you a lifetime of stories that would ease your mind. As it is, the best I can do is place a cup of wine in your hand and advise you to see the evening through. You will come to understand all of us better by the time Jovian arrives."

Rationally, Saros understood that. Yet he knew his thoughts wouldn't settle until he saw everything firsthand. Maybe Saf was onto something with the idea of wine. "What will happen when the tomb appears?" he asked. "The Elder mentioned a ritual. You said that the coven here controls when and where the lake arrives. Does that mean you... summon it?"

"In a way." Saf shrugged. "It's not so much summoning as it is directing energy. Jovian's Tomb is a potent source of magical power; without us channeling it in a certain way, it could have catastrophic effects on the surrounding environment. The Woods are already strange enough. They don't need to be further affected by ancient, untamed magic."

Saf said this lightly, as if mostly joking, but Saros did not wish to consider how much weirder Illir's Woods could be.

"Tonight is the first new moon of the year," Saf continued. "Jovian's power will be heightened, so be careful what you speak into the tomb's waters. Its magic will be vivid, blinding, perhaps overwhelming. If there was ever a time for your power to come alive, Saros, it is tonight."

Saros couldn't fathom what it would be like. He'd only ever known the pain that came with his power; to think that soon, in only a short matter of time, it would bring him alive rather than drag him to his grave... Saros hardly dared to hope for such a blessing from this god of necromancers. There was so much that could go wrong.

And if anything was going to go wrong, Saros predicted that Rune would be the root of it.

"May I offer a word of warning, though?" Saf brought his attention back to them. "Desperation is the root of chaos, Saros. You may not plan to ask Jovian to relieve you of your power, but you will still approach the tomb with a request for strength. Recall that Jovian hungered for power. He was ravenous. Nothing was ever enough, not even the ability to raise the dead. He wanted to defeat death itself, to freeze the course of nature. He wanted stasis, and he wanted control. The lake churns with his madness, and once you taste that power... I wonder if you will indeed be able to let go of it."

Their words sent a chill over Saros's skin. "I don't intend to let it get out of control," he said. "I just want to live with my power instead of dying from it."

Saf studied him a moment longer, then nodded once. "And I believe that you will. With us." A smile warmed their face. "Now, shall we return to the festivities?"

"Only for the promise of wine." Saros took their arm again.

"You read my mind."

Saf tugged him back into the throes of the festival, and now the bustling activity wasn't quite as grating as before. He and Saf strolled by merchants selling crafts, artwork, clothing, accessories, books, even small animals. Saros subconsciously followed his nose toward the food, but Saf instead directed him to a table lined with a few dozen wine bottles.

"Important things first," they said with a wink, approaching the table. "Good evening, Clari," they greeted a woman with short black hair. "We'll take two of your best."

"Nothing less for you, Saf," replied Clari, and passed them a full goblet. She poured another for Saros and gave him a once-over as she handed it to him. "You've brought a guest."

Saros resisted the impulse to shrink back. Before he could conjure an excuse for his presence, Saf saved him.

"This is Saros. He's with me tonight." Their hand tightened on his arm.

"Is that so? Well, don't let me keep you from your fun. Cheers."

Saf nodded at her and then pulled Saros away. "She seemed rather nonchalant about meeting an outsider," Saros commented as they continued their stroll amid the tents. He continued to gravitate toward the food, which Saf seemed less interested in, but this wine would go straight to his head if he didn't eat something. If it was a normal party, he'd let it. He didn't have that option here. The last thing he needed was to be inebriated when Jovian showed up.

"You're not an outsider," Saf reminded him. They turned down a path between two large tents that led out of the festival and into the shadowy trees. Their branches rustled as if welcoming Saros and Saf; leaves and buds rained down on their heads. Without thinking, Saros reached over and freed a dry leaf from Saf's hair.

They turned their head toward him, a touch startled. Their eyes tracked his hand as he moved it away; Saros found himself holding his breath in anticipation of their next move. They found his gaze again and blinked a few times, long lashes kissing their cheeks.

"You had a... er, tree stuff." Saros cleared his throat and turned his attention to his wine. He took a hesitant sip and couldn't help a surprised hum at its rich, velvety taste.

Yes, this was going to go straight to his head.

Saf laughed softly and tapped their own goblet against Saros's cup. "It's good, isn't it? These Woods are a surprisingly good environment for grape vines. You won't find wine like this anywhere else."

Saros paused with his lips on the rim of the cup. *This is Illir's Woods.* "Wait, what's in this wine?"

"Nothing *terribly* unusual." Saf looked amused. "There are a lot of things in this forest that will poison you, Saros. The grapes are not one of them."

"Is there magic in this wine?" Saros teased. "Are you trying to enchant me, Saf?"

He did not know why he said that.

But predictably, Saf grinned. "If I haven't already, I consider that a failure." They stopped walking and turned to him, lifting their free hand toward his cup. "May I?"

Saros nodded and meant to pass it to them, but they instead wrapped their hand around Saros's hand and tipped the goblet to their lips. They held his gaze until the wine met their tongue. Their eyes slid closed as they swallowed, tongue darting over their lips. "Mmmm. Exquisite."

"I thought you had the same thing." Saros eyed Saf's goblet. It looked like the same wine to him.

"Try a sip?" Saf lifted their cup, but when Saros went to take it, they didn't let go. They steadied his trembling hand as he tipped the cup to his mouth and took a sip. The wine was just as rich as his own, but with a subtle sweetness to it that Saros had not found in his cup. But how odd; he had not seen the woman pour from two different bottles.

"The Woods know us intimately," Saf murmured. "We are drinking the same wine, but there is still a hint of the Woods in our cups. It knows what we like best."

"So there *is* magic in the wine." Saros smiled. The drink already had a pleasant warmth buzzing through him, and Saf's closeness only strengthened it. He could not explain or rationalize what had drawn him toward this witch so quickly and so completely, but indeed if they were trying to enchant him, it was absolutely working.

And Saros was too starved of attention to let his logic put a stop to it.

"Where is it that you're taking me?" he asked, lifting his own cup to his lips once again. "I thought the party was back there."

"And I thought you disliked parties."

"I was starting to get used to it." Saros glanced around at the trees; their eyes quickly darted away as if they'd been guiltily caught spying. A sound like quiet laughter rustled through the branches overhead. "So this slice of solitude is for my benefit?"

"And mine," Saf said. "The ritual will start soon, and then we'll both be occupied. I wanted to snag a moment alone before all of that."

They're not subtle, are they? Saros didn't dislike the attention, but he wanted Saf to work a little harder. He sipped his wine and studied them with a wry smile. "Just as well. I was also hoping for one such opportunity."

Saf's eyes gleamed. They drew closer to him until there was hardly a breath of space between the two of them. "Is that so?"

"Mmhmm." Saros reached up and tipped Saf's cup to his lips again; Saf's dark eyes held onto his every move. He swallowed the sweet wine and heard Saf's breath catch. He waited, letting the heavy silence stretch between them, until Saf flicked an obvious glance down at Saros's mouth.

He took a long step backwards and put a foot of space between them. "I have another question for you."

Saf's mouth actually fell open for a moment, then they laughed. "You godsdamned tease." They gave him a playful shove. "You'll be the death of me. What is this *pressing* question?"

Saros resisted making a coy comment about another pressing thing or two and dragged his mind back to what he actually wanted to know. "I found something back at your cottage that caught my attention."

"Other than me?"

"Shockingly." Saros smiled. "It was a page in a book that appeared to be a spell. It said—"

"Let me guess," Saf cut in. "To Bestow the Hands of Gods?"

Saros blinked, surprised. "Um. Yes. Exactly that."

"If *anything* in my collection — other than me — was going to catch your attention, I knew it would be that. I had a feeling that spell would jump out at you. It likes to tempt people, especially when it knows they will interpret it a certain way."

Saros couldn't tell if his lack of understanding was because of the wine or because Saf genuinely wasn't making any sense.

"You thought it was a spell to make someone a necromancer, didn't you?" Saf smirked.

"What else could it be?" The stolen pages seemed to burn in his pocket. He resisted an urge to unfold the paper and read it again.

"It's a fair assumption, given what you thought you knew about necromancy," Saf said. "But aside from the fact that necromancy does not work like that, the spell's title is also slightly mistranslated. It should say, 'To *hold* the hands of gods.' It does not bestow power; it awakens what is already there, but to an extreme degree."

Saros again had to stop himself from reaching for the page in his pocket. "Would it fix my magic if Jovian can't?"

"Ah, no." Saf's expression turned serious. "It would kill you immediately. We're talking about power that is much, much greater than anything a regular person could handle."

"Then what is it for?" Saros asked. "What sort of power *does* it awaken?"

A sly smile eased across Saf's lips. "In simplest terms? That of gods."

The branches overhead rustled anxiously. Saros shoved his free hand into his coat pocket so he was not further tempted to grab the page out of his back pocket. Now he wished he hadn't taken it. Why did Saf have something so powerful and dangerous? If it was merely coincidence that it happened to be in a random book in their collection, they wouldn't know so much about it.

"Oh, don't look at me like that." Saf sighed. "I much preferred how you looked at me earlier. Would it make you feel better if I assured you I have never toyed with that spell or anything else in the book? I love a good experiment, but I'm not stupid, nor am I suicidal. I don't even know if the spell would do what it claims it does. That book is a collection of experiments developed by witches across time; not all of them have been tested, and certainly not all of them are successful. I wouldn't risk trying them and neither should any sane person, but it caught your attention, didn't it?"

"Because I thought it was something else," Saros said, but the words came out too defensively and Saf saw through it.

They smiled and drifted closer to him again. "It's fascinating. You can admit that much. The possibility of unimaginable power. The potential of it. This is the essence, the *energy* of our people, Saros. This is why we celebrate Jovian. He was not afraid to chase the impossible, and we shouldn't be, either. Though... in this case, a degree of caution is preferred."

A chill ran down Saros's back. Saf's obvious hunger for power made him uneasy, but he couldn't entirely disagree with them. It *did* interest him. All he'd ever been told was to suppress any inclination he felt toward magic. It was a forbidden fruit, kept out of his reach but not out of his sight. Now that he could reach for it, touch it, hold it, wouldn't it be sublime to drown himself in its potential? Wouldn't it be exquisite to push himself and the very powers of nature to their limits for a taste of what was truly possible?

But Jovian's story wasn't one of victory. "What of Jovian's fate?" Saros said to Saf. "What about his punishment for his hubris?"

"A tragedy," Saf said with a shrug. "And an injustice. Why would a god take down another god?" They raised their eyebrows. "So the one left standing may be the *only* one. Illir didn't curse Jovian because Jovian bent the laws of nature. Illir murdered Jovian so that he could be the one, all-powerful, universally worshiped god. If not for Illir's greed, Jovian would have ushered in a new age for witches and magicians alike."

Saf studied their wine for a second, eyes distant. "Perhaps we wouldn't be as we are today."

Saros touched their arm and they looked up. "Maybe that can still change."

"I wish I still believed that it would." Saf finished their wine with a final gulp. A drop of it lingered at the corner of their mouth, and an unstoppable impulse made Saros reach up and thumb it away. Saf stilled; their face went slack with dazed shock once again, and Saros had to admit he rather liked the way he could render them speechless with a simple gesture.

His mind spun hundreds of curiosities about them — not their magic or their knowledge of it, but *them*. He wanted to know their history, to fill in the gaps between a childhood he didn't remember and this very moment. What had made Saf? He wanted to know the person behind the charming, seductive witch, and he wished he wasn't so positive that that was a hopeless desire. He wished he wasn't so sure, despite everything, that he was going to die tonight.

He tore his attention away from Saf and looked back at the festival. Beyond the illuminated tents, the wide meadow awaited Jovian's Tomb. Would it look natural there, surrounded by the giant watchful trees that made up Illir's Woods? Or would the Woods — named for Jovian's nemesis, his murderer — resist the tomb's presence? Were the Woods truly of Illir, or had humans unfairly invoked the god's name just because they could?

Saros closed his eyes and listened. He'd followed an intrinsic feeling toward the tomb all this time, but now he couldn't feel it at all. That insistent pull was gone, replaced by a buzzing energy that made his heart thunder with anticipation.

At a light touch on his arm, Saros opened his eyes and found Saf before him. He searched for something to say to them, but it was only in that moment of silence that he realized the entire festival had gone quiet. The music had ceased and the voices had fallen away.

"We have all been fed lies about our power, Saros," Saf murmured. "Some fall victim to those lies, but others like us — the smart, the ambitious, and the desperate — refuse to accept what we are told. Because in spite of it all, we know in our hearts that those hateful words are all untrue. Tonight, we celebrate our rejection of lies and embrace the things we have been taught to hate."

Saros's pulse raced. The forest itself seemed to hold its breath; the air crackled with energy. Spots of white light flickered to life throughout the rows of tents and steadily moved toward the open clearing. Beside Saros, Saf whispered a spell to an amulet cradled in their palms and conjured an orb of white light that brightened as it rose from Saf's hands. It floated away, joining the others that surrounded the clearing. Silence reigned as the lights gradually made their way around the perimeter of the space until they formed a complete circle.

"I suggest you look away for this part," Saf said.

"Huh?" Saros craned his neck to see over the pointed tops of the tents. The coven was gathered at the edge of the clearing, positioned in a circle with the Elder in the center. She spoke out — probably a spell that Saros was too far away to hear — and at her word the white orbs flared blindingly bright. Saros flinched and covered his eyes, turning away from the flash, but an imprint of the scene remained burned into his vision. He rubbed his eyes.

"I did warn you," Saf commented. Their hand settled on his arm and he blinked until he could see them. "The lights are little vessels of pure magic. Combined, and then activated with an energy spell, they focus our power to this space. Such a potent flare of magical energy is more than enough to make this corner of the Woods light up in the astral realm. Which means..."

Saros started to turn his head over his shoulder, but Saf grabbed his chin, kissed him hard, and then gently turned his face toward the meadow. Their voice was a purr against his ear when they murmured, "Greet your god, Saros."

The air rushed from his lungs. In the middle of the clearing, surrounded by gnarled trees, a glassy black lake mirrored the starry sky.

Jovian's Tomb had arrived.

CHAPTER 11
NEW MOON VI

SAROS STARED AT THE LAKE, this impossible apparition that he often doubted he'd ever really see, and all of his doubts faded from his mind. He was here, and there it was.

He'd found Jovian's Tomb.

Cheers and shouts rose up around him, and the music came back louder than ever. The sounds of celebration rang in his ears, but underneath all of that was something else: something quieter that tugged at him like a hand gripping his clothes and drawing him forward. He closed his eyes, tuned out all the rest of the noise, and listened.

You are finally here. Come. Let me show you what you really are.

Saros's eyes flew open. Jovian— It had to be Jovian. Saf had said so, hadn't they? *Jovian will speak to you tonight. Listen.*

"I'm here," he mumbled.

"And so is he," Saf's soft voice broke through Saros's ringing pulse. "You hear him, don't you? He wants to help." They gently took Saros's wine glass from his hand. "Go to him."

But Saros didn't move. He kept his eyes fixed on the lake, afraid it would vanish if he looked away. "Jovian's Tomb was never going to take my power from me, was it?"

"Are you sure you ever really wanted it to?"

He did. For many years, he truly did. Before he understood, before he knew better, before he'd learned that he was not a freak of nature or a curse that shouldn't exist, all he had wanted was for that shameful magic to be gone.

But now he knew that his magic — his lifeblood — didn't have to be painful. It just needed room to breathe and grow with him. It needed to unfold to its true potential, and maybe then it would stop killing him.

Then maybe it wouldn't be a curse, but a blessing.

He was so tired of not understanding. He'd thought the answer was to give up what he didn't understand, but casting away his own power was no better than him being cast away for it. Everyone else in his life had rejected this magic within him; why should he?

Saros met Saf's eyes. "Yes. But I don't want to hide anymore."

Saf grinned. "That's the spirit. Well then, Saros..." They lifted their goblet toward the lake. "Claim your life. I'll be waiting."

He held their gaze a moment longer, then took a deep breath and turned to the lake. Witches danced around him, singing and laughing and shouting praises to Jovian. They praised his life, his bravery, his persistence, his determination to remain on Illir's stolen earth even as Illir tried to keep him away. Their songs painted Jovian as the tragic hero, the victim of a god's cruelty, and with every step Saros took toward the lake's black sand, he believed it more.

This was his history. These were his people. And this was his god.

"Hello, Jovian," he said quietly as he stepped onto the sand. "I think it's about time we got acquainted. If it's true that you're something like a god, that you were the first necromancer to take pride in this magic we share, then I want to know you. I want to know how you stood before a world that hated and feared you and decided not to hide, but to live.

"I used to hate this power. My family told me I was cursed by a witch when I was a young child, but they'd never say what happened or what exactly the curse was. Only that I had to be careful. That I had to stay away from other children and couldn't study magic with them. They said it might awaken something in me — something I didn't understand, and neither did they. They said I was different, that there was something wrong with me, and even though I couldn't see it, it was there. They said I'd understand someday.

"When... When I saved Rune and my power came to life, suddenly I understood. I *was* cursed. I was a monster. I was unnatural and dangerous and a disgrace to Illir. That's what they said, anyway. That's what Rune said. And I never realized how much of that sank in even as I told myself I didn't believe it."

Saros stopped before the edge of the water, boots sinking into the damp sand. The water was perfectly still, and so clear that Saros could barely tell where it met the sand. Absolutely nothing moved in those black depths, and the air didn't dare disturb the surface.

"One night can't undo a lifetime of lies," he continued, quieter. "A part of me still feels this deep, dreadful shame at what I am. I know everything would be easier if I wasn't like this. But I'm not here to reinforce any regrets. I'm not here to succumb to what *they* want. I was never quite right to them even before my power manifested. If the world wishes to call me a witch, I can at least play the part."

Saros sank to one knee and hovered his hand over the water. "Jovian, I accept your power. I accept that I am a witch and a necromancer. Please quiet this restlessness within me, soothe this magic, and show me my true gift."

He closed his eyes, exhaled, and lowered his hand. But before his palm reached the water, he felt the cold kiss of a blade against his throat.

"Not another move." Rune's voice was sharp as the dagger in his hand. He allowed Saros to turn his head to look at him, but angled the blade against his throat when Saros tried to stand. Rune narrowed his eyes. "Hello, necromancer."

"Rune." Saros swallowed. "I had a feeling I'd see you here."

"Likewise. How fitting that this cursed place shall be your grave as well."

"How did you find it? It took me years to work out this location."

"I was blessed enough to have some help." Rune smiled, but it was a twisted and wicked thing, devoid of humor. Saros looked past Rune, where two people wearing black hooded cloaks stood with a woman in dirt-stained clothes between them. Each gripped one of her arms, and she glared at Rune with a mixture of fury and fear. It was clear she was a prisoner — a hostage, maybe — and Saros turned his gaze back to Rune with a scowl.

"What are you doing here, Rune?"

"Meeting God and earning my salvation," he replied, stepping closer to Saros. He kept the blade across his throat and gripped Saros's shoulder with his other hand. "Bring the other one forward."

"Yes, Master." Footsteps shifted over the sand behind Saros, and he turned his head as much as he could to see what was happening. The other two cultists led the woman toward the lake's shore, and though she tried to free her arms from their grips, she didn't struggle much. When they shoved her to her knees, she obeyed but sent a furious glare over her shoulder.

"Is everyone else in position?" Rune said.

"Yes, Master," replied the cultists.

"Good. Begin with her. I will end with him."

Saros met the woman's gaze for a heartbeat, but he was too slow to realize Rune's intention. In one swift swipe, the cultist standing over the woman slit her throat.

She fell, choking and shuddering, onto the sand with a faint splash. Her blood clouded the glassy water only briefly before the lake seemed to absorb it.

Saros could only stare, heart pounding. Nausea swept through him and he clenched his jaw shut. Someone else must have seen, right? There were dozens of people a stone's throw away. The coven would put a stop to this before Rune went any farther. They had to. Saf had promised that Saros would be protected.

He turned his head as much as Rune's grip on him would allow, but the festival bustled on obliviously. Rune and his cult blended with the dark, invisible to the joyful, wine-drunk party-goers.

"*Fuck*," Saros hissed. He was on his own. Rune was his problem alone, just as he'd insisted he should be.

"For God," Rune said, his voice echoing across the clearing.

And all around the lake, Saros heard similar oaths.

"For Life."

"For Salvation."

"For Truth."

As each one of Rune's cultists spoke, a torch burst to life at several points around the banks of the lake. In the scarce light, he saw them step toward the water, reach out, and tip jars of liquid into the water. The sounds circled back in Saros's direction until the final cultist a few feet away from Rune had emptied their jar, and Saros felt Rune tense his hand around the dagger.

"What is this?" Saros breathed. "What are you doing? Gods, I know you haven't been yourself since that day, but what's *happened* to you?"

Behind him, Rune let out a shrill laugh. "Don't you realize it yet, necromancer? I'm the monster you created."

"Rune, pl—" Saros cut off, choking, as hot liquid filled his throat and his lungs. He brought his hands to his throat and felt it there too, slick and warm and— Blood? *Blood?* He gasped for breath but couldn't find it, and then the pain came, sudden and white-hot and consuming.

"R-Rune," he gasped. His own voice was faint and foreign to his ears. Cool sand touched his cheek and soft ground cradled his body but he didn't know how he'd gotten there. A cold touch seeped into his skin. The last thing he saw before his vision shuttered was a long, slim dagger drive into the sand beside him.

Saros suddenly felt alive.

Absurdly, impossibly, he was *alive*.

The slow and agonizing process of his life fading away had felt like a gradually-worsening coldness in his bones. A chill he couldn't shake, a numbness that started in his fingertips and spread everywhere. He didn't remember, until now, what it was like to be completely warm.

But this feeling now, this steady tingling sensation crawling through his veins, might have been warmth. He floated as if outside his body, no part of him touching anything tangible, and all was quiet and still.

He couldn't see and couldn't breathe, but no panic overtook his pulse. In fact, he realized he could not feel his own pulse at all.

"You're home." A deep voice reverberated around him.

Saros opened his eyes and took a breath. His feet settled on firm ground, but he was in no mortal place. The space around him was solid black, and now he could feel a coolness on his skin that felt more like still water than air. He tried to piece his memories together; had he submerged entirely into Jovian's Tomb? But no, he hadn't touched the water. He'd fallen...

His hand went to his throat, where a faintly raised ridge of skin marked the place where Rune had killed him.

Rune had *killed him*.

"I can't say this is how I wanted to meet you. But welcome nonetheless."

Saros looked up and saw that he wasn't alone. A man with long silver hair and a neatly kept beard floated with his legs crossed and hands on his knees. He didn't look nearly as surprised to see Saros as Saros was to see him.

The man eyed him with a hint of amusement in his clear blue eyes. "Do you know where you are?"

"Um." Saros was further surprised to find that he could speak normally despite apparently being underwater. Although, maybe he shouldn't have been so shocked that an impossible lake that existed outside the boundaries of reality operated outside the regular laws of nature.

"Last I knew," he said, "I died on the shore of Jovian's Tomb."

"Ahhh, as necromancers and other fools have a tendency to do." The man smiled, and Saros found the expression oddly fatherly. "Tell me your name and let us introduce ourselves properly."

"I have a feeling you already know who I am," Saros said, but told the man his name anyway.

"Welcome to the Tomb, Saros." The man bowed his head, long hair falling forward over his shoulders. "I am Jovian."

Saros should have suspected that, but the revelation wasn't any less of a shock. "*You're* Jovian."

"Indeed!" Then he frowned, confusion knitting his brow. "Last time I checked, anyway..."

Saros was starting to wonder if he was still actively dying and this was a weird, vivid hallucination. He shifted his feet on the smooth surface beneath his boots — and was mildly surprised to find that he was still clothed and his clothes were not affected by him supposedly being underwater. "I... Look, I'm sorry. This is... extremely strange."

"But of course it is!" Jovian laughed, slapping his knee. "Weird as all the hells, isn't it? Y'know, people always go on about how the full moon causes strange happenings, but I've never had a *new* moon pass without something bizarre occurring. I'm starting to think it's me. Maybe I'm the problem. But anyway, now that that's out of the way, I want to know something, Saros Antarian: what do you want done about this pickle you've found yourself in?"

Saros had not known what to expect from Jovian, but it definitely wasn't this. "You're asking me to choose whether to live?"

"Yes and no. And yes! I'm asking you to choose your life *and* your magic..." He brought his hands together, then apart. "Or your life *or* your magic."

So there was a way he could leave his power behind? But no, Saros didn't want that anymore. But he *did* want to live.

"You know, I have to give you some credit," Jovian said, setting his chin in his hand. "It has been a long time indeed since a necromancer such as yourself was so desperate that they spent all the time and energy it takes to successfully find me. Aside from my woodsy coven friends, only a few have made their way here, and fewer still have worked up the courage to go ahead and drink the water. But you weren't given that choice, were you? You made it all the way here only for some selfish zealot to take your life into his hands. Are you really going to let it end like that?"

Saros shook his head. A deep, hot anger began to unfurl within him. "It can't end like this."

"And it doesn't have to. If you ask me, I think you got off easier than those other fools. Personally, I wouldn't drink this water." Jovian waved his hand. "Lots of dead shit in here. Anyway, this is my realm. I make the rules. I choose who stays and who leaves. While some gods are not so lenient, I choose to give my own kind a second chance. You'd be surprised at how many turn it down." Jovian rubbed his chin and eyed Saros carefully. "So I ask you, Saros Antarian, the reluctant necromancer... What do you want?"

He wanted to live. He didn't want to be powerless. He didn't want to fade into the background of his own life. He had spent his entire life fearing and suppressing his own power just like everyone had told him to do, and now that he'd accepted it, he wanted a chance to know it.

He *was* a necromancer, and he no longer wished to change that.

But he also didn't want to be alone.

That wasn't the choice, though, was it? It was no longer between his magic *or* a family. He'd been accepted into a coven tonight, welcomed home to a place he did not know but that had always been part of him. He had a whole future ahead of him here, with people who understood him, people that were *like* him. He had so much to learn.

Rune had no right to take that away from him.

He met Jovian's eyes. "The stories say these waters strengthen necromantic power. Drinking from the lake is supposed to deepen the connection between myself and my magic. That's what I want: for it to settle. For it to become a part of me without hurting me. I want it to be mine. And I don't want to die."

Jovian smiled, wrinkles creasing the skin around his mouth and eyes. "Very well, Saros. May it be so."

Saros felt a deep tug in his chest, and warmth burst through him — so intense it almost burned. He gasped, lungs and heart seizing as power flooded him. But the sudden burn faded after a moment, and in its wake, Saros felt a rush of pleasant energy unlike anything he'd ever known. Life rushed back into his body, chasing away the stiff, sluggish lethargy that had been all he'd known for years. His heart beat faster, stronger, and he felt truly alive.

And his power, usually coiled at his core like a pit of dread, now pulsed like a second heart. No longer cold or forbidden, it thrived. Saros felt the moment it stopped feeding off his life and started to breathe on its own.

When the rush faded, Saros came back to his surroundings and couldn't help the deep laugh that escaped him. He sank to his knees, pressing his hands to the solid black floor, and through blurry eyes he realized that his hands were whole again. No more fading. No more visible bones.

He was alive.

Soft footsteps approached him, then Jovian knelt before him. "How do you feel?"

Saros blinked tears out of his eyes. "I-Incredible. I'm alive, I'm— I'm *new*."

"That's it exactly." Jovian smiled. "How ironic, too, that by dying beneath this tomb, you came to life. I love the poetry of it. But before I let you return to the surface, I wish to know one more thing." He shrugged. "Now what?"

Anything, Saros thought. He wasn't dying anymore. He wasn't running on a deadline. He could finally move forward. The world and all its secrets were his for the taking.

But first, before that, he had to do something about Rune. He still didn't know what Rune's endgame was, but now that Saros was stronger, he could stop Rune. He had to. No more blood needed to be shed on that black sand.

Maybe Saros could do something about that. He controlled death itself, did he not? And now that it wouldn't kill him to use his power...

Gods, he could change *everything*.

He looked at Jovian, then slowly got to his feet. "I'm going to fully know my power. I'm going to find its secrets and its limits. And I'll be with others like me. We'll grow stronger together, and maybe someday we won't have to stay hidden."

Jovian's easy smile vanished and his eyes darkened. "What you speak of... It's impossible, Saros. You must know nothing of the wider world. You don't know what it is like. Good deeds will not save you so long as fools learn to fear you. You can't change them, Saros. No one can, not even me. We tried — don't you remember Firelei? And Serefine? Look where that got us." He spread his hands, gesturing to the darkness surrounding them. "Don't repeat our mistakes."

"I tried to save my mother the pain of losing my father," a new voice spoke up.

Saros turned, and where there had been only dark water before, now dozens of people stood. They were faint and ghostly, all standing with their heads bowed and hands folded over their hearts.

"She was so horrified that she killed both of us in a blind rage," continued the first person who had spoken. They glanced once at Saros, then turned their head back down.

"My younger sister," added another. "She was only four. I saved her. I shouldn't have. My family cast me out and I froze to death in the woods."

"I saved my brother."

"My lover."

"My parents."

"My friend."

Their voices spoke over each other and melded together into a cacophony of names and loved ones and tragedies. Finally, the voices all came together and spoke as one: "And they killed us for it."

Saros's heart pounded. He wanted to tell them that it could be different, it didn't have to be like this forever. That just because they had suffered didn't mean every future necromancer had to. Didn't they want a better future for their own kind? Didn't they want to see change?

The shadows began to fade, but twelve remained in focus. Simultaneously, they raised their heads and looked straight at Saros. He stared back and realized he recognized one of them: the woman Rune's cultists had murdered.

She stepped forward. "You speak of change and coming out of hiding and all this bullshit like a brighter future." She scoffed. "You know nothing. Even living in hiding didn't save any of us. They found us anyway. Hunted us like animals. And if one pathetic yet determined cult can do that much, imagine the bloodshed if our lives were common knowledge."

Saros swallowed. "Is there really no other choice but to let them fear us while *we* hide?"

"No," said the ghosts, as one.

"No," agreed Jovian. He stood at Saros's side, his expression grim. The ghosts faded and disappeared, and Jovian set his hand on

Saros's arm. "I admire your optimism, my friend. But this is the way it is."

"Why does it have to be?" Saros had spent his entire life reluctantly accepting the way things were. Why should he have to continue? Why should he have to settle for *this*?

"Haven't you been listening? No one ever said it was easy for us to exist," Jovian said. "Part of accepting your true power, Saros, is accepting that you will always be an outcast for it."

Saros thought of all those witches up on the surface who'd spent a night every month celebrating Jovian. Who came together and sang his praises while Jovian himself hid in his tomb and watched as necromancers like him died day after day.

Jovian wasn't a god. He was just a coward.

Saros took a step back from him. "No."

Jovian scoffed. "No?"

"I don't accept it," Saros said. "You might be content to be tolerant of hatred, Jovian, but that's incredibly easy to say when this is your entire world. I'm not the one who has forgotten what the wider world is like."

Jovian started to reply, but his words were cut off by a deep rumble that emerged from the depths of the lake and shook the realm. He paused, and Saros frowned, and Saros did not like that Jovian himself looked confused.

"What was that?" Saros breathed.

Jovian laughed, a touch hysterically. "I have no idea."

The rumble sounded again, and Saros's attention was drawn upward as the darkness over his head wavered. Something had disturbed the lake's surface.

"Hm." Jovian scratched his beard. "You should go, probably."

Before Saros could react, the floor vanished from beneath his feet and the lake came rushing in. Saros managed to gulp in a breath before Jovian and his realm disappeared, but one lungful of air wouldn't last him long. He gritted his teeth and pushed himself through the unnaturally thick water, strong strokes bringing him gradually closer to the unsteady surface. Saros's lungs burned and his vision blurred; his long coat pulled him down, but Saros suspected the tomb itself was reluctant to let go of him. He kicked harder. Involuntarily, he released a short burst of air, and on instinct he tried to take it back in only to earn himself a lungful of water. He choked, blowing out the rest of his air, but he could see the surface and if he could just keep going, keep kicking, and stay conscious just one more second—

He broke the surface with a gasp, air and water catching in his throat. Hacking water out of his lungs, he dragged himself toward the shore.

He found Rune alone at the edge of the water. He stared at Saros as if Saros had two heads now, which Saros supposed was fair given that Rune had quite literally killed him mere minutes ago. Saros must be quite the sight to behold, climbing out of the lake's black water entirely unharmed.

"Impossible," Rune breathed. He held no weapon, and as Saros neared him, he stumbled a few steps backwards. "Y-You're dead."

"You wish." Saros stopped before him and sighed. "Can we talk?"

Rune narrowed his eyes. "What could you possibly think we have to say to each other?"

So much, Saros thought. He had nearly a decade of wishes and regrets and hopes he had been waiting to spill to Rune, but *this* Rune would not hear any of it. Still, Saros would give him one last undeserved chance. "This didn't have to be this way. We could've been so, so different. We could have been limitless, you and me."

Rune leaned closer to him. "If you had let me die that day, it wouldn't be this way." He scowled. "Your wishes are worthless. This is the way the world is, necromancer: God triumphs over evil. And if I had known back then what you were destined to become, everything that came before that day would never have happened. There can be no love for wretches like you."

"I couldn't— Wait." The thought dropped out of Saros's mind as Rune's words sank in. "What... What did you say?"

Rune hissed a low chuckle. "I tried to save you. I tried to steer you toward God so that you'd be saved from that evil inside you. We had all those discussions about life and death and the workings of the earth, yet my efforts fell on unwilling ears." He shook his head. "Now I see that I was wasting my time. God would never have welcomed someone as corrupted as you."

"Y-You can't know that," Saros stammered. "You don't... remember."

He trailed off as a smirk crept across Rune's face. The earth beneath Saros's feet opened up and swallowed him whole. Rune remembered. All this time, he had known all of it — Saros, their lives, their history, their love. And still... this. The hatred. The violence.

"Trust me, I *wish* I had forgotten," Rune said. He paced a slow circle around Saros. "I wish I had known nothing of the sinful life I had led before I met God. I wish I'd known Him sooner so that I might never have been touched by evil." He clenched his fists at his sides. "But I cannot pretend that I wasn't touched by the greatest evil known to earth. To deny the truth of it keeps me farther from my salvation. But this does not mean I can excuse it. Stranger, friend, or lover — it does not matter. The outcome was always going to be this."

Saros found it impossible to take a full breath. He glared at Rune and wanted to break every bone in his body. He wanted Rune to feel even a fraction of the pain Saros had suffered in those seven lonely years. He wanted to gut him, to hurt not only his body but his heart.

Then again, Rune might as well have not had a heart at all.

"Are you truly so weak, necromancer, that such an obvious revelation is your breaking point?" Rune continued to circle him, leather boots crunching softly in the black sand. A high-pitched ringing in Saros's ears gradually drowned out the festival noise surrounding him. "It was a lot easier to hate me when you thought you were a stranger to me, wasn't it? Easier to move on, to think of me as someone that you didn't know. I bet you told yourself I wasn't the same person that you remembered. I bet you tried to bury our past just as much as I did."

He paused in front of Saros; his smug expression only deepened Saros's anger. "Try as we both did, some things can't be buried. God had bigger plans for us, and it ends like this: His servant, cleansing himself of evil by banishing that evil from the world. As God intended."

Saros grabbed the front of Rune's cloak, hauling him an inch off the ground before roughly shoving him backwards. "Kill me again for all I care, Rune, I won't make it easy for you. Take your smug victory over my heart, but your crusade ends here. You can't win. Everyone here is more powerful than you and your delusions will ever be." He took a deep breath. "Please, just leave. Don't make me do something I'll regret."

Rune's eyes darkened. "If you do not yet regret anything, then I know I am making the right choice."

The other cultists came closer to Rune and formed a neat line on either side of him; Rune closed his eyes and tipped his head back. His expression was so sincere, creased with a sort of elation that was too genuine to be a farce. He believed in everything he was doing. Saros wanted to see it all backfire and explode in his face.

So he waited. He could have tackled Rune and snapped his neck in this moment of distraction, but despite everything Saros still didn't want to kill him. He just wanted to be done with him and move on with his life. So as long as Rune didn't do anything catastrophic, as long as this little performance resulted in absolutely nothing like Saros was sure it would, he could leave Rune alone. The two of them, in Saros's opinion, had nothing more to say to each other.

Saros backed away from Rune and the cultists until he'd stepped off the black sand. They all appeared to be mumbling to themselves or to each other, their words too quiet for Saros to hear. Rune had tears running down his cheeks. His hands visibly trembled. Saros started to turn back to the festival to find Saf or Atheris, but he froze when the music and noise from the party halted abruptly. A chorus of soft thuds swept across the clearing. Saros moved closer and found dozens of people sprawled unconscious in the mud.

Somewhere deep in the Woods, the ground rumbled.

Saros whirled back toward the lake. "What the fuck have you done?" He was too far away for Rune to hear him, but the words tumbled out of him anyway. He dashed to the nearest fallen witch and searched for a pulse, exhaling in relief when he found one. Okay, so they weren't all dead. Rune wouldn't go that far, would he?

Don't be stupid, Saros. Rune had killed at least a dozen necromancers. Of course he would go that far.

Saros couldn't let him. Rune had taken everything from him once; Saros refused to allow him to do it again.

He stormed back to the lake's shore. The cultists continued their soft chant. Rune was on his knees now, doubled over with his forehead pressed to the ground and hands clenched around fistfuls of sand. Three cultists stood over him, hands extended above him as if bestowing some sort of blessing.

Saros's certainty that their ritual would have no effect dwindled as the rumbling sound rolled through the Woods again. The trees swayed as if buffeted by a strong wind, and their eyes bulged wider than ever. Flocks of birds and other winged creatures erupted into the sky and circled in undulating swarms. The surface of Jovian's Tomb shuddered as the ground quaked, more violently than before.

"Rune!" Saros shouted, approaching him. "Whatever you're doing—"

He cut off with a grunt as one of the cultists lunged at him. Saros sidestepped the man's dagger, grabbed his arm, and snapped his bones with a flare of warm magic. The man swore and staggered away from Saros, but another cultist blocked Saros's path to Rune. The others inched closer, drawing their daggers to form a deadly circle.

He waited, weighing his options. Talking to them was out of the question; they were likely twice as delusional as Rune if they had followed his commands without hesitation. Saros wasn't interested in changing their minds. He just needed them out of the way.

Saros flexed his hands, absently marveling at the lack of aching numbness he had come to know. His power flowed freely within him, pulsing at his fingertips like a second heartbeat. He heard the steady beat in his head, too, oddly and erratically overlaid with his actual heartbeat. As he listened, another rhythmic beat joined the others, as did several more.

He glanced at each cultist's face shadowed beneath their black hoods. As his eyes settled on each one, the pulses thrumming in his head quickened.

It wasn't his heart he was hearing, he realized. It was theirs, too.

And if he could *hear* the beating hearts of other living people, he couldn't help but wonder what else he could do with them.

He shifted a step back from the cultists and clenched one of his hands at his side. He leaned into his magic and strained his ears to keep track of the chorus of heartbeats. That now-familiar warmth spread through him more quickly, sharpening his senses. A faint glow emanated from the center of each cultist's chest and gently pulsed through each body — their life forces, arguably their souls, immediately known to Saros despite his only having seen these forces outside the body. He could feel each energy as if it was his own.

Saros didn't know what to expect, but his magic was unbearably restless within him, begging for release. He focused on the cultist directly in front of him who stood protectively before Rune, and singled out her thundering pulse among the others pounding in his head. He took two quick steps toward her, effortlessly snapping the bones in her arm when she swiped her weapon at him. She cried out in pain but Saros held fast to her arm and let his magic loose.

He expected her heartbeat to drop, so he wasn't surprised when she crumpled unconscious to the ground. What he didn't expect was to see her life force flare out of her body almost as soon as she hit the sand.

Saros staggered backwards, but didn't get a chance to feel more than a flicker of horror before the other cultists swarmed him. Cloaks swished and daggers flashed in a blur around him; his magic acted for him, snapping and cracking and shattering bones at the lightest touch. Saros could not have controlled it even if he'd wanted to. He acted on one instinct alone: *survive*. Thrumming pulses filled his head, drowning out everything else, and he used the beats to direct his hits to each attacker. *Break the bones, drop the pulse.* Saros had no idea anymore if he was putting them to sleep or killing them, but one by one the cultists fell away from the fight, unconscious or disarmed or dead. When at last the final one dropped, Saros came back to his senses surrounded by broken bodies and a sharp tang of blood in the air.

Now only one heartbeat echoed his own. He turned to face Rune, and an involuntary smile crawled across his lips at the unmasked horror on Rune's face.

"Now what, Rune?" Saros stepped over one of the fallen cultists and approached him. His own voice was distant in his head, muffled beneath the deafening thump of the power pumping his heart. "Without your flock of knives, what are you?"

Rune's pulse quickened as Saros paced around him. He remained on his knees, perfectly still. His eyes tracked Saros's lazy circle. "Your actions are useless," Rune muttered. The unmistakable hitch of fear in his voice sent a warm shiver through Saros. "They were all disposable. No one can protect me but God. And He will."

Maybe it was Saros's imagination, but Rune didn't sound quite so sure of that as before.

Saros stopped behind him, and for a moment just gazed at him. If Rune was right about one thing, it was this: he had been easier to hate when Saros was able to think of him as a different person than the one who had known him all his life. But Saros had been trying to bury Rune in his past for so many years that forgetting the man he'd loved was almost easy now. It was as though the Rune from long ago had left his mind when Saros had lost the timepiece.

Now he was left with *this* Rune, who would not hesitate to kill him again if Saros let him have an inch. This Rune thought he was some kind of hero, perhaps even a martyr, and Saros wanted to see him break. Didn't he deserve it, when Rune had broken Saros all those years ago?

Having him on his knees was a start.

"There's only one god here who can save you, Rune, and it's not Illir." As if in reply, the Woods creaked and rumbled again. Saros chose to ignore that for now. "You live because I demanded it. And if you value your pathetic life, if you wish to exit this forest in the mortal plane rather than the astral one, I just need one thing from you."

He circled back around to stand in front of Rune and grinned at the fading vestiges of defiance in his silver eyes. Leaning closer to Rune, he reached out and brushed the back of his hand across Rune's cheek. When Rune tried to jerk away, Saros grabbed a fistful of hair at the back of his neck and made him tilt his head up. Rune gritted his teeth and growled.

"What do you want?" he hissed.

"I want you to say it. I want you to confess that *I* am god."

"Never," Rune snapped. "You are a *disgrace* to God."

Saros smirked and channeled his magic into Rune, but not as harshly as he had toward the cultists. He didn't wish to kill him, but a hot rush of satisfaction hit him when Rune groaned in pain. Saf's words rang in his mind: *Why cower and be the prey when I could be the predator?*

If Saros couldn't have Rune's love, he would settle for his fear.

This wasn't what he'd wanted when he'd embraced his power in Jovian's realm, but maybe Jovian was right. It was easier to see now that he faced someone who fully, truly hated him for what he was. Who was Saros to think he alone could change the world to his naïve wishes?

That optimism was a dream for another day.

Today, he was tired of the cruelty. He was tired of being chased by his ex-lover and his cult of zealots. He was done with the world and its prejudices and ignorance. People like Rune were going to paint him as a villain no matter what he did. Why not give him something real to fear?

"Come on, Rune. Three small words and this can be over." Saros let his magic strengthen, eliciting another agonized moan from Rune. "You can move on with your life, and I can move on with mine, and we will never have to cross paths again. You choose."

It took Rune a minute to catch his breath. He was trembling now, clearly fighting against whatever sort of pain Saros's magic had afflicted onto him. "N-Never." He squeezed his eyes shut. Twin tears rolled down his cheeks. He took a shuddering breath, and when he opened his eyes again, they glowed bright white.

In the Woods, something roared.

Saros didn't realize he'd loosened his grip on Rune's hair until Rune sprang forward and tackled Saros to the ground. The air rushed out of him. Rune struck him hard across the face. Blinking stars out of his vision, Saros struggled to throw Rune off, but Rune's hands closed around his throat and squeezed hard. Saros choked. Rune grinned.

Saros struggled, but his strength was leaving him as quickly as the air from his lungs. Why couldn't he move? Rune wasn't that strong. Saros reached for his magic and felt only a faint flicker of the power that had coursed through him only minutes before. Panic gripped him. *No, no, no, where did it go? Where did it go?*

I can help, murmured a voice at the back of Saros's mind.

Jovian?

I can't guarantee similar results if you die again, Jovian said. *Ask for my hand, Saros. We'll make quick work of this bothersome man.*

Saros's vision started to blur. He gritted his teeth. "Jovian, I ask for your hand."

Nice. A laugh echoed in Saros's mind, and then white-hot pain seared through his body. He screamed, and next he knew, he was on his knees and Rune lay sprawled in the sand.

But still moving. Still alive.

Saros staggered to his feet, taking in gulps of air. He could still feel Rune's grip around his throat, the unnatural strength in his hands. He took one step toward Rune and started to reach out his hand; he felt a jolt, and Rune cried out as his body convulsed.

Saros halted. *I didn't even touch him.*

You don't have to, Jovian's voice replied.

Saros blinked to clear his still-foggy vision. He realized then that he could see the astral realm — that hazy space between life and death. He was surrounded by softly glowing life forces, but he focused his attention on only one: Rune's.

Let's finish this, shall we?

Saros hesitated. He could feel Jovian's restlessness, his bloodlust, his desire to seize control of living things like he had done centuries ago. Saros lowered his outstretched hand, but at the twitch of his fingers, Rune screamed.

The sound tore across the forest clearing. Rune fully collapsed to the sand, curled on his side with his arms wrapped around his head. Heavy, pained groans accompanied the shudders wracking his body.

"Rune." Saros couldn't move. "Wait. Wait, I—" He took one halting step forward, extending his hand, and Rune shrieked.

"Stop! Jovian, stop!" Saros rushed to Rune and knelt beside him, gently taking him by the shoulders. But the moment his palms met Rune's body, he felt bones bend, shift, and break.

Saros reared back in horror. "No, no, no, I don't want to hurt him! Stop making me hurt him!"

Jovian's soft laughter rumbled in the back of Saros's mind, echoing the thing that had started to move in the Woods. *You asked for my help. I gave you my hand. Here's a tip, necromancer: don't beg for power that you don't understand. You wanted to hold the hands of gods, did you not?*

"No," Saros gasped. "*No*, not like this. This isn't what I wanted."

Wellllll... Jovian drew out the word. *It's what you got. Cheers!*

Saros felt his magic burst to life within him again, hotter and more dizzying than before. It acted of its own volition; his hands were on Rune again but he did not remember deciding to touch him. Rune's cries softened to whimpers as his strength left him, and Saros could see his life force starting to weaken.

He was dying. And it was Saros's fault.

"I don't want this," he said again. He was surprised to find his voice thick and choked up. He gathered Rune into his arms, ignoring his ex-lover's cries, and held him tightly. Maybe if he seized Rune's life force and held on, he wouldn't die. Maybe he could hold Rune together even as Jovian tried to break him.

If I recall, it was you who wanted to break him, Jovian commented.

"Let me go," Saros hissed. "I asked for your power, and I can refuse it too. Go away, Jovian."

Sorry, son, that's not how it works. Hold tight now, and see that you and I are god.

"*No!*"

Rune's body shattered in his arms. Warm, wet blood and viscera soaked him. Shards of bone scraped his skin like broken glass. He tasted the blood at the back of his throat, felt it slide in slick rivulets down his face.

Saros could do nothing more than stare in numb shock at his now-empty hands and the traces of Rune's flesh that stuck to his skin.

Admit it, Jovian spoke in Saros's mind, *you didn't love him anyway. He was too far gone. Do you really think he would ever have changed his mind? Did you truly hope for him to unravel himself from his web of foolish beliefs and decide to love you again? You would've been playing cat and mouse for the rest of your lives. I have done you a favor, Saros. No follower of Illir is a friend of ours.*

Closer, louder, the thing in the Woods bellowed. Whistling screams tore through the trees; if Saros had looked up, he would have seen them struggling to shuffle out of the way only for their roots to tangle and cause them to trip and tip and fall. He would've seen the bigger trees twist together, joining to form something with long limbs that rose up from the Woods.

And if Saros had looked behind, he would have seen the witches begin to wake.

CHAPTER 12
NEW MOON VII

ATHERIS WOKE, ears ringing, with no recollection of falling asleep. She'd been at a party — why the hell was she sleeping? How had she gotten on the ground? Now her clothes were going to be all muddy from the slush of melted snow; how was she supposed to impress anyone in these conditions?

Grumbling to herself, Atheris got up and tried to wipe the mud off her trousers but only succeeded in worsening the wet stains. "Damn." She looked around, seeking Safyre, but her worries over her clothes vanished when she found herself surrounded by bodies sprawled in the mud.

Her vision flashed red. Screams echoed in her mind — screams, cries, the wet gurgle of blood choking a cut throat. *Atheris!* someone cried. *Atheris!* But she couldn't help, she wasn't strong enough, wasn't quick enough, wasn't smart enough, and everything they had all said about her was true, and she couldn't—

"Atheris!"

She gasped and scrambled back. "No— No, I'm sorry. I'm sorry I couldn't—"

"Atheris, what are you talking about? Hey." The figure moved closer, and a few blinks brought Safyre's face into focus. Not a ghost. Not the dead barkeep. Safyre, alive and unharmed.

Atheris released a heavy, shuddering breath. "Safyre."

"Saf." They flickered a smile and lightly touched her shoulder. Their presence calmed her; she could sense their magic, potent and powerful. Her own power recognized its likeness. "You're all right. You're not hurt, are you?"

"I d-don't think so." She cleared her throat, annoyed at the wobble in her voice. She tucked her arms across her chest and looked around again, but without her glasses she could hardly tell what was a person and what was a tent. Her only hint was that the people weren't aglow from within. "What happened?"

Saf started to reply, but their words were drowned out by an eruption of noise from the Woods. Atheris and Saf turned abruptly to the lake, and Atheris's mouth fell open.

The trees were screaming. Their trunks and branches twisted around each other, growing and stretching until roots sprung free from the earth and wove together to form a giant. Atheris watched, stuck between horror and awe, as roots and branches crawled upward to form legs — she couldn't tell how many — a torso, shoulders, arms, a neck, and finally a head.

"What the *fuck*," Atheris muttered.

"My thoughts exactly." Saf met her eyes with barely-concealed panic. "We need to get the Elder. Hell, we need everyone. I don't know what that thing is, but someone woke it up and I don't think it's happy about it."

"That fucking cult," Atheris hissed. She turned to the lake, but it was too dark to tell whether any of the cultists survived. She couldn't see anyone moving, but then again she couldn't see much of anything at all. With a frustrated grumble, she started toward the lake.

"Atheris!" Saf snapped. "Don't get any closer to it!"

"I have to find Saros." She glanced back at them, and then marched on when they didn't protest again.

The thing rising from the Woods continued to grow. The trees continued to scream. Many of them had closed their eyes, and though they were all a blur in the distance, Atheris could hear them moving and groaning as if trying to run away.

In that respect, they were smarter than Atheris.

"Saros?" She stepped onto the black sand surrounding Jovian's Tomb and paused. The lake sprawled before her, its glassy surface broken by shallow ripples. A chill ran down Atheris's arms, but she didn't feel the same sort of wrongness that had cloaked the lake the last time she had seen it. It belonged here. It wanted to be here.

"And you still have something I want, don't you?" she muttered as she drew closer to the black water. "But I want my friend back first. Where is he?"

She hadn't *really* expected the lake to reply, but this was Illir's Woods. Anything was possible.

It wasn't the lake that answered, though. A familiar, hushed voice called to her: "Atheris?"

She turned, heart jumping. Several feet away, visible to her only as a vague splotch against the dark, someone knelt in the sand.

"Saros? Saros!" She ran to him, and when he came into clearer view she nearly lost her footing as a wave of relief struck her. He was okay — through all of that, he was okay. Atheris went to fling her arms around him, but Saros scrambled away from her.

"No! Don't come any closer! Don't touch me." He staggered to his feet and backed off, holding up his hands as if afraid she would hurt him.

Atheris halted. "Saros, it's me. What's wrong?"

"I know." He clutched his hands tightly against his chest. "I know it's you. I'm glad you're all right. But you need to stay away from me. Please." His shoulders heaved with each heavy breath. "I don't want to hurt you, too."

"Saros, what—" Atheris drew closer to him despite his protests, and realized now that he reeked of blood. His face was spattered with it, and his clothes were stained with dark splotches. Atheris pressed the back of her hand to her nose. "Saros... what happened?"

"Stay away from me!" His voice cracked on the words. "Atheris, please. *Please*. I can't— I can't control him. I don't want to hurt you."

What have you done? Atheris clutched her amulets. The trees groaned. The thing growing out of the Woods swayed on its crooked legs. Atheris glanced at it, then back at Saros. "What is that?"

"I don't know. Rune..." He winced. "Oh, gods, Rune..."

Goddamn cultist. "What did he do?" Atheris flinched as the tree monster roared. "Whatever. We need to get out of here. Saf is getting the other witches to do something about that, but we need to move. Come on." Without thinking, she reached toward him, and when he lifted a hand to warn her back, a shock of white-hot pain struck Atheris like lightning. She doubled over and then collapsed to her knees, but everything hurt. Her bones threatened to splinter and snap. Her skull felt close to bursting, throbbing with crushing pressure as if she'd been dragged to the bottom of the sea.

And as suddenly as the agony had hit her, it lifted. She lay gasping in the sand, colors swirling in her vision. Cool air dried the sweat and tears on her face. Her body shivered in the aftermath of such intense pain, and when her eyes cleared she realized there was someone next to her.

"Saros?" She blinked until the figure's face came into focus and found it to be Saf. "Oh. Gods, what happened?"

Saf helped her sit up and set a hand on her shoulder, but their attention was fixed somewhere behind her. Atheris turned her head; Saros knelt several feet away, staring at her with horror.

"He accepted the Hands," Saf murmured. They darted to their feet and pulled Atheris up with them, steadying her when she swayed. She still felt strange, like she'd been taken apart and put back together but not quite right. Saf turned to her with their hands on both of her shoulders. "Are you okay? Does anything still hurt?"

Atheris managed to shake her head. "What was that?"

Saf glanced away from her, grimacing. "Necromancy. Unchecked and uncontrolled."

"Saros did that?" Atheris looked at him, her odd and unlikely friend. Saros was a lot of things — grumpy and withdrawn and often irritable — but he wasn't violent. He wasn't cruel. Atheris would even dare to say that he loved her, in his own way. He'd nearly died to save her life; he wouldn't have hurt her.

"No," Atheris said to Saf. "He wouldn't."

"I don't think it was him who chose to," Saf said quietly. "I don't think he had a choice at all."

"What do you mean?" Atheris cringed as a scream howled through the trees again. "Okay, and seriously, what is that?"

"The Woods," Saf said. They gripped her arm and pulled her toward the festival. "Come with me. We'll take care of it. The Woods are hurting, but our magic can soothe the pain. Are you strong enough to help?"

"I think so." Saf's explanations offered little clarity for the situation, but Atheris was too disoriented to argue. She was still stuck on the impossibility that Saros had hurt her. She glanced back at him once more; he hadn't moved but for sinking his head into his hands.

Damn it, Saros, what did you do?

Atheris followed Saf back to the Woods, where the rest of the coven waited in a flurry of anxious murmurs. They gradually quieted as they took notice of Saf's arrival, and an older woman with coarse white hair stepped forward to approach them.

"Safyre. I am relieved to see that you're safe." She squeezed their arm. "I'm relieved at all of us being safe. But what has occurred here cannot be ignored or swept under the rug. The Woods need us. Anyone with amulets on your person, follow. If you do not carry amulets, I ask that you stay here. We will need all the strength we can obtain, and I fear those of you relying only on your inherent magic will be at risk."

She didn't leave time for anyone to argue. A group of about a dozen witches broke off from the crowd and followed the woman toward the lake. Atheris watched them go, then turned to Saf.

"What can I do?" She pulled her amulets out of her shirt and spread them across her palm, then watched Saf's expression shift as they studied the talismans. She noted a flicker of recognition in their eyes, but less shock than she expected.

"You can help us tremendously," Saf said. "But be careful. Those amulets are itching to unleash their power. I do wonder if..." They gathered the wavy length of their hair into their hands and let it spill down the front of their shoulders, then combed their fingers through it. They surfaced a bead the size of their fingertip from their curls and unwove it from the twine keeping it braided in place, then pressed their thumb to the surface. Seconds later, the stone's color changed from muddy brown to bright orange.

Atheris gaped at it. "That— That's..."

Saf smirked. "Perhaps those talismans of yours will be happier with their lost companion."

"What the *fuck*," Atheris hissed. She fisted her hands to stop herself from snatching the talisman from Saf's hand. "That's Firelei's fucking amulet... Holy shit, Saf."

They offered it to her, raising their eyebrows expectantly. "It has been safe with me for over a decade, but I believe it's time for it to return to its family."

Atheris couldn't bring herself to move. "How did you know?"

"I saw the other two when you first came to my cottage. You fiddle with them — a nervous tic. I recognized them immediately, of course, and I know our history." Saf smiled. "Only a descendant would have two of the three amulets." They flipped the amulet into their palm and extended their hand to Atheris. "Take it. It's yours. And you are going to need it."

As if to nail the point home, the thing in the Woods screeched.

Saf winced. "All right, let's go. We deal with that thing first, and then we can take care of Saros."

Atheris had no idea what to expect, but she grabbed Firelei's amulet from Saf and hastily secured it to the cord around her neck with the other two as the two of them hurried after the rest of the coven. She felt a flare of energy as the amulets connected with her magic and faintly wondered if the three of them combined would be too much for her to handle. She'd never used the other two before; they were trophies rather than tools to her, and part of her feared their power.

But if there was ever a time to let that magic loose, it was here. She reckoned these amulets would be the only thing powerful enough to quell whatever monster had awakened in the Woods.

The witches that had gone ahead with the older woman stood in an arc at the edge of the lake. The tree monster had nearly doubled in size and was now fully formed: its hulking, long-limbed body was crowned with moose-like antlers made of entire trees. Its form was humanoid in the vaguest sense, but its head was an equine skull with long, curving fangs. Its lanky arms ended in jagged claws that effortlessly sheared across the treetops it passed.

"Right. So. What the hell."

"It's a guardian," Saf breathed. They stared up at the creature with unmasked awe. Not even fear — just wonder. "Whatever that cult tried to summon, this is what they got. If they wanted a god, well..."

"If I had to guess, they were hoping for Illir," Atheris said. The creature took a lumbering step closer to the lake that sent the ground quaking. It *was* majestic, in a dreadful sort of way, but Atheris was eager to see it put back to sleep.

"In the minds of some, this very well might be him." Saf gripped their own amulets in one hand and kept the hem of their gown off the ground in the other. "But he doesn't belong here."

"It's his Woods," Atheris pointed out.

"No, in this *realm*. Gods — or at least, entities that we designate as gods — are beings of the astral realms. It's why Jovian can only touch the mortal world under certain conditions. An astral entity in the mortal realm can be catastrophic. That's where we come in." Saf jingled their handful of amulets and met Atheris's eyes. "Are you ready?"

Atheris tossed up her hands. "Are *you*? Look at that thing, Saf, and tell me you are in any way prepared to face it."

They smirked. "I was mostly asking out of courtesy. None of us are ready. Come on, then."

Atheris and Saf joined the other witches in their line before the lake. Atheris copied their poses, with one hand gripping her amulets against her chest and the other raised with thumb and forefinger extended. She exchanged a glance with Saf, who nodded once before turning their attention to the lake.

The coven's leader spoke the command: *"Ra Arisszun."*

In her shock, Atheris nearly missed her cue to repeat the spell in unison with the other witches. *Universe magic?* She'd only ever heard this spell described as myth — pseudo-magic, a sort of power that shouldn't exist and sure as hell should never be used.

But with everything else going on, Atheris reasoned that this might as well happen too.

She didn't have time to overthink it; at the spell's command, magic flared to life within her, conducted by the amulets she gripped in her hand. A visible pulse of power shot across the lake and collided with the forest monster; it reared back with a howl, taking out numerous trees with its flailing arms. It stumbled, but did not fall.

"Again!" commanded the coven leader. "*Ra Arisszun!*"

"*Ra Arisszun!*" shouted Atheris and the others. The air buzzed with power, and this time when the spell hit the creature, it flew backwards and crashed to the ground. Atheris nearly lost her balance as the earth shook. She waited, heart pounding, but though the creature growled and moaned, it did not get back up.

Slowly, softly, the Woods calmed and came back to life. The trees blinked their eyes open and glanced around at each other; a hushed breeze rustled through their leaves as they huddled closer and intertwined their branches. Dots of color bloomed as the forest's bioluminescence returned. Birds whistled and critters howled.

Beside Atheris, Saf sighed and dropped their arms to their sides. "It will return to the Woods now. We're safe."

The other witches eased their stances and gathered together, sharing embraces and words of comfort. The coven leader approached Saf and wrapped them in her arms, then turned to Atheris and offered a hand.

"I regret that we have only just met." Her voice was softer now; it soothed Atheris's frayed nerves. "I welcome you, child. What is your name?"

Atheris took the woman's hand. "Atheris Fay, Elder."

"You've done us a great service, Atheris Fay." The Elder bowed her head. "I commend you for your help. Tell me, of which coven are you?"

Atheris hesitated. She had not been formally excommunicated from her coven, but it had been years since she had been a part of it. It felt wrong to claim membership to a community that had tossed her out.

She met the woman's soft eyes. "I'm afraid I have no coven, Elder."

She expected the Elder to be suspicious of her for that, but her gaze turned sympathetic. "My apologies if I have opened a wound. Tell me, what can I do to repay you for your help tonight?"

Atheris hadn't thought she'd been all that useful, but if this powerful witch was offering, she wasn't about to turn her down. "Well... I wonder if you can help my friend."

Saf gently touched her arm; she glanced at them and they shook their head once, nearly imperceptibly. Atheris frowned but turned to the Elder again when the older woman squeezed her hand.

"Of course, child. Anything. Take me to them."

"Thank you." Atheris started across the sand; Saf caught up with her and leaned close. "What is it?" she whispered to them.

"Be careful what you say to the Elder," Saf murmured. Their voice so close to her ear tickled something in her chest. "She is kind, and she is powerful, but she has the interest of the coven at the front of her mind."

Atheris resisted casting a glance over her shoulder. "What are you saying?"

It took Saf several seconds to reply. When they did, Atheris could hear the pain in their voice. "Saros may have crossed an unforgivable line."

Dread curled in her stomach. Saf's words roiled like a storm in her mind as the three of them approached Saros, who had not moved from his slouched position on the ground. Atheris didn't stop walking until he came into clear view; he looked up at her and Saf and the Elder with utter defeat in his mismatched eyes. Deep lines of exhaustion and devastation creased his face, and that spirit that Atheris had come to know behind his eyes had been extinguished. Her heart broke for him.

"It's you." The Elder failed to hide the surprise in her tone. She moved a step closer to Saros, and he visibly tensed. "What has happened?"

Saros's eyes flicked to Saf, then lingered on Atheris before flicking back to the Elder. "I..."

"Something took hold of him," Atheris said. Three pairs of eyes landed on her. "He lashed out at me, but there was not a trace of *him* in there. He's been possessed, or something. Can you help?"

The Elder's eyes widened. "Possessed? No, that's impossible. That can only mean…"

"Damn it, Atheris," Saf muttered, but there was no anger behind their words. Only despair.

"What?" She turned to them. "All I said—"

Saros suddenly started laughing, and the mirthless sound combined with the wicked grin on his face made Atheris's blood run cold. "You foolish, *foolish* witches. The necromancer doesn't need *help*. The necromancer is everything he was always meant to be."

"Jovian," the Elder hissed. She strode closer to Saros. "Leave him be. You are not meant to be of this world."

Atheris swallowed her shock. *Jovian* was possessing Saros? Was *this* the result of Saros approaching the tomb?

"I *was* of this world," Jovian growled through Saros's voice. "I could have changed this world and made it better. It was *in my hands*." He raised Saros's hands, palms-up, then clenched them into fists. "It was taken from me once. I will not allow it to be torn from me again."

"Then you leave me no choice." The Elder lifted both of her hands toward Saros and spread her fingers, touching her forefingers together.

"No! Elder, wait." Saf darted forward and gripped her arm. "Elder. *Grandmother.* Please, don't do this. It's not his fault. He didn't—"

"The only way this could have happened was for him to have accepted the Hands of Gods," snapped the Elder. She turned a shockingly cold glare toward Saf. "You know that this is the only way, Safyre. I will not risk this coven, these Woods, or this *world* for one man."

Atheris pressed her hands over her mouth. This woman wouldn't kill him, would she? *Could* she?

"Elder." Saf was begging now. "Please. He doesn't deserve this."

"Back away, Safyre, and let me do my work." She tilted her head up. "Anyone willing to hold the Hands of Gods is too dangerous to have in our coven. He is unstable, inexperienced, and hungry for more than he ought to possess. You see the proof here before you."

Saf had started shaking their head when she'd started talking, and they shook it more vigorously now. Tears spilled down their cheeks. "Give him another chance. *Please.*"

"*Give him another chance,*" Jovian mocked. "Yes, Elder, don't be so hasty. Don't you wish to see what sort of power I can bring you? Didn't you, too, wish to frighten the silly mundane humans into submission?"

"Shut it, Jovian. *Enough,* Safyre. Back away." The Elder took a long stride forward, flinging an arm across Saf's chest when they tried to follow. They stumbled back. She glared over her shoulder. "Do not make me ask you again."

Saf looked ready to fight, but then the tension bled out of their shoulders and they abruptly turned on their heel and marched past Atheris. She reached out to them but her gesture was ignored. She let them go.

She turned back to the Elder just as she spoke a command Atheris had never heard before: "*Ra Aduzen.*"

"Wait!" Atheris lunged forward, but it was too late. Saros screamed and his body convulsed; his spine arched backward and shudders shook him violently. His pained shouts scraped Atheris's ears; she didn't realize she'd started crying until she lifted a hand to her mouth and felt tears drip onto her fingers. Her mind scrambled for a spell to help — something for pain, for life, anything to counteract the coven Elder. But in her desperation, her thoughts wouldn't clear, and it was over before she could help.

Saros lay flat on his back in the black sand with his hands resting on his chest and his head tilted to the side. Atheris ran to him and fell to her knees beside him; his face was slack, his eyes closed as if he was sleeping. Atheris pressed a trembling hand to his throat and held her breath.

Somehow, miraculously, she felt a faint pulse.

She gasped out a sob and sank her forehead to his shoulder. *He's alive. He's alive, and that means he can be okay.* It wasn't the end.

"He's not here."

Atheris tensed at the Elder's voice. She sat up, but kept her hands on Saros's chest. "What did you do to him?"

"The only thing I could possibly have done." The Elder folded her hands at her waist.

"Somehow I doubt that." Atheris sniffed. "What do you mean, he's not here?"

"His body is here, of course, and will remain in stasis," the Elder said. "But the rest of him — his soul, his consciousness, his *being* — is in the astral realm. And there it will stay, until the coven decides that he is no longer a danger."

Tears spilled down Atheris's cheeks. "So for all intents and purposes, he is dead."

"No." The Elder lifted a shoulder in a casual half-shrug. "His soul will be confined to the Woods, so he will not be far. He is bound to the Woods and to the dark, so if you visit at night and avoid the moonbeams, you may find him. But he will not be able to speak with you."

Atheris shook her head. "All he wanted was to belong here. You gave him the promise of community, of *family*, and then you... you threw him out just like his other family did, for no fault of his."

The Elder did not reply. Atheris rose to her feet. "If this is how this coven treats its witches, Elder, then you will not be seeing my face here again."

The Elder didn't appear bothered. She bowed her head once, then silently turned and retreated from the lakeshore.

Atheris buried her face in her hands and let out a long breath. Then she wiped the tears from her cheeks and strode toward the lake. At the threshold where the black crystalline sand met the glassy water, she stopped and opened her palm.

One black, one white, and one orange amulet gazed back at her. Serefine, Thalia, Firelei. These ancient, coveted pieces of magic were her ticket back to her family. She should have been elated. She should have been sobbing with gratitude that finally — *finally* — she had found what generations before her had failed to find. So why didn't this feel like a victory?

These talismans weren't treasures to her. Not anymore. They were just rocks. Old, pretty rocks that had caused her more trouble than they were worth.

Atheris raised the amulets to her lips and kissed the smooth stones, then hurled them into Jovian's Tomb. They hit the water with a deep, hollow *plunk*.

She turned away from the lake only to find that Saf had returned.

They knelt in the sand beside Saros, gripping his hands. Atheris approached them and slumped to her knees.

Saf glanced up. They didn't try to hide the tears that glistened in their eyes. Their voice was raspy when they spoke. "I'm sorry."

"No, I am." Atheris shook her head. "This was my fault. I shouldn't have asked for her help, but I— I didn't know what else to do. I should have just listened to you."

Saf reached over Saros's body and touched Atheris's arm. "Don't blame yourself. You just wanted to help him. I wish..." They trailed off with a sigh.

Yeah, Atheris wished, too. She studied Saros's face; he looked calm, at least. Part of her could believe, maybe, that he'd wake up eventually and she would have her friend back.

"God damn it, Saros." Atheris swiped her hand across her cheek. "I'm sorry."

What else was there to say?

EPILOGUE
WAXING CRESCENT I

Saros thought he knew what regret felt like. He was wrong.

He had always found comfort in darkness, in silence, in the solitude and stillness of night. It was preferable over the busy, noisy daylight hours, which he feared he wasted if he didn't do something productive or meaningful with his time. But the night was for solace, for introspection. He never thought he'd tire of it.

But it had been a month now, a full moon cycle as of tonight, and Saros missed the sun. He missed the blue daytime sky, and the warmth on his skin, and the clatter of ambient noise in his little village. He missed Zenith.

And he missed Atheris.

All he had now was the night and the Woods. A benefit, he supposed, of being stuck in the astral realm was the ability to wander anywhere in Illir's Woods without fear of injury. He didn't need to eat anymore, so he ran no risk of consuming poisonous fruit. The odd creatures in the Woods did not see him as a threat, nor did they consider him prey, so they left him alone. Most surprising was the discovery that gravity didn't affect him here, either. He drifted rather than walked, more ghost than man.

One way or another, he was always going to end up like this, wasn't he? He'd been a ghost for most of his life. This was no different.

Or so he tried to tell himself.

Why didn't I try to fight harder? One of many regrets surfaced in his thoughts. This was the time of night when the events of last month, without fail, vividly plagued his memory. The night was waning, and soon he'd fall asleep until the moon rose once again. But of course, his mind wouldn't let him rest until it had spun through everything that had gone wrong and led him here.

All things considered, though, it could be worse. The only real thing he had to worry about was staying out of the light. He'd learned rather quickly that sunlight burned now, and he did not wish to find out what would happen if he let too much light touch him.

Still, why hadn't he fought? Why had he let this become his fate?

He was supposed to get his life back. He was supposed to have a community — a coven, a *family*. He was supposed to learn his history and build a home here. What had happened to all those shiny promises?

Why didn't he deserve that, after he'd suffered for so many years? Why should he have *had* to fight for it?

And what good would it have done, anyway, to try to resist his sentence from the Elder? He had seen how she had all but shoved Saf out of her way when they had tried to stop her. If Saros had so much as lifted a finger, Jovian would have taken over and caused more unnecessary harm.

He still had not forgiven himself — or Jovian — for hurting Atheris. So despite everything, the Elder had been right to send him here. If it was the only way to break the tie he'd forged with Jovian, Saros would have taken the same measure.

It wasn't ideal, but he would get used to it.

Or so he tried to tell himself.

"IT WAS A *BINDING* SPELL," Saf said for the millionth time. They paced the length of their library, ruffling their already-disheveled hair. "It's not just a simple blood spell, so *using* the blood command won't reverse it because it's—"

"Because he's not in his body, yes, I know." Atheris sighed and tossed her quill down on the table, then plopped into a chair. She bent forward until her elbows hit her knees and dragged her hands through her hair, then took off her new glasses and rubbed her eyes. "We've been at this all night, Saf. We should rest."

"Do you want to free him or not?"

Atheris bristled. Were they really going to have this argument *every* night? "Saf. Don't make me say it again. Seriously, it's like we're following a script. I say 'We should sleep because we pulled another all-nighter' and you say—"

"We can't give up on him, Atheris."

"That." She watched them pace. Their leather slippers scuffed almost soundlessly over the rugs and across the wood floor. Atheris had come to understand a lot about Saf this past month, and looking at them now with their hunched shoulders and wild hair, she was pretty sure they were cracking.

Was this how they had been for all those years they'd spent searching for Saros, waiting for him to return?

Atheris sympathized with them, but she couldn't handle seeing them like this much longer.

"Hey." She glanced at the window; it was still mostly dark. They had time. "Saf."

They barely spared her a glance. "What."

"Do you want to go see him?"

Saf halted. They turned a hesitantly hopeful look toward her. "What?"

"I doubt he's far." Atheris rubbed her hands together. "We still have about an hour of darkness. Do you want to—"

"Let's go." Saf swept out of the room faster than Atheris could blink. Smiling to herself, she replaced her glasses on her face and followed.

. . .

Saros was easier to find than Atheris had expected. She and Saf rode into the Woods on Zenith's back, and thanks to Zenith's senses and the Woods' cooperation with Saf's commands, it was only half an hour before Zenith halted with a decisive *mrrp*.

Atheris and Saf hopped down from Zenith's back onto spongy moss and soft grass spread out in a small, serene grove. A massive weeping willow presided over the clearing, its leafy strands blowing gently in the breeze. The other trees gazed curiously down at Atheris and Saf, but a few flicked eager glances to a certain corner of the space.

Saf lingered by Zenith's side as Atheris wandered around. "Saros? Are you here?"

For a few moments, only the rustling trees replied. Then Saf gasped, and Atheris turned.

Saros appeared beside the weeping willow. He was hazy and ghostlike, rendered in bluish light, but otherwise looked perfectly himself. Even his fancy festival clothes had stayed with him.

Atheris found herself too choked up to speak. She raised a hand and waved; Saros stared at her, so perfectly still that for a moment she feared that the Woods was showing her only an apparition and not the real Saros. But then his mouth moved in the shape of her name, and then Saf's when he turned to them. Yet no sound accompanied the motion.

Saf moved a few steps toward Saros, slowly at first and then in a rush. They reached for him and Saros reached back, but when Saf went to take his hand, their fingers passed through his.

Both of them drew away, looking equally dismayed. Atheris had sort of expected as much, but a part of her had hoped for a surprise.

She approached Saros next and flickered a smile when he met her eyes. "Hey."

He nodded back.

Atheris was no stranger carrying on a one-sided conversation with him, but despite a month of wishing she could talk to him, she now had no idea what to say. She glanced awkwardly around the shadowy grove and finally decided to draw Saros's attention to Zenith. "She's been with us, in case you were worried. We're taking care of her, but I can tell she misses you. I'd let her stay if she could, but..." Was that even possible?

Saros shrugged. Clearly he didn't know, either, if familiars could pass to and from the astral realm at will. He held out his hand toward Zenith and snapped his fingers; her ears perked up and she rushed over, but when she tried to nose his hand, she wasn't able to make contact, either. She released a soft, saddened noise.

Saros looked at Atheris again, now with a wrinkle of confusion between his brows. He pointed a finger at her, then darted it to Saf and then back again. *Us?* he mouthed.

Atheris nodded. "I've been staying with Saf these past weeks. They've taught me lots more than Evyrmyre ever could, so..." She shrugged. Returning to that stuffy, pretentious academic world was less appealing with each day.

"Besides," she went on, "Evyrmyre can't give me a way to help you."

Saros raised his eyebrows, but the glimpse of hope in his expression quickly soured to doubt. *You can't*, he mouthed.

"Not *yet*," Atheris corrected. "But we will." She stepped as close to him as possible without stepping *through* him. His ghostly form flickered when he tipped his head down to meet her eyes.

"I promise," she said.

"I told you that you wouldn't be alone anymore," Saf added, "and I meant it. We'll find a way. We just need time."

Saros still looked incredulous, but finally he nodded. His eyes were warm with gratitude that Atheris knew he wouldn't know how to put into words even if she could hear them.

He flickered again. The sky was lightening; they were running out of time. Saros met Atheris's gaze and offered his hands.

She hovered her own palms above his, as close as she could get. Tears stung her eyes. "When you're out of there, Saros Antarian, I'm going to hug you so hard, it'll break all your bones. And I mean that affectionately." She sniffled as Saros cracked a smile.

Reluctantly, she moved a few steps back from him to give Saf some space if they wanted it. They moved forward, and after a moment of hesitation they pressed a kiss to their fingertips and then extended their hand toward Saros. He pressed his own hand to his heart.

Atheris watched him grow fainter as the dawn broke; he cast a nervous glance at the sky and then retreated to the shadows beneath the trees. In another few seconds, he was gone.

Zenith meowed and padded ahead as if to follow him, but stopped beside the weeping willow where he had disappeared. Her tail swished and her ears twitched, and after a minute of apparent deep thought, she strode into the trees. Atheris blinked, and Zenith was gone too.

Her heart sank. She'd come to love the little feline since she'd known Saros. Zenith belonged with her human, of course, but Atheris hoped she hadn't seen the last of her.

Saf lightly touched Atheris's arm. "She'll come back when she wants to. Don't worry, she won't forget us."

Atheris nodded, but couldn't yet tear her gaze away from the foliage.

"Atheris." Saf drew her attention to themself. A gentle smile warmed their face and chased away some of their sorrow. "We'll see him again, too."

Bolstered by that promise, Atheris followed Saf back through the Woods. "Right." She strode ahead of them. "Come on, then. We've got work to do."

ACKNOWLEDGMENTS

Four years ago, I decided to write a book about a necromancer whose character arc was a descent to villainy. Little did I know how much I would fight with that book to make it a reality. I often joked about "the goddamn necromancer book" that wouldn't get out of my head but also wouldn't let me write it. But today, you hold that book in your hands, and as with every book, I could not have made it here, to the Acknowledgments page, alone.

Firstly, I want to thank Maggie: you were the first person to help springboard the idea for this book, and though you may not remember that conversation, I am still grateful for all of the creative encouragement you have given me over the years.

Next up, I owe eternal gratitude to my brilliant beta readers: Juniper, Artemy, Tabitha, and Payne. All of you left the *most* unhinged comments on this manuscript, only to then give me some of the most insightful feedback I've ever received. Thank you, thank you, thank you for everything you've done to help make this into a cohesive, book-shaped thing.

One million additional thank-yous to Juniper for the absolutely stunning cover art. I am honored to have your beautiful art wrapped around this weird little story and scattered throughout its pages.

Thank you to my family and friends for all of their continued support in my publishing journey.

And lastly, though they'll likely never see this, I feel obligated to shout-out Kamelot, whose music was endlessly, obsessively on repeat while I wrote this book. They're at least half the reason I made it through the final draft, and this book exists because of the *Silverthorn* album. So yeah, thanks for the vibes!

ABOUT THE AUTHOR

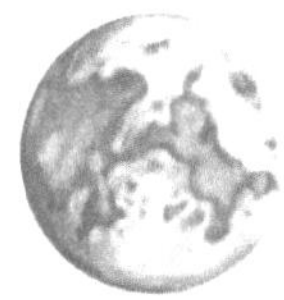

T.L. Morgan is the author of several fantasy novels, including the Windermere Tales series. When they're not writing, Talli enjoys drawing, playing D&D, and meandering through bookstores. They can also be found lurking in the stacks of local libraries.

Find out more about Talli's books on their website, tallimorgan.com.

instagram.com/undernightfall